A Worthy Wife

A Worthy Wife

Barbara Metzger

Thorndike Press
Waterville, Maine USA

Chivers Press
Bath, England

This Large Print edition is published by Thorndike Press®, USA and by Chivers Press, England.

Published in 2003 in the U.S. by arrangement with NAL Signet, a member of Penguin Group (USA) Inc.

Published in 2003 in the U.K. by arrangement with the author.

U.S. Softcover   0-7862-5427-0 (Paperback Series)
U.K. Hardcover 0-7540-7295-9 (Chivers Large Print)

The text of this Large Print edition is unabridged.
Other aspects of the book may vary from the original edition.

Set in 16 pt. Plantin by Al Chase.

Printed in the United States on permanent paper.

British Library Cataloguing-in-Publication Data available

Library of Congress Cataloging-in-Publication Data

Metzger, Barbara.
    A worthy wife / Barbara Metzger.
        p. cm.
    ISBN 0-7862-5427-0 (lg. print : sc : alk. paper)
    1. Bigamy — Fiction. 2. Large type books. I. Title.
PS3563.E86W67 2003
813´.54—dc21   2003048371

A Worthy Wife

To the wonderful and loyal Regency readers, especially anyone who has ever taken the time and trouble to send a note or an E-mail of interest or appreciation. It matters! Thank you.

Chapter One

The bride was radiant in ivory satin. The groom was splendidly stalwart in scarlet regimentals. The little stone church outside Bath was filled with flowers and weepy females. Aurora Halle McPhee was getting married!

The bells of Bath might not be ringing in celebration, but Aurora's heart was certainly pounding loudly enough, and her stomach was doing somersaults. Clutching her bouquet in trembling hands, she glanced up at her husband-to-be through lowered lashes, while the vicar droned through the marriage ceremony. The most important day of her life, Aurora reflected, and she'd be lucky if she recalled half of it. Then again, lucky did not half describe her good fortune. Lieutenant Harland Podell was marrying her! Aurora knew she was a merely passable female of undistinguished birth and unimpressive dowry, who'd never been out of Bath since her parents sent her home from India as an infant, shortly before their deaths. Adopted by her aunt and uncle

McPhee, amateur naturalists, she had no lofty connections, no Town Bronze, no expectations of making any grand match. Why, she was more like to wed an amphibian than make her bows at Almack's. Yet the dashing lieutenant had chosen her. Some ten years older than her nineteen, he had arrived from London scant months ago, recuperating from an injury. He'd declared his heart was mortally wounded at the first sight of her blond beauty, and only her company could alleviate his pain. How could she resist, a sheltered young female not long out of the schoolroom? And why should she? The lieutenant was darkly handsome and polished and well-bred, casually mentioning this or that well-known acquaintance. He regretted that the Duke of Wellington was too busy to meet the Belle of Bath. Aurora had no regrets whatsoever when she accepted his proposal of marriage soon after. Why, dear Harland had even shaken Uncle Ptolemy's hand, the one recently holding an ailing bullfrog. If that was not a true judge of gentlemanly character, Aurora would eat her hat. Of course, her stomach already felt as if she had, silk flowers, beaded ribbons, and all. She really wished Reverend Mainwaring would get on with the ceremony.

After what seemed an eternity to Miss McPhee, the vicar looked out over the congregation. "If anyone here" — he cleared his throat — "knows just cause why these two" — he paused to put his finger in the book, marking his place — "should not be joined in holy matrimony" — he wiped his nose — "let him speak now or forever hold his peace."

Aurora let out a deep breath. She could hear Aunt Thisbe's muffled sobs and a few of her schoolmates giggling, even over the hammering of her heart as they all stood waiting for the awkward moment to pass and the vicar to proceed.

But the noise hadn't been the beating of her own pulse, it had been something from a bride's bad dream, or a worse novel — someone pounding up the church steps, slamming open the heavy wooden doors. "I'll speak, by God," shouted a tall, reddish-haired stranger as he strode up the aisle, his caped riding coat flapping like the wings of Lucifer himself, and his boots leaving a trail of mud on the white carpet runner placed there.

The ensuing silence could have filled Westminster Abbey, much less the small stone church. Then they all heard a thud as Aunt Thisbe's prayer book hit the floor, and a louder thud as Aunt Thisbe followed.

"B'gad, she's fainted," Uncle Ptolemy cried, then turned to the broad-shouldered intruder, who was now halfway to the altar. "Sir, who the devil are you and what is the meaning of this heinous commotion?"

The gentleman — and everyone recognized his bearing, his tailoring, his very arrogance as aristocratic, if not noble — pointed one gloved finger at Lieutenant Podell. "I am Windham, and that dastard is already married to my sister, by Zeus. If that's not just cause, I don't know what is."

Uncle Ptolemy fainted.

Aurora shook her head and turned to her almost-husband for reassurance. "How absurd. The man is obviously escaped from Bedlam. Or else he is one of your army friends playing a prank. Tell him to go away, Harland, do."

But Harland was turning as red as his uniform coat, looking over her shoulder for the nearest door. He never made it. The stranger grabbed the officer by the neck and lifted him clear off the ground, shaking Podell until gold braid and buttons went flying. "Tell them, you cad. Tell them it's true."

"T-true," Podell gasped, then tried to raise his arm to point to Lord Phelan

Ramsey, the family friend who had brought the infant Aurora back from India. "But he —"

Lord Phelan rushed up and struck Podell in the jaw, a not so difficult maneuver for the much smaller, older man since Windham still held Podell, dangling. He dropped him now, half-conscious, to the floor.

"Yes," Lord Phelan shouted, "I introduced you to my precious goddaughter, to my everlasting regret. Never has a man been so deceived."

A man? Her godfather's outrage was nothing to Aurora's. When the lieutenant would have scrabbled an escape through the tumult and the titters of Aurora's girlfriends, the bride hauled up the small marble urn from in front of the vicar's lectern. She emptied it of orange blossoms and trailing ivy, then bashed her misbegotten bridegroom over the head with it. After which she dragged herself and the urn behind the lectern, where she cast up her accounts in as ladylike fashion as possible, while the wedding wrecker, Windham, ordered everyone to go home.

"But," Aurora whimpered, only loudly enough that half the exiting congregation could hear, "I need a husband."

The vicar fainted.

Damn, thought Kenyon Warriner, Earl of Windham. He hadn't been in time to keep another gently bred female from being ruined. He'd ridden from London as fast as he could as soon as someone in his club asked if the Podell chap calling the banns in Bath was any relation to his sister's deceased husband, and was he going to the wedding. He was going, all right. If Podell was not deceased, he'd wish he were when the Earl of Windham got through.

Now Kenyon almost kicked the ofttimes groom before he remembered he was a gentleman, and ladies were present — ladies in delicate conditions, blast the bounder to perdition. Besides, Lord Phelan was tying Podell up with his own cravat, before they decided what to do with the scurvy cur. Calling the magistrate was the last choice, for everyone's sake. Lord Phelan stuffed one of Podell's gloves in the villain's mouth, so they did not have to hear any more of his filth, the long-nosed gentleman declared.

Kenyon took his quizzing glass out of his pocket and examined the young woman more closely. She was paler than her ivory gown and as wispy as a flower stem, but she did have starch in her backbone. She was young and pretty, and her dress was of excellent quality, if not precisely modish by

London standards. The current high-waisted style concealed her current dilemma nicely, he considered. She was tenderly ministering to her aunt, while her uncle and the vicar shared the fortifying contents of the earl's own flask. Kenyon took a long swallow when the flask was restored to him. He wiped his mouth and said, "*I'll* marry you."

Aurora fainted.

When order had been restored, the gawkers removed, the wedding party revived — except for Podell, who had been clobbered again by Lord Phelan for trying to escape — they all gathered in the vestry. And they all turned to the earl.

"Harland Podell married my sister, Brianne, a year ago," he began, "while I was abroad on a diplomatic errand for the government."

By this everyone understood that such a misalliance would never have taken place otherwise. Uncle Ptolemy nodded. "Being responsible for flighty young females is a devilish business."

To spare Miss McPhee's blushes, Kenyon continued. "He declared that he could not sell out of his army commission, not in time of war, not even for her. And a battlefield was no place for a lady, of course."

"Just what he told us." Aunt Thisbe sobbed into her sodden handkerchief. "We were so pleased to have our dearest staying on with us after the wedding, we never thought to question his credentials."

"He had none, madam — credentials, that is. When I returned, I found Podell gone, along with all of my sister's handsome dowry. She was of age, so there was no refuting his claim. That was about a year ago. Soon after the wedding, she received notice from another officer that Podell had been killed in action. My subsequent inquiries at the War Office, trying to reclaim my sister's portion or her widow's benefits, showed he had been cashiered out of the army five years before. The officer's signature was a forgery."

Uncle Ptolemy tsked. Aunt Thisbe wept louder. Aurora was too numb to do more than nod.

Lord Phelan was cursing beneath his breath. "I suppose you searched for him, Windham, what?"

"Yes, I had men scouring the countryside. That's how I discovered that Brianne wasn't merely the victim of a scurrilous fortune hunter, but that her husband was a bigamist besides, making her own marriage illegal. Podell's family had sent him to Jamaica after he was drummed out of the army. He married a plantation owner's daughter there and sired two children. He might even have other wives. I'll find out as soon as the dastard wakes up enough for me to question."

"I'll help with the interrogation," Lord Phelan volunteered, holding up his fists and hopping around like a spindle-shanked, bantam-weight pugilist.

Windham turned to the young woman's uncle. "The man is a proven coward. I'm sure he'll tell us what we need to know without such drastic measures. And I am certain no one wishes to involve the magistrate's office in this matter."

"Oh, dear, no. There will be talk enough as is!"

The earl nodded his agreement. Then he turned to the beleaguered bride. "Honor demands my offer, Miss, ah, McPhee," he began, although no one could possibly hold him responsible for her present situation, except in his office of bearer of ill tidings. "I already have an heir of sorts, so there could be no embarrassment to the succession, and I have been thinking of acquiring a new wife anyway. This merely expedites the decision.

Furthermore, you might be of comfort to my sister, proving that she is not the only gudgeon — ah, gullible female — to fall prey to such a plausible vulture. She was disconsolate at Podell's supposed death; she is distraught at his deceit."

Aurora could well imagine. Yet finding consolation for his sister seemed a poor reason for wedding a stranger, a mere nobody. He knew nothing about her, or had the least inkling if they would suit at all. Why, the earl spent more time selecting his waistcoats, Aurora supposed. "I am honored, my lord. But there is no need —"

"There is every need," Vicar Mainwaring put in, putting down the cup he held, which held the remains of Windham's flask. No one had thought to offer Aurora a drink, more's the pity. She could barely stand, much less decide her entire future.

Windham seemed to recognize her confusion. "You'll have at least an hour to think about your decision, for it will take me that long to procure a special license. If you don't choose to accept my offer, simply go home."

"An hour?" the vicar echoed. "More like a week to get all the papers in order. Bishop Hollingsworth doesn't approve of skimble-skamble weddings."

The earl tapped his gloves against his muscular thigh. "Nonsense. Bishop Hollingsworth is my mother's uncle. He's been after me to remarry this age." He turned to smile at Aurora, a warm smile full of humor and understanding and sympathy. "You see, Miss McPhee, there are many advantages to our wedding, besides the obvious. Do consider carefully."

After he left, while everyone was clamoring about her future, Aurora sat wondering what the earl considered the obvious: his devastatingly handsome looks, his wealth, social standing, the power to move bishops, if not mountains — or merely the natural charm he showed to one and all. A woman could well enjoy basking in the sun's rays for the rest of her days, Aurora reflected.

But where was the advantage for Lord Windham? He'd have a bride without having to present himself at the Marriage Mart, but his wife would be a Bath miss with more hair than wit, who'd gaily tripped down the primrose path to her own ruin. He'd likely have no handkerchiefs left either, she realized, seeing how she'd shredded the one he'd handed her. But his lordship did not seem to care. Aurora supposed an earl was beyond worrying over petty matters such as soiled linen and soiled reputations. And his own sister was in a worse state, having actually married the blackguard bigamist.

And what choice did she have, after all? Everyone would know that the marriage had been interrupted. Soon they'd know she was ruined beyond redemption, and Aurora would be cast out of all decent society. Most likely her dear aunt and uncle would be ostracized along with her. They'd be miserable without their friends at the Amateur Naturalists Society, and they'd have her on their hands forever, for no honorable man would make her an honorable offer, not that she'd ever trust her judgment of a man's character again. No, she was and forever would be an embarrassment to the loving relations who had adopted her as their own daughter, giving her their name. What a repayment for their affection.

As for his lordship, his very offer proved him honorable and kind. His devotion to his sister also spoke of his loyalty and steadiness of character. He was a tad intimidating, Aurora reflected, but he would keep her safe from scandal — and everything else. His class often married by arrangement instead of affection, although not usually penniless brides of nondescript ancestry and dicey reputations. Still, if he was kind enough to offer, she'd be a fool not to accept. And Heaven knew she'd been enough of a fool for one day.

"Nonsense, my girl," Lord Phelan argued. "No reason to take up with any London swell. Why, I'll marry you m'self. Yes, that's what I should have done. Would have married your mother, by Jupiter, if my blasted brother George hadn't interfered."

Since Lord Phelan was old enough to be Aurora's father, no one paid attention to his offer. The vicar merely poured the contents of Lord Phelan's cup into his own. "Too much excitement, old fellow."

Aunt Thisbe was weeping, this time at the thought of her little girl becoming a countess. Uncle Ptolemy kept fumbling in his fob pocket, checking the time. No, he was checking the toad.

What a fine match his lordship was making!

Chapter Two

The bride was haggard in crumpled satin. The groom was heroically handsome in his buckskin breeches. Windham's auburn hair was freshly combed, and he had found time to get his boots shined. Still, he smelled of horse, which somehow made Aurora feel better. The earl was a mere man, not a visiting deity.

Instead of her wedding bouquet, which had been trampled in the earlier debacle and kept too long out of water at any rate, Aurora clasped a paper sack of peppermint drops. Lord Windham had returned with it, along with the special license, to settle her stomach, he'd said. Aurora clasped that small kindness to her heart, for courage.

While the vicar wended his slow way through the wedding service once more, Windham patted her hand and whispered, "I promise not to beat you, you know. My first wife died of the typhus. I was not even in the same country at the time."

She managed to give him a shaky smile in return, at which he said, "Good girl. I knew you had bottom," and turned back to the vicar.

The most momentous day of her life, Aurora thought, and she was liable to recall his praise above all. For sure she heard not one sentence of the Reverend Mr. Mainwaring's speech, until he got to the part about just cause and speaking now, and oh, dear, Uncle Ptolemy was poking Lord Phelan in the ribs, to keep him still. The vicar went on, and Aurora sighed in relief. When he got to the part where Aurora had to repeat her vows, though, she could not utter the words. Likely a peppermint drop had glued her tongue to her teeth, for she could not open her mouth. The silence in the near-empty church was like a stone gargoyle, hovering. Then Lord Windham raised one eyebrow at her, and one corner of his mouth, and she found the will to whisper: "I-I do if he does."

Windham winked at her. "She does."

Aunt Thisbe sighed in relief.

The bride's mouth was sticky from the peppermint drops, and the groom's was quirked in a smile, but the kiss sealed the marriage. It was done.

The vicar sighed in relief.

Windham signed his name in the church

21

registry with a flourish. He raised his quizzing glass to watch Aurora sign almost as if he were checking to see if she knew her letters. She frowned at his enlarged eye — of a lovely forest green color, but horridly magnified — and muttered, "Odious affectation."

The earl chuckled, but put the looking glass away in his pocket. "I can see I'm to live under the cat's paw."

Aurora gasped at her own audacity. Heavens, they'd been wed for less than a moment, and already she was turning into a fishwife. It must be all the high drama of the day, that and his gentle smile that led her to such indiscretion. "I swear I am not a managing female, my lord."

Windham merely shrugged, as if a gnat had apologized for lighting on his shoulder. "It's too late now, my dear, one way or the other. And perhaps you might call me by my name now that we are officially man and wife? It's Kenyon, if you missed it during the ceremony."

Aurora had, but she'd checked the registry after he'd signed. "Kenyon. And I —"

"You're Lady Windham," Aunt Thisbe gushed, embracing her once more. Uncle Ptolemy was shaking the earl's hand, and Lord Phelan was making certain Podell was still securely tied.

At the earl's suggestion, they all agreed to send the makebait back to his first wife in Jamaica, after getting a signed confession from him. No one wanted a public trial, least of all Aurora or the earl's sister. With Podell out of the country, Lord Windham convinced them, other women were protected, and the scandal would more quickly fade from memory. The earl did make sure the blackguard understood his ultimatum: if Podell ever returned to England, he would face criminal charges, a military tribunal, and Windham's Mantons. Lord Phelan offered to take charge of the prisoner until Kenyon could make arrangements in London to have the shabster shipped off.

Since the wedding breakfast would have been long since spoiled, and the invited guests long since gone about their business, no one could argue with the earl's plan to cut short the nuptial celebrations. He wished to leave for the City as soon as he could hire a proper vehicle and collect his new wife's trunks. "I apologize," he told Aunt Thisbe, who'd been eager to show him off in Bath as if he were a rare butterfly she'd just added to her collection. "But I left London in such a rush that I must return with all possible haste. I was in the midst of negotiating my brother's return from a French prison hospital when I got word of Podell's latest villainy. You will understand my concern with completing the arrangements, I'm sure. And I'll also see to inserting notices of the wedding in all the papers, and visit with the solicitors concerning Miss McPhee's — ah, Lady Windham's, ah, your niece's settlements and such."

The man never seemed to do anything at a leisurely pace, it appeared to Aurora. In no time at all she found herself dressed in her new traveling ensemble, seated in an elegant carriage with fur throws and hot bricks and a picnic hamper, and her new husband, who was ordering the driver to spring 'em. He settled himself opposite her, sprawling exhaustedly against the cushions. "I instructed the coachman to stop for the night halfway to Town. No reason to get to London after midnight. The Black Dog is where I usually stay, but you might wish to rest before then."

Stop for the night? It occurred to Aurora that he was expecting to spend the night with her . . . and informing her that she should rest to prepare herself! Good grief, no amount of rest could prepare her for such intimacies with a perfect stranger, unless it was the eternal sort! Of course she'd made her bed, and now had to sleep in his. Dear heaven. Aurora popped another peppermint drop in her mouth to keep her teeth from clattering in fear.

"I say, you aren't going to be ill again, are you?" Windham asked, almost as nervous at the thought. "Are we traveling too fast? I'll tell the fellow to stop at the Golden Thistle in Bycroft."

Stop sooner? "No. That is, no, the carriage is so well sprung, I swear I could ride straight through to London."

He relaxed again. "Well, I for one am looking forward to a hot bath and a comfortable bed, the sooner the better."

Aurora swallowed the candy whole, almost choking on it.

"No, tomorrow afternoon is soon enough to reach London," Kenyon told her with a yawn, leading her to hope that he'd be so tired he might forget he had a wife. "I'll still have time to send notices to the papers and see your family's solicitor concerning your dowry."

"My dowry?" Now Aurora had a new concern, that he expected her to be bringing him a vast fortune. Surely he understood that the McPhees were minor gentry, living modestly on annuities and investments.

"I'm afraid that I —"

"Never fear, as I assured your uncle while you were changing, I intend to see that your monies are put into a secure trust for your children."

Children? Her children would be *his* children, may the saints preserve them, and her. But monies? "Uncle must not have been listening. He does tend to let his mind wander, especially when the ground starts to thaw. Otherwise he would have informed you that the sum is so small it needs no legal safeguards. Why, I doubt my dowry would keep an infant in nappies for a year."

"Nonsense. Podell only battens on heiresses. You must have a healthy bank account somewhere."

"I assure you, there is none. I keep the accounts for my aunt and uncle, and I know to the shilling that there is no fortune. Aunt Thisbe was constantly bemoaning her inability to see me presented at court."

"Then the money had to come from your parents in India."

She shook her head. "By all accounts my father never rose above his post as one of the East India Company's minor clerks. He died before amassing anything but debts, and my mother shortly before him. If not for the generosity of the British colony there, I understand, she'd have been buried as a pauper."

"Then what the deuce could Podell have been after?" Kenyon wondered.

Aurora drew the fur rug and her pride more closely around her. "Might it not occur to you that he loved me for myself, not my family's wealth?"

"No."

She gasped. "That is plain speaking indeed."

The earl seemed to recollect himself, and his company. "I say, I did not mean to insult you, Miss . . . ah, my dear. It's not that Podell couldn't have held you in the greatest esteem, but that his motives were never so pure. My apologies — I must be even more tired than I realized."

With that, the earl settled into the corner of his side of the carriage and pulled his hat down over his eyes, as if he intended to nap right then — on her wedding day! This might not be the glorious celebration Aurora had imagined in her schoolgirl's fantasies. Gracious, this was not even the bridegroom she'd pictured in her fondest dreams. Yet this was the only wedding day she was liable to have, and this the only husband. Till death did them part. That much she remembered the vicar saying. Granted,

Windham had ridden *ventre-à-terre* to save her from Podell's clutches, and he had sacrificed himself on the matrimonial altar, but still! How could any person of sensibility sleep on such a momentous, cataclysmic day?

Aurora cleared her throat — and got no response. She rustled the paper sack still in her hands, and he did not even twitch. So she spoke up. "You must have loved your first wife very much."

Now *that* got a reaction. Kenyon sat up so fast his hat went flying across the coach to land near Aurora's feet. She picked it up and brushed the nap with her fingers. He was examining her through his quizzing glass, most likely because he knew she disliked it so, but she would not lower her eyes, nor her expectations of a reply.

He let the glass fall back on its ribbon and muttered, "What the deuce are you nattering on about, woman?"

"I am not nattering, my lord. I never natter. I am merely trying to understand you and your actions better. That is the foundation for a successful and comfortable relationship, do you not agree?"

"I agree only that we will have a lifetime to develop an understanding, so there is no reason to begin at this precise moment." He tried to dispose his broad shoulders more comfortably against the cushions.

Aurora was not giving up. Her aunt and uncle had never ignored her conversation; she saw less reason for this gentleman to do so. If he was a surly, uncooperative sort, she decided, 'twere better to know it sooner, rather than later. Of course it was too late to matter, but a woman should know all she could about the man to whom she was wedded. His favorite foods and how much starch he liked in his neckcloths could wait. "You must have loved her a great deal. That's why you showed no hesitation about entering a marriage of convenience."

"Which is growing less and less convenient," Kenyon muttered, turning his head to the window. His bride was nattering — no, she did not natter. She was babbling on, almost as if she were speaking to herself, or to the hat he wished were covering his weary eyes.

"If one had no hopes of loving again," Aurora persisted, "what difference could one's choice of bride make? I see."

Kenyon saw houses and trees flashing past the window, and no rest in sight. "Whatever you say, Mi— my dear."

"Was she very beautiful?"

"Exquisite. Elegant, refined, a daughter

29

of the French aristocracy."

Everything she wasn't, in other words. Aurora couldn't help the kernel of self-pity that lodged in her throat. "I . . . I see."

He peered at her across the carriage, instantly sorry for his brusqueness. Miss McPhee must be feeling all the anxiety of a fledgling sparrow, shoved out of the nest to face the cold, cruel world. She was about as innocent and defenseless, and he was a beast to tease her so. "Her parents fled to an estate near my parents'. We were thrown together a great deal."

"And you fell in love." She sighed.

So did Kenyon. "I fell into lust. Genevieve and I were discovered, on purpose, I have always suspected, and our parents saw to the rest. Two such ancient families must not let a hint of scandal besmirch their noble bloodlines. After the wedding, of course, we discovered that we had absolutely nothing in common. I preferred my government work; she preferred the society of other French emigrés in London. Our paths seldom crossed. Then she ran off with her French lover, a deposed duke. So much for avoiding scandal. Other than the embarrassment, I did not mind overmuch. So you can wipe the stars from your eyes, my lady. There was no deathless devotion, no bond reaching beyond the grave."

She solemnly handed back his hat, nodding. "Yes, I understand now. You were hurt so badly, your pride so shattered, that you swore never to love another. That's why you were willing to take an unknown bride."

He frowned at her through narrowed eyes, then took out his quizzing glass to further discompose her. "And you, Miss — my lady wife, have been reading entirely too many novels."

"And you, sir, do not know my name!"

Aha! She'd finally succeeded in putting the gentleman out of countenance, for there he was, blushing like a schoolboy. Aurora supposed her husband's nearly red hair made him more susceptible to such humbling moments of common mortality. Now *there* was an important fact for a wife to know about her husband! Feeling much better about their horribly unequal match, she grinned at his discomfiture.

"Wretch," he murmured, smiling back. "I tried to look at the license after you'd filled in the names, but the vicar took the deuced thing away to record before I had the chance. And then I was distracted when you signed the registry."

Aurora giggled. "I was too busy deciphering your signature to notice. I didn't hear a word the vicar said either. It's Aurora, my lord. Aurora Phoebe Halle McPhee."

"Aurora. Dawn. That's lovely." He reached beneath his seat for the hamper and pulled out a bottle of wine. He poured some into the two glasses he also found wrapped in a towel, and offered one to her for a toast. "To a new dawn for both of us."

"And golden days ahead," she added, clinking her glass against his.

"And nights."

Oh, my.

Chapter Three

The Black Dog was well groomed. Smaller and less noisy than a regular posting inn, it catered to a more select clientele. The carriage bore no crest, and the pale young female was not one of the earl's usual dashers, but Windham was instantly recognized, of course, and treated like royalty. Better, in fact, for Prinny was known to let his accounts lapse. The Earl of Windham was known for his pleasant manner and open purse.

Aurora was whisked past the public rooms into another world. There were area rugs on top of the carpets. She would have stopped to admire the artwork on the walls, positive most were by painters she recognized from books, except servants lined the hallways. They were ready to unpack her luggage, the innkeeper announced as he bowed her into a parlor nearly the size of Bath's Pump Room.

One of the maids led her to the adjoining bedchamber, which was filled with flowers in vases, fruit in baskets, biscuits on platters — and no Earl of Windham in dishabille, thank goodness. Somehow sharing a lifetime with the gentleman seemed easier than sharing a bedroom. Nibbling on a macaroon, for she had not eaten anything all day except for the peppermint drops, Aurora looked at the selection of books and journals left on the bed table — all the latest from London — and knew how she'd spend the night. She was trying to decide where to start while the servants brought a copper tub, hot water, warm towels, a tea that could have fed the entire Amateur Naturalists Society, and a message from the earl. He would be pleased with her company at dinner in their sitting room, at nine.

At nine? Many nights, in Bath, if there was no assembly or lecture, the McPhees were abed by nine. She supposed she'd have to get used to Town hours, Aurora realized, along with a great many other things — but not tonight.

"Please inform his lordship that I am far too exhausted from the day to be good company," she instructed the messenger. "And the lavish tea will surely satisfy my appetite until breakfast in the morning. And . . . and I bid him good night."

Much relieved, Aurora settled back in her

bath, with a book in one hand and a raspberry tart in the other. This business of being a countess wasn't half bad.

When her bags arrived with the newly hired maid from Bath, Aurora donned her new nightrail, the wedding finery that Aunt Thisbe had so painstakingly embroidered for her. The maid would have commented otherwise, and Lud knew there was enough grist for the gossip mills already. Well, Lord Windham would get to see Aunt Thisbe's skill another time, Aurora reflected as she used the footstool to climb onto the enormous canopied bed. She brought the book with her, but did not get much reading done, as she rehearsed the talk she'd have tomorrow on the way to London with his lordship. Her husband. Kenyon. She rolled the name around her tongue like a peppermint drop. It was a nice name, for a nice man. He'd sympathize with her sentiments, Aurora was sure, once she explained that he simply could not expect her to commence certain wifely duties until they knew each other better. He'd know which ones.

Aurora understood that her husband had shared this suite before; from the inn's maidservants' sideways looks, the surprise quickly erased, she understood that none of his previous guests had been such milk-and-water misses. Those women he was wont to entertain might want to share their beds with strangers, but Kenyon hadn't married any of them. She supposed she could study how to be more dashing, more attractive to a top-drawer gentleman like Windham, although that poltroon Podell had not found her lacking. Well, she'd learned Latin and Greek. Surely she could learn about the ways of a husband and wife, given enough time. Given Windham's decidedly attractive looks and heart-melting smile, Aurora doubted she'd need much time at all before she welcomed the intimacies of the marriage bed. Perhaps a month.

Or perhaps not.

Kenyon tapped lightly on the connecting door and then entered Aurora's bedchamber without waiting for her reply. He carried a tray with a bottle and two glasses, and he was wearing a long velvet robe sashed at the waist. Aurora wondered if it was borrowed, or if the earl kept a wardrobe at various inns across the kingdom, for just such occasions. How many such occasions could there have been, unless he had taken a page from Podell's book and had brides stashed around the countryside, too? She swallowed a nervous giggle and lowered her eyes. Goodness, his feet were bare! Aurora could not recall ever seeing a man's naked toes before in her entire life. She shivered to think of what else he was not wearing beneath the velvet robe. She looked at her own hands, as a safer site for her eyes to rest. Her knuckles were white around the book, and her fingers trembled.

Kenyon seemed to be enjoying her inspection, by the devilish grin he flashed her, all white teeth and dimples. "What, cat got your tongue again, my dear? Too bad you found it in the coach, or I would not be so late coming to you. I fell asleep after my bath. My apologies for leaving you alone so long."

"But . . . but I said good night."

"Did you? The maid did not deliver any good night kiss."

"I should hope not!"

He laughed and placed the tray on the bedside table, as if he were planning on staying. "I thought we might chat a bit, get to know each other better, as you suggested in the carriage."

"I was thinking the precise thing. For after breakfast tomorrow. I . . . I was just about to blow out the candle now."

"Were you?" He sat on the edge of the bed and leaned over to blow out the candle. "If you prefer . . . ?"

"No! Don't do that. You'll need it to . . . to see your way out." She edged away from him across the mattress, which he unfortunately mistook for an invitation to join her on the bed. His weight started to pull her sideways, toward him. Aurora dropped the book and clutched the opposite edge of the mattress.

Windham chose not to notice that his bride was about to fall off the bed altogether in her efforts to put as much distance between them as possible. He busied himself filling the glasses. "I thought we should share a toast to our wedding."

"We already did that in the coach, remember?"

"Ah, but that was wine. This is champagne, specially chilled. Here, you'll enjoy it, I am sure." He brought the glass to her mouth, and the bubbles brushed her lips.

"No, I never —"

"Nonsense. It is your wedding night. You can be a little daring." He tipped the glass so she was forced to swallow, then he reached inside his robe and pulled out his quizzing glass on a ribbon around his neck. "I say, what the deuce is that thing crawling across your chest?"

Aurora pulled the covers up, mortified that he'd been staring at her nearly transparent lawn nightgown. "It's a great crested newt, *Triturus cristatus*. Aunt Thisbe embroidered it there, for luck, don't you know." At his blank look, she added, "A salamander."

"If I recall my mythology, the salamander is the elemental of fire. A fitting emblem for a night of love."

"No, no!" Aurora was horrified to hear her voice squeak like a wood mouse caught in the talons of a hawk. "That is, Aunt Thisbe simply adores newts. It's her specialty, you see."

"She cooks them?"

"Heavens, no. She collects them and studies them, makes sketches for the society's journals and such."

Windham was using his looking glass to study the bow tying her hair in its night braid on her shoulder. Uncomfortable under his gaze, Aurora pursed her lips and pointed to the gold-handled quizzer. "Do you sleep with that dratted thing, too?"

"Only when there is someone to impress," he teased, pulling the ribbon over his head and laying the piece on the nightstand. Somehow, while they were speaking, her glass had gone empty. Windham refilled it and offered it to her again.

"But I am not used to —"

"You are not used to being my wife, either. This will help you relax a bit."

Relax? May as well ask that dangling wood mouse to relax. She took the glass rather than have him hold it so close, so close that she could almost taste the wine on his lips. She took a sip to cool her heated thoughts. Then she squeaked again. His lordship was untying the bow of her braid, spreading the wavy blond locks in his hands, combing them smooth with his fingers. "Sh," he whispered, studying his handiwork. "I am only making you more comfortable."

More comfortable? She had never been less comfortable in her life! Aurora took another sip of the champagne, which was quite good, once one got used to the bubbles. With enough moisture, her lips managed to move. "Well, as long as you are here, we might as well have the talk I was saving for the carriage ride tomorrow."

He propped his head on one elbow. "*Now* you want to talk?"

"We'd better. You see, I have decided that we should not . . . not . . ."

"Not?" Windham drank from his own glass. Aurora could see him laughing at her over the rim.

"Nothaveintimaterelationsuntilweknow

eachotherbetter," she said in a rush.

"That's what you decided?"

She nodded, thankful that he understood.

"Odd, I thought matrimony was to be a partnership, not a one-sided affair. Barring that, I always supposed that the husband had some say in his marriage. Perhaps I got that impression from hearing you swear to love, honor, and obey. Just this morning, wasn't it?"

"I said that?"

"Oh, yes. I might not have caught your full name, but I particularly noted the bit about obeying."

Aurora took another swallow. "Then I suppose we could discuss the issues and come to a mutual agreement. That's more equitable, don't you agree?"

"Much." He was sifting her hair through his fingers again, breathing the scent of the rosewater rinse. "Lovely."

Yes, it was, but Aurora made herself say, "There is no reason we should rush into the, ah, physical aspects of our marriage."

"Am I rushing, my pet? Sorry. I do tend to move quickly once I have decided my direction. I was never one for shilly-shallying. You'll get used to it."

"I thought a month."

"No."

"Perhaps a sennight would be enough if we spent a great deal of time learning about each other's habits and such."

"No."

She frowned. "I thought this was to be a discussion."

"Very well, Aurora mine, we shall discuss the matter at hand." Since his hand was now stroking the back of her neck, Aurora could not decide if he was teasing. He was not. "The primary issue is the issue of our union. I prefer our progeny to be products of my own seed, no matter how remote the possibility."

"Of course you do, but —"

"But you will permit me the delusion, won't you?"

Since he was nibbling on her ear in a most interesting manner, Aurora feared she would have permitted Kenyon to delude himself into believing she was Venus Aphrodite. She nodded, not quite sure what she was agreeing to.

He refilled her glass — how many times had that been? — and blew out the candle so the only light in the room was from the glowing embers in the fireplace. Then he removed his robe. Aurora pulled the sheets over her head, but he only laughed and got under the covers with her. He did stay on his side of the bed, but soon he was presenting the glass of champagne to her lips once more.

"Oh, I don't think —"

"Sh, love. Don't think. Just sip, and relax."

Relax with a naked man in her bed? Was he daft? No, he was kissing her! "But Harland and I —" she began when she could speak again.

"Forget about Harland," he whispered, pressing his warm lips to hers once more. "We'll make new memories."

Chapter Four

People kissed with their mouths open? Heavens! And heavenly. But the shock of the thing, and the shock shimmering down to her own bare toes, made Aurora gasp. At least she wasn't squeaking like a mouse anymore.

Kenyon pulled away, one brow quirked in query.

"Harland never did that."

"Podell was a prig," the earl murmured before readdressing himself to turning Aurora's composure to consommé.

His tongue felt like cool silk, like the champagne bubbles, like nothing she had ever felt before. His kisses were making odd parts of her grow warm and tingling. No, his hand was on her breast. *That* was why she tingled. Then he followed his hand with his lips. Good grief, Aunt Thisbe never intended her embroidery for that! Aurora gasped again.

He stopped.

"Harland never did that either."

Kenyon just growled in response and kept

savoring her salamander — her breasts. His other hand was tugging at her gown, raising the hem over her calves, her knees, her thighs, her — *Holy herpetologist!* She gasped even louder.

"I know," Kenyon said with a sigh, "Podell never did this either. Besides being a loose screw, he was a poor lover, my pet. A gentleman always makes sure of his partner's pleasure. You are enjoying yourself, aren't you?"

Enjoyment was not quite the word she would have used, if she could have formed a coherent word. Delirium? Euphoria? She'd think about that some other time.

Kenyon seemed to take her garbled reply as assent. "Good, for I do not need to hear any more about what Podell did or did not do." He raised himself over Aurora, his body between her thighs, with his lips over hers to stifle whatever comment she was about to make. He rocked forward, murmuring his own pleasure into her mouth. Forward, forward he thrust, moaning softly, until he encountered an unmistakable barrier. "Bloody hell," he shouted, leaping off the bed. "He sure as Hades didn't do *that!*"

Windham stormed over to the buhl table near the window and hefted a decanter to his lips. Stunned and stupefied, Aurora could not help noting the smooth planes of his back, the chiseled muscles of his thighs and calves, the perfection of his posterior. And she'd fretted over his bare feet! She did slam her eyes shut when he turned back to the bed, though.

"You can look. I have my robe on again." He was holding a glass out to her again, too.

"But I do not drink strong spirits."

"Drink it, my lady wife, and tell me if you will, how, barring Wise Men, mangers, and miracles, you are bearing Podell's child whilst still a blooming maiden!"

Aurora huddled in the blankets. "A child? I never said —"

"You said you were ruined, by Jupiter!"

"That's what the lieutenant told me. We . . . we kissed and . . . and embraced on the balcony at Lady Featheringill's musicale, and one of the servants surprised us. Harland said the talk would be all over Bath unless we announced an engagement. I'd be labeled fast. Not a suitable companion for my friends. Not invited to their parties. Not partnered at the dances. Not —"

"I get the gist of his threats." He raised the decanter to his mouth again. "And you believed the mawworm that a few stolen kisses could blight your life?"

"He said he loved me, and he would

simply be speaking to Uncle Ptolemy that much sooner."

"And then, when that wedding turned into dust, you found an even riper plum to pick, to settle your affairs. You would have done anything to escape the narrow confines of Bath society, wouldn't you?"

Aurora stopped cowering in her corner, in light of his unjust accusations. "What, you think I set out to trap you? How could I know that you weren't wed? That you'd be so deuced impetuous you'd offer for a woman whose name you didn't even know?"

He paced to the fireplace and tossed on another log with such vehemence that sparks flew. He hopped back, swearing, and rubbed his bare feet. "You leaped at the offer quickly enough, dash it."

"Unfair! You gave me no time to decide. If I'd had the least suspicion that you were such a bully and bad-tempered to boot, you can rest assured I would not have —"

"I gave an hour to a lady with no choice but one if her babe was to have a father. Did you feign the morning sickness, too?"

"Morning sickness? Oh. No, I . . . I am afraid I become ill under severe distress. I've always had an uncertain digestion, which is why I rarely drink more than a sip

47

of wine. As a matter of fact —"

"Oh, no!" He raced for the wash basin, just in time. "Damn, why the devil can't you be like other women and just cry?"

When Aurora awakened, the fire was still burning and her husband was still there. He was sprawled in a chair dragged near her bed, his bare feet resting on the covers inches from her nose.

"How do you feel?" he asked, instantly alert at her first movement.

"Oh, much better. The feeling never lasts."

"Good." He held out a glass. "Just water. Would you like me to call for a maid? Tea? Perhaps some lemonade?"

Aurora did not want the servants bustling around with their curious stares. "Nothing, thank you. The water is fine."

Kenyon nodded, wishing to broadcast the bumble-broth of his wedding night as little as she. He pulled back the covers on the side of the bed and began to shrug out of his robe.

"What are you doing?" Aurora yelped.

"What does it look like I am doing? I am preparing to spend the rest of my wedding night in the arms of my bride, as expected."

"No."

"No?"

"That's right, no. The servants will know you have been here, so there is no reason for you to stay." He had a bedroom of his own; let him spend what was left of the night there.

"There is every reason, woman. I intend to finish what we started."

"No."

"Dash it, stop naysaying me at every turn. We already had this discussion." He reached for the sheets again.

Aurora held them down with her hand. "And your reasons are no longer valid. You wanted to ensure the paternity of your sons. That is no longer an issue, and never will be, for I would not be an unfaithful type of wandering wife, no matter the state of my marriage. My concerns, however, are magnified a hundredfold."

"What, that we don't know each other? I believe I am getting to know your idiosyncracies, by George. You can make book I'll never offer you champagne again."

Aurora ignored the sarcasm. "You do not trust me. I think you might not even like me. I cannot share such intimacies as you expect, not without some degree of affection or respect."

Kenyon ran his fingers through his already mussed hair. "Deuce take it, woman, you just did share such intimacies, and enjoyed every minute of it. I am the identical man who had you gasping not an hour ago."

Hoping that he couldn't see her blush in the dark, Aurora persevered. "No, you're not. That man might have cared for me. You will not share my bed until you believe that I did not — that I would not — act as dishonorably as you accused."

"My apologies. I was angry. I realize you could not have known my circumstances when you made your decision."

That was fustian, and they both knew it. His very bearing proclaimed wealth and breeding, even if his name wasn't known the breadth of the land. "No, but you still believe I willfully deceived you, that I set out to ensnare you. That is what I cannot accept, your estimation of me as a conniving, scheming jade." Like his first wife, though she didn't say it. "I would feel besmirched, sharing your bed under those conditions."

"Oh, Lord," he muttered, retying the sash of his robe with an angry snap that almost ripped the fabric, "save me from sanctimonious, self-righteous sapskulls. But what, my dear, is to keep me from forcing my attentions upon you? I would be within my rights, you know, as your husband."

She shook her head, sending blond curls every which way. "No, I cannot believe you would use your strength against a woman."

Of course he wouldn't. "But there are other ways of . . . persuasion, if you will. I could make you quiver with desire until you asked me, nay, begged me to make you mine." He was brushing her hair aside, off her face.

She slapped his hand away, knowing where that could lead. "But you are too much the gentleman to take a woman against her will. And it would be against my will, my lord, even if you told my body otherwise."

He stepped back and stared at her as if she were one of her Uncle Ptolemy's specimens, pinned to a board. "Your pardon, but I need to get this clear. You trust me enough not to exercise my God-given rights, but you won't let me, because I don't trust you?"

"Precisely. You see, I knew we could come to an understanding."

He slammed the connecting door on his way out. Aurora thought she heard him mutter, "Now I think *I* am going to be ill," but she could be wrong.

The maid woke Aurora late in the

morning, saying that she'd let her sleep as long as possible, on his lordship's orders, but now my lady had to rise if they were to make London by nightfall. Certain that the earl would not like being kept waiting, Aurora hurried through her morning toilette and into her traveling ensemble, which was freshly sponged and pressed. Her hair, however, could not be as quickly repaired. The maid pursed her lips, but thankfully made no comment as to how the neat braid had turned into a brier patch.

While the woman worked, Aurora made plans. She was going to make her husband trust her. More, she was going to make him love her. She could recite the Latin names of thirteen varieties of liverworts and lichens; surely this endeavor could not be more difficult, especially when she had such promising material to work with.

Her husband was impetuous and subject to fits of temper, likely due to a spoiled upbringing and toadying associates. Other than those minor, easily correctable faults, Kenyon was kind and considerate and honorable, the perfect gentle knight of every woman's daydreams. That he was also the heroically sculpted embodiment of every woman's secret night dreams was another factor in his favor. Why, if she did not watch herself, Aurora feared, she'd be more than halfway in love with the man, after less than a day.

He had not tried to change her mind, even though both of them knew his kisses could scatter her wits like so many *Ephemeroptera,* mayflies. And he'd sat with her through her embarrassing affliction, made her comfortable, watched over her, ordered every amenity for her comfort. He was predisposed to care for what was his — she understood that well enough from the care he took with the hired horses — but she truly believed he held a tiny spark of feeling for her. She would breathe that flame into a veritable fire of fondness, see if she didn't. And she'd be a countess to make him proud, a worthy wife to the Earl of Windham. Oh, he could not help coming to love her.

Unless he strangled her first.

Lord Windham had not slept a wink the entire uncomfortable night, which made two days and nights without rest except for that brief nap before dinner. Worse, he'd had too much too drink, too much of his wife's rattle-brained reasoning, and not enough physical gratification. Not nearly enough of that. None of that. Damn, even this morning he was feeling like a randy schoolboy who'd got into the headmaster's liquor cabinet.

And there was his wife, his bride, his bête noire, tripping into their sitting room as bright as her namesake in her lemony outfit and cheery good mornings. Her hair was neatly twisted under a ruched bonnet, with only a few curls left to escape, to torment a man.

Totally oblivious to his migraine, megrim, and general bad mood, Aurora was filling her breakfast plate with enough food to sustain a herd of Herefords. The place in front of the earl was empty except for a cup of black coffee, as bitter as his ruminations.

She made him feel old. He had eleven years more in his dish, but it seemed an eternity. He'd long ago lost that youthful optimism, where every day offered a new, better adventure. All his days seemed alike, offering nothing but new headaches, especially if he kept drinking as he had last night. Aurora McPhee was young and innocent, and she deserved to have her golden dreams come true. She deserved a young man to love her wholeheartedly, with no reservations, no restraints.

He announced, therefore, "I have decided not to announce our wedding in London. Bath society can wonder, but the servants here are well paid not to gossip."

Aurora spilled her chocolate. As she mopped at the tablecloth, he went on. "I thought it would be better to wait until I spoke to my solicitor to see if there was any possibility of an annulment."

"You can do that?"

"I have no idea. My man of affairs will know. Or he'll find out. There is a better chance, of course, if the marriage is not consummated, so you will have your wish to be relieved of the burden of my presence. I thought to install you at my aunt's home in Mayfair. She can take you around, introduce you to the *ton*, help you gather a stylish wardrobe, at my expense, of course. No one will speak of the incident in Bath. Did I mention that my aunt is Duchess Havermore? No one will question her sponsoring a new protégée, either. Her Grace has so many nieces and godchildren that she herself can hardly keep track. And if we can annul the marriage, I am sure she can find you an eligible *parti*. A husband of your choice, that is, who will show you the proper —" He jerked his looking glass out of his coat and surveyed his bride's suddenly ashen coloring. "You are not going to be sick again, are you?"

"No." But she put down her fork. "I do think I have lost my appetite, however."

Chapter Five

The earl was finally going to get to sleep. After a polite offer to share the pile of journals and newspapers she had taken from the inn, which he just as politely refused, Aurora sat mumchance in the carriage on the way to London. She glanced out the window; she glanced at the magazines. She did not glance at Lord Windham, not even once.

Kenyon had expected an argument over his admittedly unilateral decision to seek an annulment. He'd supposed there would be tears and recriminations, the type of scene he most loathed. Hell, he'd even prepared for her casting up her accounts again, with an empty milk pail packed in the hamper. Then he'd wondered if she would try to bargain with him, rather than lose her chance at being his countess. Lud knew Aurora held all the right cards for negotiation, for he'd consummate the marriage in the carriage, in a flash, in a fever, if she crawled into his lap. Pigs would take wing and fly first. Why, the only way she could sit any farther away from him was riding up with the driver. She was most likely glad of the chance to be rid of him, to have a London Season, to meet the man of her dreams — the *young* man of her dreams.

Satisfied that he was doing the right thing and that Aurora was content, Windham pulled his hat over his eyes and went to sleep.

He didn't want her. He didn't even want to discuss the London journals with her.

He'd never wanted her, of course. He'd never wanted any wife, or he would have had one long ago. Aunt Thisbe thought his first countess had died four or five years previously, surely enough time to find a suitable bride if he had any desire to step into parson's mousetrap again. Now he obviously couldn't wait to leap out of it, the way he had the driver springing the horses.

Aurora couldn't blame him. Quite simply, she was not worthy to be Windham's wife. Why, her lack of sophistication had already driven him to drink, and she'd proven herself anything but demure, dignified, or docile, qualities an earl must require of a bride. She'd made him angry, to boot, by booting him from her bed. No, she could not blame him for wishing to be rid of

57

her. Neither could she let him see her tears. Windham was too nice a man to burden with guilty feelings. He'd pity her. Heavens, he might even pity her enough to reconsider, and then he'd be miserable for the rest of his days. No, Aurora could not do that to such a fine gentleman. She kept her eyes firmly on the magazine in her lap. So what if it was a journal on sheep shearing? If she wasn't going to be a countess, the saints knew she needed another career.

How could he think that she should be presented to London's beau monde, and by a duchess, no less? She'd be nothing but a *Phoxinus phoxinus,* a minnow in a pool of glittering goldfish. No, she did not belong among London's upper elevations. But the scandal in Bath would be devastating to her aunt and uncle if she had the funds to return there, which she did not. She had no other relations she could beg for sanctuary, no friend to invite her for a long visit — like a lifetime.

Perhaps the duchess could help her find a position. Yes, that's what she would do, Aurora decided. She'd throw herself on the mercy of this unknown woman, who'd much rather find her a job, Aurora was certain, than find her part of the family.

Windham would not like her going out to

work, Aurora knew. It would neither suit his notions of what was right nor satisfy his sense of responsibility for her welfare. But if he dissolved the marriage, she reasoned, he had no say in her disposal. The blasted man could not have it both ways. And she was glad to be getting out of such an uncomfortable marriage anyway, Aurora told herself, biting on her handkerchief lest she start sobbing. She'd be much better off, gainfully employed, than wed to a man who snored!

London was filthy. The very air was dark and dirty. No wonder so many Londoners came to Bath for their health. The sickly on the street corners, though, could never afford the spa, and the wealthy in their gold-trimmed carriages, their furs and lace, seemed hale enough to Aurora. And there were so many carriages! All were traveling at top speed, it seemed, as if the Quality had to hurry lest they miss a moment of frivolity. It was a marvel that the coaches were not constantly crashing into one another. From the shouts and curses, perhaps they were. Her head was spinning from the sights, sounds, and smells — and Windham's smiles at her openmouthed astonishment. At her first sights of the buildings of Mayfair, she took the houses for royal palaces, government offices, or museums. The earl expected her to live in one of those mansions?

Their carriage pulled up at one of the most imposing.

"Havermore House," the groom announced, letting down the steps.

For all her gentle birth, her mother and Aunt Thisbe having a marquess for an uncle, Aurora thought she'd be more comfortable going around to the rear entrance like a servant or a tradesman. Her gloves were soiled from the newspapers' ink, her hair was coming undone, and her lemon-yellow traveling costume that had seemed so fine in Bath now appeared to be frumpish and out of fashion.

"You'll do," Windham said when she appeared reluctant to leave the safety of the carriage. His casual compliment helped stiffen her resolve as she walked beside him to the servants' entrance, since the knocker was off the front door, and no one answered the earl's raps and shouts. Only a carpenter was in the kitchen when they arrived there, hammering away at high shelves he was installing. Her Grace had gone to her daughter's lying-in in Ireland, the man reported when they managed to gain his attention, and might stay through the summer — until the house renovations were completed, anyway.

Damn, Kenyon cursed as he led Aurora back to the carriage. What the devil was he to do with her now? He knew no other dowagers well enough to ask such a favor, and he was not about to leave the chit with any of the willing widows of his acquaintance, not that they'd be willing to take in a beautiful young innocent.

He definitely could not take her to his own town house. Warriner House had been bachelor quarters since Genevieve had run off. Aurora's reputation would not survive the night, especially since there was not one female servant in the place to lend the minimum countenance. Besides, his brother's army friends were liable to wander in at odd moments, knowing they'd always find a clean bed and a hot meal. Those choice spirits were liable to consider her dessert.

The Clarendon and the Pulteney were out, as the premier hotels would not accept an unaccompanied young female. His own company would, of course, label her a lightskirt. Hell and thunderation. He couldn't just leave her at some lesser establishment either, for who knew what dirty dish would accost her, or convince the gullible little peagoose to run off and get married? He finally chose the Grand, a newer hotel near Green Park which, while respectable, might not be so nice in its requirements. Besides, he was less likely to run into anyone he knew there.

The concierge did not bat an eyelash when the earl requested facing suites, not attached. "Miss McPhee's aunt will be joining her, along with her maid," Kenyon explained. A leather purse pushed across the registration desk made further explanations, such as the aunt's name and direction, unnecessary.

Aurora was simply glad to be out of the coach. Her rooms were well appointed and clean, and far more expensive than she could possibly afford. Without the duchess to help her find a position, she had no idea what to do. When Windham announced he was going to call on his solicitor, therefore, Aurora said she'd go along. Perhaps she'd locate an employment agency along the way.

"No, this is my affair. You'll do better here."

The annulment of her marriage was none of her concern? "If I cannot go along with you, I'll just take a walk in the park, I suppose."

"By yourself? Your maid is not even here yet. Gads, woman, do you know nothing? A female never goes anywhere unescorted in London."

"Of course I know that. I intended to ask that nice footman who carried up my valise to go along. I am sure no one would dare molest me, he was that tall and broad-shouldered."

Kenyon took her with him to the solicitor's office.

Mr. Juckett was an older man with spectacles perched on his hooked nose and tufts of white hair rimming his bald head. He had diplomas on the wall and law books on every inch of his desk. And he was no help at all.

When Kenyon introduced Aurora as Miss McPhee, the young woman who had last fallen into Harland Podell's coils, the lawyer looked at her with sympathy. "Ah, when you rode out in such a hurry, I had hoped you'd be in time to save the unfortunate female from such an unhappy hobble."

"Yes, well, we need to know about getting her marriage annulled."

"But I thought you understood, my lord, that a bigamist's subsequent marriages are immediately null and void, by virtue of being illegal, the same as your sister's. It's as if it never took place, and any children of such a union are declared illegitimate by virtue of their parents not being wed. I am sorry, miss," he said to Aurora.

She tried to explain that it wasn't that

marriage they were trying to have set aside. "You see, another gentleman kindly stepped forward with a special license in time to avert a terrible scandal."

"Good for him. And for you, too, miss, I am sure."

"But then Miss McPhee decided they wouldn't suit," Kenyon put in, and went on in a hurry before she could interrupt. "The second marriage was not consummated either, of course, so there is no question of children."

"I see." The solicitor polished his glasses, perhaps hoping to make good on his statement of understanding. To his mind, the female should be happy with a husband, any legitimate husband.

Mr. Juckett wiped so hard at his spectacles, Aurora feared he'd wear the lenses away. "My lord, if I might speak to you in private?"

Aurora raised her chin. "It is my marriage" — with a glare to Kenyon for not acknowledging his own participation in the event — "so I would hear what's discussed."

Mr. Juckett looked for guidance to Lord Windham, who shrugged. The solicitor cleared his throat. "Yes, well, that's a common misapprehension, it is, that . . .

that non-consummation is proper grounds for annulment. But what the law means is that . . . ah, consummation shall be impossible to complete."

"Of course it is, with him staying across the hall."

Kenyon chuckled, which earned him glares from both Aurora and Mr. Juckett. The solicitor addressed Aurora, although his bald pate turned scarlet in embarrassment. "Physically impossible, as certified by examining physicians in the female's case."

"Oh, dear," Aurora whispered, knowing she would fail such a test, if she did not die of mortification.

At the same time, Kenyon declared, "Miss McPhee shall not be subject to such indignities."

Mr. Juckett nodded. "Then the man must give a sworn avowal that he is, ah, incapable of fathering a child."

Kenyon groaned. He'd have to declare himself unmanned? Hellfire and damnation! And enough opera dancers could refute the claim. "Impossible."

"There is the insanity clause." The solicitor steepled his fingers. "If you wouldn't mind having yourself declared insane, Miss McPhee, you might still have the marriage set aside."

"Gammon, man, Miss McPhee may be addlepated for getting into the fix; she is not attics-to-let."

Aurora did not know whether to be pleased or insulted. She did know she was not alone in this sinking ship on the sea of matrimony, nor was she the only one fit for Bedlam. "Please, sir, there has to be another way."

Mr. Juckett rubbed the bridge of his nose, thinking. "Tell me, miss, did your parents agree to this marriage?"

"My parents are long dead. My aunt and uncle formally adopted me years ago, and, yes, they witnessed the marriage ceremony."

"And did you give your own true name?"

"Of course."

He shook his head. "Then I am afraid you were legally married, and married you shall stay."

The earl sighed and stood. "Then, Mr. Juckett, I take great pleasure in presenting you to Aurora Warriner, Countess of Windham." While the solicitor bounded to his feet, bowed, and babbled out his felicitations, Kenyon placed a sheet of paper on the man's desk. "Here is the notification for the newspapers, if you would be so good as to see it inserted. And begin drawing up settlements and such. I have the name of the McPhee family's solicitor here in London. I am sure he'll be in touch."

And then they were in the carriage again, married again.

The poor man was stuck with her, Aurora lamented, trying to keep the grin from her face. How sad.

The poor puss was stuck with him, Kenyon despaired, hurrying her into the hotel before he did a jig right there in the street. Too bad.

Chapter Six

A gentleman of three decades should not have to go courting. He should indicate his interest by a smile, a soft, not quite accidental touch. The lady in question should answer the unspoken question with a nod, or a gentle brush of their bodies, a promise of what was to come. So Kenyon's relationships had always developed in the past.

But marriage was not mistressing, and a wife was not affair fare, so a-wooing he would go. The earl was not about to scribe love poems to Aurora's earlobes, dainty and delicious though they might be, nor to her honey-colored, arched eyebrows. He'd not shower her with costly baubles — although he did wonder if he could match her sunny-day-skies eyes to sapphires — or pay her flowery compliments. His bride would sniff at Spanish coin. What was left? Dancing attendance at shopping expeditions and social dos? Lud, he was too old for that nonsense.

Win her he would, however, now that he'd wed her. Kenyon merely needed to prove himself worthy of Aurora's regard, by proving that he trusted, respected, and revered the mutton-headed Miss McPhee. He had absolutely no idea of where to start, except it shouldn't be in London's fish bowl. He was not about to have the entire *haute monde* witness him making a cake of himself over some starchy-scrupled snip of a female. He'd have to take her to Windrush, his family seat in Derby, where only his sister and his lifelong retainers could watch him try to wheedle the widgeon into his bed.

He couldn't bundle her off on another journey today, Kenyon decided, although she'd been a regular Trojan on the way from Bath. Aurora didn't chatter or complain that he slept, or suffer carriage sickness. His first wife, Genevieve, had always insisted on stopping every half hour, and being entertained between times. Miss McPhee just might turn out to be a restful sort of female, when she was not turning his life upside down. And once he overcame her maidenly misgivings.

There were other reasons he could not leave London on the instant — the marriage settlements, for one, and discovering information about his brother for another. Besides, Kenyon needed to spend some time at his own house, making arrangements for his trunks and valet and horses and messages. He could make a start in the few hours before dinner.

Kenyon decided that he'd also make a start in showing Aurora that he had confidence in her intelligence and her honor by leaving her alone at the hotel, her proper Bath maid having arrived.

"But what shall I do?" Aurora wanted to know. "I have read all the papers, and Baggins has unpacked all the boxes."

"You could work on your embroidery, I suppose," he offered, since every lady of his acquaintance had a workbasket or tambour frame nearby.

"I gave up on needlework ages ago. Aunt Thisbe is the only one in the family with any talent in that regard."

Yes, Kenyon thought, she had enough talent to drive a man to lascivious thoughts over lizards! "Well, what about the lending library? You'd enjoy taking out a subscription, I'd wager. Or you could go shopping, as long as you take the maid along." No female had ever turned down that pastime, to his knowledge. Still, his bride was looking like an abandoned kitten. "I realize you had a large circle of friends in Bath to visit with and none here, but why don't you go have calling cards made up, for the time when you do meet some proper people?"

Dash it, she was just shaking her head no. "Confound it, Aurora, do what any other well-off woman does — go spend your blunt. Purchase a new wardrobe or practice good deeds. I shall return by dinner."

He was halfway out the door of her sitting room when a small voice stopped him in his tracks. "But I have no money to spend."

Damn, damn, damn! Any other female would have had his purse in her hands hours ago. He'd forgotten Aurora's innocence and inexperience, again. How could he be so insensitive as to make her ask, nay, nearly beg him for funds? Kenyon pulled a leather pouch out of his coat pocket and handed it to her. "This is for incidentals only, gratuities to servants and the like. For anything else you wish to purchase, merely direct the bills to me. Later we'll establish an allowance so you don't have to come asking for pin money."

The purse weighed as much as a *Sciurus vulgaris*, a red squirrel. "It's too much."

"It's nothing. I'll fetch more from the town house when I instruct the servants to clean the place from top to bottom, pending their new mistress's arrival." All traces of feminine apparel, exotic scents, or inebriated soldiers would have to go. "Don't

71

worry, I can stand the nonsense."

"But I can't take your money."

The earl took her by the shoulders, trying to decide whether to kiss her or shake her. Instead, he merely said, "You are my lady, Aurora, my wife. You will never want for anything as long as I live, or after, according to the marriage settlements I am having drawn up. What I have is yours."

So she purchased a horse that was too old to pull its master's wagon, a cart full of wilted flowers from a girl who was coughing too badly to hawk them to passersby, a tray of meat pastries for the one-legged veteran and his ragged friends on the corner, and a boy.

She didn't mean to purchase the boy, not precisely, just hire the street urchin for the afternoon, but he declared he was hers now, not belonging to anyone else, which meant he was Windham's too, Aurora supposed. She was sure Kenyon wouldn't mind, for Ned Needles was such a handy sort of boy to have around. Ned had approached her when she and Baggins left the hotel, offering to find her a hackney or direct her to the best bargains in lace, the nearest glovemaker, or the prettiest selection of gowns, sewn by two sisters who were supporting their ailing parents and nine younger siblings. That's why they called him Needles, he'd explained, to Baggins's severe disapproval, 'cause he could find anything. Anything she needed in all of London, Ned was her man for locating it.

Smiling, Aurora had handed the ragamuffin a coin for his recommendation of a lending library, and in no time at all she was being bowed into Hatchard's, where her husband's name placed a world of books at her disposal. Despite her new friend's promise that he could show her all the sights, Aurora selected a few London guidebooks for now, which Ned was waiting outside to carry for her. And to tell her about Gunther's ices, which they then had to sample, to Baggins's disgust. But it was Ned Needles who bargained with the drayman over his decrepit horse, and who hired the one-armed soldier to lead it back to the Grand Hotel. He even knew a deaf printer who'd have her calling cards delivered before she could say Jack Rabbit. Ned also set a fair price for the flower girl, else Aurora would have emptied her purse.

"No, m'lady, you can't go givin' all that blunt in one swoop. There be lots of folks what need a share. I'll find 'em for you. The ones what be honest beggars, don't you know. Coo, you need me, lady, else you'd

73

get diddled proper."

And Ned needed a bath and a pair of shoes and a place to stay and reading lessons, he was such a bright boy. Why, he could grow up to be a Bow Street Runner with his aptitude, and Windham's sponsorship.

"Bloody hell, he's a waif off the streets!" The earl did not appear pleased with his new dependent. "And filthy to boot. And the management of the hotel is complaining of the lines of beggars waiting outside for you, and —"

"They were waiting for you. I had no idea what to do with all those people in search of positions."

"What am I, an employment agency?" Windham was trying to hold on to his temper; shouting at the peahen was not his idea of turning Aurora up sweet. Was it just a few hours ago that he'd promised himself he'd woo his bride into submission? 'Twould be a miracle if he did not wring her neck! Pasting a smile on his face, he asked, "And just what the deuce am I supposed to do with a horse that can barely hold its head up, much less pull a cart?"

They were having dinner in the sitting room of Aurora's suite, and she could tell Kenyon wasn't really angry because he kept smiling at her. And he *had* sent a lot of the unemployed soldiers over to his town house to help with the cleaning, since they'd be moving sooner than he'd planned, with the hotel management's encouragement. He even got Ned to agree to a bath, by banishing him until he was clean and free of vermin. Truly her husband was a kind and generous man, despite his blustering. He was beautiful, besides, in the formal evening dress that his valet had brought from Warriner House, handsome being much too insipid a word for such magnificence. Of course Aurora had found him attractive in the altogether, but she would not think about that, not for a month. They should be good friends by then. She would also not dwell on the fact that his valet had unpacked the earl's bags in the other bedchamber of her suite, not the one across the hall.

Finished with his soup, Kenyon brought his quizzing glass to his eye. "This hotel is never going to be a success at this rate. All the flowers are wilted." Then he studied the young person waiting to take the covers off the next course.

Noting his raised brow, Aurora took a drink from her water glass and said, "That's Judith, my maid."

Judith bobbed a curtsy. Kenyon nodded

politely, but addressed his wife. "Correct me if I am in error, but isn't your maid, Margaret Baggins, a proper, gray-haired woman of middle years?" He knew dashed well she was, for he'd hired the woman precisely because of her respectability.

"Oh, Baggins found that she missed Bath, my lord. She found London agitating to her nerves."

London or Lady Windham? he wondered. From the evidence awaiting his return to the hotel, Aurora's afternoon had been enough to daunt the staunchest soul. But Aurora was going on. "Happily, Ned Needles found me Judith, who had been employed as abigail to two sisters making their come-outs this Season. Wasn't it lucky that she was available?"

Lucky wasn't quite how he would have described the young woman's availability. With his looking glass now dangling from its ribbon, he drawled, "Were you aware, my pet, that your new maid is increasing?"

Aurora leaned forward. "Ssh, Kenyon. She'll hear you."

He edged his chair nearer to hers conspiratorially and whispered back, "I think she knows it."

"It wasn't her fault. The two young ladies had an older brother, the bounder. Judith was tossed out, while the libertine was merely sent back to university. That's not fair!"

"It never is," Windham agreed. "But how do you intend to right the wrong done to the girl? You do know you cannot keep her on as your dresser, don't you?"

"Of course, but I could not let her go to the poorhouse, could I? I thought you'd have the answer."

"I suppose I should be warmed by your confidence in me, my dear, but I have already saved one damsel in distress. That's my limit. I'm not taking a page from Podell's book, not even for you, Aurora."

"I didn't mean you should marry her, silly. I just thought you might know of some kind family that would take her in for a few months or something."

"I suppose she may stay on long enough to travel to Derby with us, if that's what you wish. There is always an empty cottage or an old pensioner who needs assistance with chores."

"I knew you could make things right!" Aurora leaned over the table and kissed his cheek.

"Hmm, I wonder how you'd show your gratitude if I found a home for your pet pickpocket, Ned."

Aurora laughed, blushing at her own daring. "Needles is no thief. And he found his own home. He's going to be my page."

"Fustian. Pages went out of fashion with the Middle Ages."

"Chivalry lives on," she told him, patting his arm before reaching for her fork, "so why not page boys?"

She thought of him as a knight in shining armor? Kenyon's heart swelled. So did other organs, to think the night might yet end amorously. He moved his chair closer still.

"So how was your afternoon?" Aurora asked hurriedly, before he could press her further.

Kenyon sighed, but addressed himself to the veal roulades instead of the delectable morsel at his side. "Not quite so eventful as yours, I daresay. The doddering old fools at the War Office have no news of my brother's release, and your family's solicitor confirms that you have no fortune. Had no fortune, that is, for mine is enough for both of us. At least I thought it would be, before you set out to give it all away." He quickly held up one hand. "I am teasing, my dear." He was also intending to get her out of Town before London's underworld discovered what an easy mark his mutton-headed wife was.

"You're truly not upset about my lack of dowry, Kenyon?"

He raised her hand — the one not holding the fork — and kissed her fingers. "A good heart is worth more than all the gold on earth. On the other hand, I still cannot help wondering about Podell's motives. Don't fly up in the boughs, my dear, but the man was a confirmed cad and a wanted criminal. He'd not have chanced a public wedding, with the banns being called three times and published for all to see, unless he expected a windfall in return, no matter how fond he might have been."

"I have been thinking of what you said earlier, too, and I have to conclude that Harland never truly loved me, despite his oaths of eternal devotion. A man truly in love wouldn't lie or cheat or chance destroying his beloved's reputation the way he did. But I had no fortune for him to be hunting, so I have concluded that he . . . he simply desired me."

Now Kenyon made the biggest mistake of his life, after marrying Genevieve and trying to ride that man-hating stallion when he was seventeen. He regarded his pretty young wife through his quizzing glass, noting the demure, high-necked gown that hid a sweet but far from voluptuous figure, the clear complexion innocent of cosmetics, the honest blue eyes, and he laughed.

Which was indeed a very big mistake, unless he had been wishing to create a new style of neckcloth: the *trône d'asparagus.*

Chapter Seven

"Go away. I don't want to see you."

"Then how are we going to get to know each other, my pet?"

"I don't care if I ever get to know you, you insensitive clod. In fact, the more I do know of you, the less I like, so you would do better on your own side of the door."

"But I cannot apologize through the wood, Aurora. Besides, you missed dessert. I brought a bowl of strawberries and cream."

"Fresh strawberries?"

"Large, ripe, juicy ones. And fresh, sweet cream — perhaps from the cows right nearby in Green Park."

Aurora opened the door, accepted the tray, and would have shut the door in his face if her hands were free. As if he could read her mind, Kenyon stepped inside the room before she had the chance to close the barrier between them again. He noted the angry spots of color still staining her cheeks, as if a child wearing mittens had played in the rouge pot, and said, "I do sincerely apologize, you know."

She put the tray down on an occasional table and went to stand by the fireplace, away from him. "And I regret acting so childishly, throwing food at you. I don't know what came over me." Of course she did; it was the realization that she could never be the wife he wanted.

"No, I should never have laughed. But I was not belittling your desirability, my dear. Lud knows I harbor lustful thoughts of you myself, after the sampling last night."

"No, your honor demanded to brand me as yours, as you explained then. You'll beget your heirs, doing your duty, without ever believing that any man would develop a . . . a burning passion for me."

"Widgeon." He followed her to the fireplace and took her in his arms. When she did not resist, he kissed her, stealing her breath, if not her wits. "There," he said, his own breathing none too steady, "you could incite passion in a dead man, I'd swear." He placed her hand over his chest, where his shirt was open at the neck, his cravat and coat having been sent to the laundry. "Feel the heat? I do not burn for every attractive woman I meet. You did that."

Aurora snatched her hand away, but not

before noticing that the hair on his chest was darker than the hair on his head. It felt different, too — springy, and, yes, warm. Not as warm as she was feeling, though. She clasped her hands together, making sure they did not trespass where her mind was wandering. The heat had to be from the coal fire, so she moved away from the mantel, but that way was the bed. Oh, dear. "But if I, ah, elicit licentious thoughts in a gentleman like yourself, then why do you insist that Lieutenant Podell had other motives?"

Kenyon smiled at her nervous pacing and helped himself to a strawberry. "Because if all he wanted was your body, my dear, he would have taken it. The man had no honor, no principles to stop him from having his pleasure."

"What, like that dastard cornering Judith on the servants' stairs?"

"Oh, he would not have resorted to ravishment. Podell was contemptible, but he was a coward at heart. No, you would have surrendered your maidenhood in a hurry if he'd asked."

Now she was affronted again. "I never!"

"So I discovered, but you would have."

"How could you think I am that kind of woman!"

He took another bite of the fruit. "You

were the one who declared yourself ruined, remember."

"Yes, but I only permitted him such liberties because he said he loved me, and I expected an offer any moment. I would never have permitted a gentleman such license otherwise, you may be sure."

"Fustian. You are a passionate woman. We proved that last night, too."

"You plied me with champagne."

"No, my lady wife, your blood runs warm in your veins, though you are not aware of it yet. A practiced rake could seduce you in a moment, despite your scruples, and without rendering you disguised."

"Never." Now if Aurora were more sophisticated, she would have known not to issue such a challenge. Then again, she would have known that the whole conversation had been a trap. "Never," she repeated.

The gauntlets were down. He smiled, a knowing grin. Such a look a fox might have worn when the rabbit left his last bolt-hole. Windham's green eyes were alight with dancing sparks, but Aurora would not back down. So when he said, "Let's sit on the chaise, eat our strawberries, and discuss it further, shall we?" she had no choice but to follow.

She sat as far from him as possible,

smoothing her skirts so not even an inch of fabric brushed against his satin breeches. Of course she could not help noticing how the smooth fabric molded itself to his well-muscled thighs. She inched over till she was in peril of falling off the sofa. But now she could not reach the strawberries on the table next to him.

"Oh, would you like one?" he asked, selecting a large berry, dipping it in the cream and holding it out. She reached for the fruit, but instead the earl brought it to her lips, brushing it against them, leaving a trail of cream for her to lick off.

He licked his own lips, as if in anticipation.

"I don't think . . ."

He ignored her. "Sweet, hmm? But not as sweet as your lips." He still held the berry, offering it to her again. She took a bite, and he ate the rest. Staring at her mouth, he licked the juice from the corner of his own mouth while she watched. "Hmm. Soft and moist and delicious."

Aurora swallowed, loudly.

Then he selected another berry. But this time he wiped the cream off with his finger and sucked on it, reminding her of how their tongues had met. She almost choked on the berry he finally fed her.

Kenyon slowly licked the cream off his next strawberry, making those contented humming sounds. Aurora could only watch, recalling how he had kissed her breasts through the fabric of her nightgown, licking as . . . as though he was licking the strawberry. Heavens!

He held the next one an inch from her lips. "Think of how good it will taste, how your tongue will wrap around it, keeping the flavor. How satisfying it will be. The anticipation is often the best part, isn't it? You can almost feel the sweetness spread from your mouth to your throat and down to those hidden depths."

Aurora couldn't take her eyes off his lips as he finally put the strawberry in her mouth, then withdrew it. And again, almost as if — "I think I have had enough strawberries. Any more and I am liable to get spots."

"Any more and you're liable to let me make love to you here on the rug in front of the fire." Kenyon reluctantly wiped his hands on a napkin. He'd made his point, but wasn't cad enough to press the advantage. "Admit it, Aurora. I could have seduced you tonight, without ever laying a finger on your rosy skin. You are a warm-blooded woman, so why are you denying us both the pleasure of that comfortable bed?"

Because she didn't want to be seduced; she wanted to be loved and cherished and esteemed. Because she did not want to be like every other woman he had lain with, her wedding lines notwithstanding. Aurora couldn't say any of that, of course. What she did say was, "I thought this was a discussion about Harland and his motives."

"He was not after simple sexual gratification."

There was nothing simple about it that Aurora could feel — and she was still feeling quivers down to her knees. But he was wrong; she might succumb to strawberries, but Harland had never made her feel like this, not by half. "What, then?"

"There has to be money somewhere. Perhaps from your father's family?"

"The Halles sent Papa out to India just before disowning him, I'm afraid. He had gambling debts, you see. I have avoided wagering my entire life, lest I become addicted to it, as he was reputed to be."

"Perhaps he gambled on something and died before he could collect? Podell might have discovered it somehow. Someone else in India might have known."

"The only one I know was Lord Phelan, but he was only there a month before contracting malaria. He left and took me and a nursemaid with him, I understand, because my mother was ill. He would have told me long ago if I was any kind of heiress."

"Someone else, then, someone who made a practice of knowing every tidbit about every Englishman in India. Did you ever meet Lady Anstruther-Jones? Her husband was an official of the Trading Company, and she was the unofficial British hostess."

"I left India before my second birthday; I really don't recall anything but the heat."

"No matter, Lady Anstruther-Jones will see us anyway. She enjoys chatting about her India days. I'll send around a note tomorrow morning, asking if we can call, shall I?"

Aurora shrugged. "If you wish, but I swear it's hopeless. You'd do better to drag Harland back and ask him."

"He should be halfway to Portsmouth by now, on his way to catch the next ship for Jamaica. Lord Phelan was going to escort him to make sure the loose screw didn't slip away, so perhaps your godfather learned something more. He said he'd call on us as soon as he returned to Town. We'll visit the viscountess tomorrow. If anyone knows anything, she will. Meantime, the evening is still young. I thought we might . . . might . . ." He'd been going to suggest cards or something, but Lud, she didn't gamble. "Discuss color schemes. That's it, I want to redecorate the master suite at Warriner House and need to know your preferences. I brought some fabric swatches back with me."

Goodness, Aurora thought, if strawberries could rouse such a fever in her blood, imagine what havoc silks and brocades could wreak. She quickly yawned. "I'm sorry, my lord, but that will have to wait for morning, also. I'm not used to Town hours yet, you know, and I am much too tired. It's been a long day, hasn't it?"

And it looked to be a longer night, but Kenyon was not giving up. He gave her a chaste good night kiss on the cheek, and then he intended to give her thirty minutes to prepare for bed. He changed into his nightshirt meanwhile, then paced in his own bedroom, peering at the clock.

Before twenty minutes had passed, he heard a scratch on his door. Thinking his valet must have suicidal tendencies in returning after he'd been dismissed for the night, Kenyon yanked the door open. "What the devil do you —"

The devil indeed! There stood his wife in a sheer gown, limned in the glow from the firelight. Speechless, he could only watch as she took a few steps into the room, turning slowly. He'd wager that she didn't know how the light behind her made her nightdress almost transparent, from the dark peaks of her breasts to the darker triangle between her thighs. He'd lose.

Aurora knew precisely what she was doing, licking her lips and shaking her head till the blond tresses flowed down her back. She waited only until she was positive she'd stirred his interest, by the stirring of the front of his white lawn nightshirt. Staring pointedly at the pointed evidence, she smiled and skipped back to the door. "You see, my lord, two can play the game. I have managed to seduce you, without even saying a word."

He had to laugh. It was either that or cry. The chit had bottom — and top, and everything in between. Playing knight errant hadn't been an error after all, it was appearing, though she'd lead him a merry dance. Well, she'd had her jig; now it was time for a nice, slow waltz.

He waited until the sounds of movement stopped, when her maid called good night and the hall door shut with a click. Then he tiptoed back across the darkened sitting room toward Aurora's bedchamber. Before he got there, though, he discerned a lump on the floor. He went back for his quizzing glass. Devil take it if he wasn't going to have to pay for a new carpet, with all the to-and-fro.

Closer inspection revealed the lump to be a half-grown, half-starved boy. There was Ned, asleep on the floor in front of his mistress's closed door like a faithful watchdog. And there went Kenyon's hopes.

Ned's hair was still wet, and his cheek was red from scrubbing. The earl went back and fetched another blanket to cover the lad. Returning one more time to his own cold, empty room, Windham wondered, had he ever really wanted a restful wife? *This* restful?

Chapter Eight

A female of a certain age was entitled to a certain number of eccentricities. An old woman of infinite wealth was forgiven an infinite number of whims. Lady Anstruther-Jones was of the latter class of character. Hortense had been concubine to an Oriental prince, favorite in a sultan's harem, and first wife to a tribal chieftain before marrying her India nabob viscount. Or else she'd been a vicar's daughter from Devon. No one seemed to recall, or care. With Anstruther-Jones gone to his final reward, the lady was finally able to indulge herself. Now she was titled an Original. Her notions of gracious entertaining, for example, were an eclectic blend of rites and rituals from any number of ancient societies, or guidebooks.

One never wore shoes in her house. Silk slippers were offered to guests in the entry hall in summer, thick woolen socks from Yorkshire mills in winter. Granted, the lady had white fur rugs, but the rule held for the bare-floors areas, too. And no one sat on chairs. Guests couldn't, for none were available, only thick cushions. Ladies as well as gentlemen were invited, nay, encouraged to smoke, as their hostess was never without a long pipe carved out of ivory. No one called without an invitation — or left without a token of her esteem. Her regular guests quickly learned not to admire anything in the house, for they'd be leaving with it. To refuse was to insult Lady Anstruther-Jones, which meant social disaster, since Hortense had become one of London's luminaries, despite barely leaving her house. No matter that you were expected to reciprocate with a present of equal value, you graciously carted away the elephant-foot umbrella stand or the brass gong that rang so loudly the windows shook — next door. Exchanging gifts was a tradition from the East, Hortense always claimed, but it could have been East Anglia. Finally, as Lord Windham explained to Aurora, one never, *ever*, arrived without a gift in hand. Hence their shopping expedition.

Lady Anstruther-Jones had responded to Kenyon's note with an invitation to pay a morning call, which meant sometime after noon. Of course she would be delighted to meet with Windham and his wife, since they were the premier topic of conversation now that the notice of their marriage was in the papers, and Lady Anstruther-Jones was the premier gossip.

Not wishing to waste an opportunity to get into his wife's good graces, and not daring to leave her alone to get into more scrapes, Kenyon was therefore taking his lady shopping, just what he least enjoyed. "I suppose it will have to be jewelry, though the old dragon must have a lairful of gems by now. I cannot imagine what else she could want or need. I never bought you a wedding gift, either." He reluctantly headed the curricle toward Rundell and Bridges, where he'd doubtless stand around for hours, until it was time to pay for Aurora's choices. Since she seemed to possess nothing but a string of pearls, he expected to spend a great deal of time and a great deal of money. She was wearing her mother's wedding ring, for he'd refused to allow the one Podell had purchased to touch her finger. That should take another hour, judging from his past experience in purchasing finery for a female.

"I knows a place what has pretty gewgaws the old lady might like," Ned offered helpfully from his tiger's place behind the driver's bench.

Kenyon clamped his jaws shut. He hadn't

wanted the boy along in the first place. Just what he needed, a diminutive duenna. Now he was to be bear-led by a barely civilized brat, one who hadn't the least notion of what was due a lady of Quality like Lady Anstruther-Jones or Lady Windham. "I'm sure Rundell's will suffice."

"I don't know about no soft ice, but No More Morris has sparklers what should turn the old bat up sweet so she tells you what you wants to know. Real pretty, they are, and half the price of what those top-lofty, thieving jewelers in Mayfair charge. That's why they calls 'im No More Morris. 'E sells stuff for what it's worth, 'n no more."

"Paste, I am sure," Kenyon scoffed, but Aurora was all for going to look. "No reason not to save money," she said from lifelong habit learned at her Scots uncle Ptolemy's knee.

"An' No More Morris wouldn't cheat no friend of mine. He's a collector, don't you know. Only has the best."

And he only had two gold balls hanging outside his ramshackle, rundown shop. The other had fallen to the ground, some time in the last century. "It's a deuced pawn shop!" Kenyon complained as Ned went to the horses' heads.

"But not a fence, guv'nor. I wouldn't

bring 'er ladyship to no criminal ken, don't you know. All the folks what bring their merchandise to No More has swallowed a spider, legitimate. Most are swells, too."

Aurora needed a translation.

"Your protégé seems to believe that all the goods herein come from the homes of the upper classes, those who find themselves temporarily financially embarrassed."

She nodded, taking his arm as they walked through the narrow door and hoping he would stop fretting about leaving his cattle in Ned's hands. "Debtors. I should think that selling off their heirlooms is preferable to going to Fleet Prison. At least their creditors might be paid."

Kenyon wasn't listening. "Great gods, is that a Tintoretto?" He had his quizzing glass out, examining the dark canvas in its heavy gold frame.

While he and Mr. Morris enthused over the painting's provenance, then moved on to examine what might be a Turner in better light, an unknown Madonna of the Italianate School, and a vase that No More wouldn't swear to being Ming, but looked to be a perfect match to one at Warriner House, Aurora wandered around, ignored.

The shelves were crowded and dusty, the

glass cases of jewelry so dirty she had a hard time viewing the contents, and the light so bad that she mistook a sleeping cat for a marble sculpture. Mr. No More Morris might be a collector, but he was no house-keeper.

Not knowing Lady Anstruther-Jones, of course, Aurora had no idea of the woman's taste, but couldn't find anything that she thought might be a suitable gift. The diamonds resembled crystal chandeliers, the pearls were the size of birds' eggs, and the emeralds looked like they belonged on Cleopatra's breastplate. No woman of refinement would wear such gaudy pieces, except to a masquerade.

Perhaps a well-traveled, elderly lady would like an antique book. Aurora picked one off a pile on the floor, only to have the gold-leafed cover come off in her hands. She sneezed, from the dust or the cat, and her husband looked up, as if suddenly remembering her existence. "One of these will be perfect for the viscountess. Why don't you pick out a necklace for yourself while Morris shows me what he has in the back room?"

There was more of the stuff? Aurora sighed, then dutifully regarded the jewelry again. She'd rather have the cat. On top of one of the cases, though, she spotted a gold filigree butterfly on a wooden base. Lifting it, she saw that a key on the bottom made the butterfly sway and turn to a tinkling little tune. Aunt Thisbe would adore it. Aurora held onto the music box, thinking to show Ned, so he could return for it once she had an allowance of her own and could afford to buy gifts for her aunt and uncle.

Kenyon and the proprietor returned to the shop's front room, both carrying stacks of paintings and portfolios. When Mr. Morris went back for the rest, and string to tie them with, the earl grinned at Aurora. "Can you believe I found a Leonardo sketch? I'm sure it's his, with the mirror writing. It's a lovely piece on its own, even if it does turn out to be by one of his students. And the price was too good to pass up. What a find this place is! I'll have to apologize to Needles, and make sure he doesn't tell anyone else about it. Did you find something you like?"

"Just this, for my —"

She held up the music box, but a collection of snuff boxes caught his eye. He had to squint to see them in the poor light. "Fine, fine, whatever you like, my dear."

Just then a shelf full of clocks started to toll the hour. Some chimed, some gonged, one had a little bird that warbled, and another was in the shape of a ship that rocked. They did not all finish at the same time, either. But they did remind the earl that they were expected all the way across the City. "Confound it, we'll be late if we don't hurry. Morris, add her ladyship's purchase to my bill, and send the lot to the Grand Hotel." He tucked the small Italian Madonna under his arm and led Aurora out to where Ned was waiting with the curricle.

"All right 'n tight, m'lord. I walked 'em just like you said."

"Good lad. We'll have to see about fitting you with a suit of livery."

Ned's thin chest swelled with pride. So did Aurora's. "Thank you, Kenyon," she said when Ned had scrambled up behind and they were under way again. "That's a better present than anything you could have bought me."

"What did I buy you, actually? I'm sorry I got so caught up in the artwork. I have been looking to add to the family's collection of paintings for years, without finding much of interest."

"I understand. I get that way in bookstores." She wound the music box to show him how it worked, but he could only spare a glance, since they were in traffic.

"That trumpery bit is what I bought you for a bride gift?"

"Actually you bought it for Aunt Thisbe. I thought it would go nicely with the butterfly collection."

"Thunderation, you must think me the worst kind of nip-cheese. Blister it, I meant to buy you something pretty this morning. A new wedding ring, at least. Now there's no time to get to the jeweler's."

"I don't mind, truly. I like wearing my mother's ring. I have so little of hers, you see, not even many memories."

As hard as it was to credit that a female was content with an insignificant gold band, Kenyon had to believe those guileless blue eyes. Still feeling guilty, though, he vowed to send for the Windham diamonds before another day had past. His loving first wife had financed her elopement to France with all of the other family pieces, but she'd left the diamonds at least. His sister had worn them for her come-out. Aurora should wear them for her introduction to the *ton*.

Meanwhile, he leaned back and called to Ned, "Bonnets. Where can I find bonnets in a hurry?"

"But there's no time, Kenyon, and I have two new hats already," she protested.

His grimace was opinion enough of her

headgear. The yellow ruched affair she wore yesterday had made her look like a dandelion, and today's was a blue coal scuttle. "Master Needles?"

"Left at the corner, guv, then straight for ten blocks. Mam'selle Marie will . . . will suffice."

His lordship's lips were twitching at Ned's quick study, but he asked, "A Frenchwoman?" After Genevieve, the entire breed was suspect.

"Mary Maloney. She be as French as Yorkshire puddin', Earl. But the gentry morts come down heavy for Frog legs."

"Frog legs?" Aurora thought of her uncle's beloved batrachians.

"He means the ladies will pay more for the cachet of French fashions."

"That's right, m'lord. Mary gets good cash for spoutin' a few mercies and wees."

"*Merci*'s and *oui*'s," Aurora said, correcting him.

"That's what I said. Turn here, m'lord, and down that alley. Mary can't afford no street-front rent, but she matches the styles of them what does." He hopped down to take the horses' leads. "You tell her Needles sent you, and that 'er ladyship is aces wiff me."

Aurora didn't need a translation. "Why,

101

thank you, Ned."

She didn't need three new bonnets, either, but she got them, nevertheless. "The Countess of Windham cannot be seen in the same hat every day," her husband declared. Besides, he was having fun. Picking out bonnets was not nearly as exciting as selecting Lady Anstruther-Jones's gift, but Kenyon was finding a challenge in creating his own masterpiece. Some brims shielded Aurora's fine, high cheekbones; some ribbons clashed with her eyes; a few permitted too many gold curls to show, which might tempt a man into touching them. His favorite was the tiny jockey-style cap with the blue feather that curled down, almost to the corner of her mouth. No, he really liked the straw bonnet with the silk forget-me-nots peeping under the brim. The lace-trimmed satin, though, lent her a sophistication and maturity befitting a married woman. Aurora was laughing as he and Marie discussed her finer points. It was good to see her so carefree.

"We'll take them all," he announced. "And parasols to match."

Aurora thought parasols were as silly an affectation as his looking glass, but naturally she did not say that. "Oh, I don't burn, so I have no need for a sunshade."

The parasols were not for the sun, it seemed, but to protect her from the stares and scrutiny of the gabble-mongers when they drove through the park.

"Surely no one would be so rude."

"Ruder," Kenyon swore, and Marie agreed. "They'll all be on tenterhooks to get a glimpse of the new countess, especially after word of the unconventional wedding arrives, which it will, every dowager and debutante having a bosom bow in Bath. You'll be happy to shield your face from their inspections. On the other hand, don't use the parasols too much. I want everyone to see what a beautiful bride I have."

He thought she was beautiful? Aurora floated to the carriage, not even noticing which new bonnet she wore.

Chapter Nine

"And remember, don't admire any of Hortense's treasures overmuch," Kenyon warned Aurora as they passed through the doorway of Lady Anstruther-Jones's house. "She'll simply give you a fan or a hair comb if you don't express interest in anything grander, and that will be fine."

In the marbled entry a footman took Kenyon aside to remove his boots, while a maidservant showed Aurora into a bamboo-papered chamber where she was offered a selection of soft-soled silk slippers. She chose a pair with turned-up toes, feeling that the more exotic, the better. She was a *Troglodytes troglodytes,* a common wren in the midst of peacocks. She might borrow a plume or two.

The butler who then bowed them into Lady Anstruther-Jones's presence wore a jeweled turban, the maids who sat on pillows near their mistress, ready to pour tea or serve the honey cakes, wore flowing robes of rainbow hues, and the viscountess herself wore an abbey's worth of gems at her throat and wrists and ears. She was a tiny woman for all that power, all that wealth, Aurora thought, and dwarfed by the ballroom-size room she inhabited. She was not rendered insignificant by the high ceilings or the thick white carpets, however, not with her loose saffron yellow pantaloons, which were eminently sensible for sitting on the floor.

"Don't even think of ordering a pair," Kenyon whispered, as Aurora gaped at the sight of a female in trousers, bobbling her curtsy and missing the introductions altogether.

She must have made the correct response, though, for they were invited to sit on adjoining pillows at some distance from their hostess. Aurora saw no way of doing so gracefully. She tried kneeling, then sinking sideways, only just managing to land on the pillow. Kenyon and her ladyship were sitting cross-legged, she saw, but her dress's skirt was just too narrow. With her feet sticking out in front of her like a jointed doll on a shelf, she fretted about her ankles showing. And the gaudy slippers made her feel like a court jester, not a courtly lady.

Sensing her anxiety, Kenyon spoke softly, for her ears only. "Relax. You outrank the old besom now."

So she did! Aurora wriggled her toes, just for the fun of it. She need not have fussed anyway. Lady Anstruther-Jones held a cane and wore spectacles with black lenses. The viscountess was blind, and they had brought her a painting!

Aurora scowled at Kenyon, who shrugged. "I haven't visited in ages, and I never heard why she stopped doing the social rounds. I'm not the one *au courant* with all the talk; she is. And her loss of sight hasn't kept her from knowing everything there is to know."

"But the gift!"

He looked at the smiling virgin in his lap, and could swear she was laughing at him — the Madonna, not his maiden bride, who was horrified that her very first call as Lady Windham was going to be a disaster.

Thinking frantically, Aurora gestured for a maid and sent the girl off with a message for Ned, who'd been sent to the kitchens while the horses were stabled. The maid returned with a bow, and with Aunt Thisbe's butterfly music box.

Lady Anstruther-Jones adored the little bibelot. Her long-nailed fingers could trace the filigree wings she'd never see again, and could play the music she'd never more perform. She wound and rewound the trinket while Kenyon paid his respects and their hostess asked after his sister, and if there was any news of his brother.

Aurora meanwhile, was able to look around. She didn't even worry that she was staring, for Lady Anstruther-Jones couldn't tell. And remembering Kenyon's instructions, she bit her lip to keep from exclaiming at the marvels in the room. To one side, ceiling-high palm trees were covered with lush blooms and trailing vines, just like a jungle. They couldn't be real. But why would there be so many windows in the roof, if not to let in the sun? Surely Lady Anstruther-Jones did not require light. Newfangled oil lamps stood in every corner of the room, and small braziers glowed from the trees' branches, hung with pots of steaming, scented water. She could feel her hair curling from the humidity, so the indoor forest must be real.

The black leopard near Lady Anstruther-Jones must be stuffed. No one would keep a panther in their parlor, would they? She prayed that, if it was not stuffed, at least it was satiated. A huge egg, which Aurora could only surmise was *Struthio camelus,* an ostrich, from her aunt's ornithology volumes, stood on a lotus pedestal closer to hand. Aurora had never seen an egg half so large, nor so intricately painted and carved. The gilded sides were hinged open, and an entire little village of ivory and jade figurines cavorted inside. Aurora had to cough to cover her gasp of admiration. Lud, Kenyon would kill her if she went into raptures over such a priceless piece. He'd have to sell Windrush to pay for a correspondingly valuable gift. She let her eyes move on, though she was aching to examine the egg more closely. How Aunt Thisbe would love to see such a thing.

One wall was hung with a collection of weaponry: curved blades, heavy swords that could have been at the Crusades, rapier-thin ones with blued steel, daggers with jewel-encrusted hilts, spears with feathers twined to their shafts. Aurora wouldn't have been surprised to find Excalibur among the masterpieces of the armorer's art. She *was* surprised Kenyon didn't pay them any attention, since most gentlemen seemed entranced by instruments of war. Perhaps he'd seen them enough times before that they had lost their fascination.

Aurora let her eyes move on, to cabinets filled with porcelains so delicate she could see light coming through behind them, to shelves loaded with figurines carved from precious stones, to piles of fabrics embroidered with stitches so fine fairies must have sewn them, and on and on and on. The room was almost as crowded as No More Morris's, without the dust. Aurora only wished she could get up and examine everything at her leisure. For once she wished she had Kenyon's quizzing glass. Instead she had to sit and listen while he told some faradiddle about her being a young friend of his sister's, whom he'd known for an age. Lying through his teeth, Kenyon said he'd been waiting to offer for her hand, but she'd grown weary, the impulsive puss, so he had to ride to Bath and snatch her out of another man's arms.

"You know how females get romantical notions. My darling wanted to be carried off over my saddle bow, but I convinced her to settle for a carriage."

Lady Anstruther-Jones nodded. "That's the Banbury tale you want me to tell, eh? It's a pretty one, though not very believable. Thought you'd do better than that. No matter, now you can tell me why you have come. On second thought, you have been doing all the talking, Windham. Let me hear from your bride. Miss McPhee, was it? Any relation to the Somerset McPhees?"

"Through the cadet branch only, ma'am, via Scotland. There is no communication between the families. My relations are from

Bath. They are amateur naturalists."

"Dabble in pond scum, do they?"

Kenyon grimaced. This was going worse than he'd hoped. But Aurora clapped her hands together. "Oh, you've heard of them! Aunt and uncle will be so proud! They feared no one read those scientific papers they work so hard over."

"I do keep up with the journals, don't you know. A female can't know too much. Remember that."

"Oh, yes, I have always believed it so, but not just for females. Education is never wasted, not even on men, and never finished."

Lady Anstruther-Jones nodded, setting her jewelry to clamoring like Mr. Morris's clocks. "That's right, I heard you were a bookish sort. Caused a near riot at Hatchard's yesterday, did you?"

Kenyon groaned. Of course Hortense would have heard about the melee in the midst of the *belle monde*.

"It was nothing like a riot," Aurora was explaining. "The man was abusing the poor old horse, right outside the bookseller's door as I was leaving the establishment. I went back in to seek help. The proprietor would not come to the unfortunate animal's aid."

"So you did, eh?"

Aurora caught herself nodding, which her hostess could not see, so said, "It was quite simple, really. The man only needed to be able to purchase another beast so he could work for a living to feed his family. Lord Windham had been generous, so I was able to pay the man the price of a younger, stronger horse."

"In view of all the other patrons, eh?"

"I was not aware anyone was watching. Certainly no one came to help move poor Magpie from the street. That's what caused the congestion, which caused various drivers to become irate, which, ah, caused the Watch to be sent for."

"Irate didn't half describe it, from what I heard. But they are always watching, the creatures with nothing better to do than find fault. They'll see anything you don't want them to. Remember that, too, missy."

"Yes, ma'am, I will."

"You like animals, do you?"

Worried over saying the wrong thing, and ending up with the stuffed leopard, which she was positive had been lying on its right side before, not its left, Aurora was noncommittal. "My aunt and uncle taught me to respect all of God's creatures, Lady Anstruther-Jones, from the tiniest to the

111

largest. I believe it is our duty to look after them, for, like poor Magpie, they cannot speak up."

"Good. I never could abide anyone who thought animals mere dumb brutes, made to serve mankind and nothing else. Shows a hard heart and a closed mind. Don't fall into that trap, missy."

"Oh, no, I won't."

"Good. I always say you can judge a person by how they treat beasties." The viscountess turned unseeing eyes toward Kenyon. "Is she pretty?"

Without pause, he answered, "No."

Aurora would have sunk to the floor, except she was already there.

"She's not pretty," the earl was going on. "She's beautiful, like springtime, full of golden sunshine and blue skies."

Ah. Aurora wiggled her toes in joy.

"And her mind? Gel's got to have a head on her shoulders if she's to keep a man's interest."

"Her mind?" Kenyon stroked his chin, pretending to think. "Quite frankly, her mind is totally incomprehensible to me." That may have been the only honest words to leave his mouth, except for calling Aurora beautiful.

Lady Anstruther-Jones slapped her leg

and laughed out loud. "Good, good. You'll never grow bored, then. Seems like you did something right for a change, Windham, after that mess you made the first time around. And you, missy, count your blessings. You've landed one of the finest catches in all of England."

"Yes, I know."

Kenyon shot her a look full of curiosity, but Lady Anstruther-Jones went, "Hmph! I can smell April and May from here. You take care not to lose that tender regard, Windham."

"Yes, ma'am. I'll try my damnedest."

"See that you do. Smoke?" She gestured for one of the serving girls to fill her own pipe when Kenyon and Aurora both refused. When it was lit, she nodded again. "Very well, you have my blessings on this odd alliance. I'm the last one to insist on an equal match, great wealth to high titles. Bah, better for everyone to spread the blunt around. Besides, desert nomads wouldn't breed a camel to its cousin the way Englishmen do, trying to keep the blue blood in the family. Now, what do you really want?"

Kenyon didn't bother trying to hide his motives. The old witch would see right through any fustian anyway, blind or not.

"Information, of course. My wife had relatives in India about twenty years ago. They are both dead now, but we were hoping you might tell us something about them."

"Elizabeth and Avisson Halle," Aurora elaborated. "She was Elizabeth Balcombe before her marriage."

Lady Anstruther-Jones flipped through the pages of memory. "Yes, I remember Elizabeth Balcombe. A lovely gal, somewhat in the manner you describe your wife, Windham. She came out to India with Halle when his parents tossed him out, though no one ever knew why. It seems everyone in London thought she'd marry George Ramsey, Lord Ratchford, or his brother Phelan, but that never came to pass. Ratchford was the better *parti,* by far. I knew Halle better, of course, for he worked for my husband, if you could call the pittance he did work."

"Could he have amassed a fortune there?" Kenyon wanted to know.

"What, looking to claim an inheritance for your new wife? I thought you were too well to pass for that nonsense. You'll grow cold at it anyway, for the man couldn't hold on to a shilling if it was glued to his thumb."

"We understood he gambled."

"He gambled and drank and whored. We

all felt sorry for Elizabeth, especially after her daughter died."

Kenyon and Aurora looked at each other. "Her daughter died?"

"That's right, an infant. Less than two, to my recollection. I have the letter she wrote to thank me for my condolences. Never threw anything away. My girls can find it if you want." Lady Anstruther-Jones puffed on her pipe, sending smoke rings to the tops of the trees. "Elizabeth was always a melancholy sort of female, never robust. She seemed to lose heart after the little girl's death, and passed on not long after."

"And their other child? Who took care of her?"

"Other child? I don't remember another child, boy or girl. No, I would have known because my maid's sister was their nursemaid. There was just the one, and Elizabeth doted on her, more's the pity."

Aurora could not understand, could not think what questions to ask. It was Kenyon who persisted. "And Halle? What happened to him? Could he have had a lucky streak, or a windfall at business?"

"Him? He took up opium, like other weak-willed wastrels before and after. That would have taken any brass he got his hands on. He died a few months after Elizabeth, to no one's regret. We had to take up a collection to bury the ne'er-do-well. No, if you're looking for a fortune, you'll have to seek elsewhere."

Kenyon thanked her, somehow, and got them through another few minutes of Lady Anstruther-Jones's reminiscences and advice, invitations to call again, and congratulations on the marriage, while Aurora caught her breath. White-faced and trembling, she managed to exchange parting pleasantries as if nothing of moment had been discussed. Finally the curricle was brought round and Kenyon handed her in.

He couldn't speak of what they had learned, not with Ned hanging over the back of the seat, but he could deuced well glare at his wife and the burden she carried. "Damn, I told you not to find favor with anything!"

Her nerves stretched as thin as the ribbon holding his cursed quizzing glass, Aurora snapped back, "What was I supposed to say when it landed in my lap?"

"Anything, by George, but 'Oh, what a nice monkey'!"

Chapter Ten

"No, I refuse to believe it." Aurora needed both hands to hold her teacup steady. They were in the sitting room of their hotel suite, trying to make sense of Lady Anstruther-Jones's information.

"Hortense may be many things, but she doesn't lie. She'd lose all credibility if she fabricated her stories." Kenyon was pacing between the fireplace and the window, window to fireplace. He was giving Aurora the headache, atop her other woes. He was also in the way of Tarlow, his valet, who was carrying the earl's belongings back across the hall, into the other suite.

Aurora waited for the valet to leave with his latest armload of folded shirts. "I cannot accept that Aunt Thisbe would have taken in any but her own sister's child."

"She might have believed what she wanted to believe. A childless woman with the opportunity to raise an infant after years of barrenness? She would have turned a blind eye to anything."

"No. Aunt Thisbe is a scientist, a searcher for truth. She would not have practiced such a deception." Her cup rattled in its saucer.

"Then why was she so quick to change the infant's name? The adoption was not necessary if the McPhees were legal guardians."

"I can understand why, if my father's name was in such ill odor. Perhaps he had creditors who would have dunned Uncle Ptolemy. Either way, Aunt Thisbe spent hours telling me stories of her sister, so I would remember the mother I never knew."

"Very well, she did not know," he conceded. "She thought she was taking in Elizabeth Halle's daughter. But face facts, Aurora, that daughter was dead. Someone else saw an opportunity to get his by-blow out of India, and leapt at the chance."

"No, again," Aurora insisted. "I have my mama's letter saying that she was sending me to Aunt Thisbe. She was not well enough to raise an infant, she wrote, and conditions in India were too unhealthful for a child. We always assumed she knew she was dying and wished her baby's well-being secured before it was too late. She loved me, my mother did. It's in her letters, along with the tearstains. I've cherished that knowledge my entire life and you shall not steal it from me."

It was bad enough to learn that her father was a wastrel, but Aurora had always known that, in her heart. Aunt Thisbe and Uncle Ptolemy had shielded her from the worst facts, but Aurora had heard the truth in their voices when they referred to him as "that dastard Halle." But to think that the pretty young girl in the portrait with Aunt Thisbe was not her mother? That her beloved aunt and uncle were not even blood kin? Aurora could not bear the idea.

"It's not I who would take your birthright from you, Aurora. It's everyone who knows the truth." He poured himself a glass of cognac, wishing he could offer one to his wife, whose voice was beginning to quaver.

"Birthright? I have my birth certificate."

"And Lady Anstruther-Jones has a letter from Elizabeth Halle herself saying the child was dead. You have *that* child's birth certificate, not your own."

"No! I am who I am!"

"Dash it, Aurora, you don't know who you are! You could be anyone, though the blond hair and blue eyes would point to English parents." He turned and saw his valet making another trip. "Dash it, Tarlow, put that down and have done!" he shouted when the gentleman's gentleman would have edged past him with his traveling lap desk. The valet carefully placed the heavy cherrywood piece on a table near Aurora and fled.

"Shouting at servants is not going to alter the situation," Aurora chided the earl.

"Tarlow is used to it."

Lord Windham resumed his pacing, but still heard her sotto voce: "I daresay he is." He took out his quizzing glass to stare her down, but Aurora's eyes were closed. She refused to watch his furious pacing or listen to his logic. "My mother must have had a reason for her deception, she must have! I wonder if Lord Phelan knew. He helped bring me home, Aunt Thisbe always said."

"Or his brother. What was Ramsey's brother's name? Ratchford?"

"George, Lord Ratchford, died some years ago. The only times I ever saw him or the son who inherited the earldom were when Ratchford Manor was thrown open for public days. I cannot imagine any connection, other than that the Ramseys and the Balcombes were neighbors. I never even knew either of the brothers had a *tendre* for my mother until this week."

"But Ramsey would know. Thunderation, I should not have been so quick to let him disappear with Podell. At the very least, I could have shaken some answers out of your sham soldier."

Aurora's eyes snapped open. "You think there is a link between Lieutenant Podell and my parents in India?"

"If there is, it's Phelan. The whole argle-bargle is too smoky by half. Would you mind if I traveled back to Bath tomorrow to see what answers I can find? You could stay here, seeing the sights, while I went." And she could make micefeet of her reputation and his fortune. "On the other hand, would you mind coming along? Your aunt and uncle would be more forthcoming, I think, with you present."

"I would be glad to go. My whole world is turned upside down, and I won't feel sane until it's righted." Aurora felt better now that they had a starting point, a plan of action. She needed the safety and security of her old home, to touch the familiar. She needed the comforting reassurance of her aunt and uncle, for she was certainly not getting any solace from her husband. Why, he hadn't taken her hand to help her from the carriage, letting the hotel's footman do the honors. And he hadn't so much as smiled at her once since they'd left Lady Anstruther-Jones's house. Worst of all, his valet was moving his belongings across the hall.

"Are you still angry about the monkey, Kenyon? The groom did say as how your curricle could be restored. And Ned is out right now, ordering a cage and finding how to feed the little creature and care for it. I promise Sweety won't be a problem to you."

"Sweety? The simian is a spawn of Satan, and I could purchase this whole blasted hotel for what I'm having to pay in damages. What the devil were you thinking, woman, letting a monkey loose in the lobby?"

"I wasn't thinking anything until *you* shouted for the manager, demanding he change your rooms again. You frightened poor Sweety into jumping out of my arms."

"Poor Sweety?" he shouted, then, struggling, managed to moderate his voice. "Poor Lady Wystanly's poodle. Poor Mr. Harris's toupee. The poor chandelier, the poor carpet, the poor ornamental fountain that will never come clean. And poor me, who has to pay for the entire mess. And a restorative holiday in Brighton for the manager. But, no, I am not still angry about the monkey. Your Ned and Sweety can both don Windham livery and little red caps and go begging on the steps of Whitehall. I would not care."

"Then why are you in such a pique?"

"Madam, if this is a pique, Trafalgar was a picnic. But you do not understand, do you? Let me explain. If you are not Aurora Halle McPhee, then we are bloody well not married! That is the name on the license, the name the vicar gave when you made your oath. Our marriage, which has now been published throughout the kingdom and entered into the Anstruther-Jones arsenal, can be set aside in an instant. We can ignore the discrepancies, of course, and soldier on, except for the children — our children, which we'd dashed well create if I stayed in this room one more night. Those innocents would be illegitimate, and I will not have it, do you hear?"

The Prussian dignitaries in the next room heard.

"But nothing is proved, and no one needs to know."

"Phelan Ramsey knows the truth, I'd wager, even if your aunt and uncle do not. Who's to say that five years down the line, or ten, he'd not decide to try his hand at blackmail? Or else he might let something slip while in his cups, or to his cronies at a card game." Kenyon laughed bitterly and threw his empty glass into the fireplace. "First my son, then my wife. The devil take it, am I destined never to know who anyone is?"

"You have a son?"

"I told you I had an heir, right at the church."

"You said you had an heir of sorts. I thought you meant your brother."

"Think about it — my brother wouldn't be in line for the succession if I married you and had a son. Remember, I thought you were carrying Podell's child, so I could not have offered for you unless I had an heir of my own, lest your misbegotten babe step into my title. Podell's get as Windham would have six generations of Warriners spinning in their graves. I was praying for a girl — the odds are even at least — in case something ever happened to Andrew."

"You have a son," she repeated. "Andrew? Where is he?"

"At school, of course. He's eight. No, he must be nine by now. I don't know. My secretary keeps track of those things. But don't go getting all teary-eyed over him. He's not one of your foundlings. He has everything a boy could need."

"Except a father who loves him, it seems. How far away is his school? How often do you visit?"

"He stays with a respectable family when school is not in session. They have children of their own, and write that they think very highly of Andrew. There is no reason for him to travel to Derby. And I rarely know whether I'll be there or in London, at any rate. This is less disruptive for the boy."

"For the boy or for you, my lord? My word, I suppose whole school terms can go by without your seeing him."

It was more like whole years, two since the child had been sent to school, almost never before that. Facing away from the condemnation he knew he'd see in her face, Kenyon said, "I refuse to discuss my relation with my son, Aurora. It is no concern of yours."

"How can you say that, when he is now my son, too?" She set her cup aside and fumbled in her pocket for a handkerchief to blow her nose. "But of course you do not believe he is yours, do you? What, do you think Genevieve played you false?"

"Hah. I know the jade played me false. She ran off with her lover, remember? But no, I thought the boy was mine at the time of his birth. If nothing else, Genevieve was born knowing the importance of bloodlines and successions. She did not set out for London and her various affairs until after the heir was begotten, as far as I know. Of course she could have been carrying on with the servants in Derby, but I like to think she was too proud for that."

"Then why do you question Andrew's birth?"

Still facing away, leaning on the mantel, the earl stared at the fire. "It's not his birth that I question, it's his identity. Genevieve took my son to London with her. She must have loved him, which is the only thing I have ever admired in her character. Either that or she hated me so much. Her French emigré lover's wife had died in childbirth, about the same time Genevieve gave birth to Andrew. That infant survived, and when my wife got to London, she played at being mother to both boys. At first I thought she was consoling *le duc*, then advising him about nannies and such. About that time, D'Journet decided to throw his lot in with Napoleon, hoping to get back his lands. When he returned to France, Genevieve went with him, with both infants. She took all the Warriner family heirlooms she could carry, to buy favor with the emperor. My money was going to England's enemies, and she must have known how that galled. My brother was risking his life defending the kingdom, and my wife was supporting the Corsican upstart."

"She was French. Perhaps she looked at it differently."

"She was a traitor to her lawful husband and to the country that had sheltered her. And it was all for naught. D'Journet quickly realized that his cause was hopeless, that Napoleon would never reinstate the dukedom, that France could never return to the old ways. At least when he recognized that his very life was in danger, he sent my son back."

"With Genevieve?"

"She chose to stay with *le duc*. She would have been ostracized in England, perhaps even charged with treason. But she would not sacrifice her son. Or D'Journet's."

"She sent both boys?"

"Yes, those were her terms. My heir would be returned, if her lover's son was also brought to safety. I can't begin to explain the dealings with smugglers and spies, all the bribes I had to pay merely to send a message, but I agreed. I swore to be father to both children."

"And?"

"And it was a rough passage. The smugglers' ship was shot at by a British man of war. The boat capsized in the storm and only a handful of the brigands managed to cling to the hull until they were rescued. Knowing how much I was willing to pay, one of the smugglers saved a boy."

Aurora stifled a sob. "Andrew?"

"Or Henri. There was no way of knowing. The child was too young to understand the question. He answered to both names, having been raised in the same cradle. And he was distraught over the separation from the only parents he'd known, his brother and his nursemaid, in addition to the horrors of the journey. He did nothing but cry, then he took sick. He would have died but for my old nanny. I tried to pray for his recovery, I swear. Then word came that the duke and his mistress had perished when their castle was stormed. I would never find out the truth."

"So you claimed the boy." Tears were rolling down Aurora's cheeks by now, but Kenyon was looking inward and did not see.

He nodded. "I claimed the boy as Viscount Windslow. He has Genevieve's look, her dark eyes and pointed chin. That's all I could judge by. But I will never know, will I? Just as we will never know what child came home from India."

Kenyon turned and saw that Aurora was crying, and he wished more than anything to take her in his arms and soothe her, but she was not his to hold, to comfort. Until this mess ended, he did not dare. He was going to be a laughingstock, she was going to be a social pariah, and neither was going to find the happiness that had seemed so close. "Don't cry, my dear," he told her, wanting to weep himself. "We'll go to Bath and straighten this hobble out. We can always get married again, when we know the answers."

Jumping to her feet, she stamped her foot. "I am not crying because I am not the real Aurora Halle McPhee, you dolt. I am crying because I am married to an autocratic, overbearing, unfeeling brute who didn't even think to tell me that we have a son. I am crying because the man I thought was almost perfect is actually a pompous prig who doesn't trust me enough to know who I am." She pounded her fist on the top of his nearby lap desk. Then she flipped the lid back, knowing what she would find. She reached in and pulled out the proof. "You don't believe me, you don't approve of me, and you don't even like me enough to admit that you wear spectacles!"

Chapter Eleven

Monkeys were like men, appealing, amusing, and often impossible to live with. Sweety wanted out of his cage; Windham wanted out of his marriage. The monkey was unintentionally destructive; Windham was well nigh to breaking her heart. Aurora had Ned find a collar and lead for the monkey. She did not know what to do about the earl.

If she claimed to be someone else, some magnate's mischance, he would be free. But what about Aurora's honor, her mother's memory? She could not do it, not even for Kenyon. She had to prove his theory wrong, that was all. So, while her maid, Judith, was packing for the Bath trip, again, and Windham was making a call at the War Office about his brother, again, she and Ned started looking for the truth.

A great many of Ned's acquaintances knew someone who had a friend whose cousin had been in India two decades ago. The ragged, toothless, vacant-eyed individuals were not, necessarily, the type of clientele the Grand Hotel wished to welcome through its elegant front portals. A loose box in the livery stable out back was set aside for Lady Windham's use, therefore, with a barrel for a desk and a bale of hay for a seat. The one-legged soldier stood guard, and Sweety checked the callers' pockets for concealed weapons, pilfered goods, or treats. Those with seemingly valid information, or sad stories, went away with one of Windham's coins. Others were sent off by Ned with a flea in their ear for bothering his lady.

No one knew anything of Elizabeth Halle or her child. That would have been too much to hope for. Two of the men had heard of Avisson Halle, though. Another had actually been a clerk at John Company before being charged with embezzlement, which he swore was a false charge. The picture of her father that emerged was even blacker than Lady Anstruther-Jones had painted. Not only was Halle lazy and incompetent, a gambler and a womanizer, but he grew violent when in his cups. Aurora was beginning to understand what her mother had done, the sacrifice Elizabeth had made to keep her daughter safe, knowing she would not be around to protect her in the future. She could not simply send a man's child back to England, but a dead child was mourned and forgotten. Aurora's mother had loved her enough to give her up when she had so little time remaining, like Andrew's mother.

Aurora could not prove any of her suppositions, of course, but she felt better in her own heart and that, she felt, was a great accomplishment for one morning. Oh, and she hired the embezzler as Windham's secretary.

The worst part of wearing his detested spectacles, the earl decided, was having to see the injured look in Aurora's blue eyes. Might as well mow down a field of bluebells. The worst part of having a bride of uncertain antecedents was that none of it was her fault. Kenyon could not blame her for being born on the wrong side of the blanket, nor for being so innocent she tossed her cap over the windmill for Podell. Even the monkey was not her fault. Lady Anstruther-Jones's Indian butler had confided that the shrewd old stick had been looking for a way to get rid of the plaguesome beast. Why clutter up the Thames when she could cause chaos in Windham's household? Kenyon wondered what he could present the witch with in return. Perhaps Needles could find a viper for the viscountess.

The earl was having no luck finding anything. Whitehall still had no word of his brother's release from the French prison hospital, so he went on to the Home Secretary and the Registrar of Records. The blasted government ran on paper, with everything recorded, filed, dated and initialed three times at least. Why, then, could no one find a death notice for Aurora Halle?

Perhaps because the child was not born in England and did not die there, a harried clerk complained. But Windham handed over another coin and told the lackey to keep looking.

The East India Company clerks worked for higher bribes. *Baksheesh,* they called it. He called it extortion. He could travel to India himself for half the cost of finding the information he wanted. Eventually one of the ink-stained underlings found the records of Avisson Halle's brief employment.

" 'Dismissed for dereliction of duty,' " the clerk read. "That usually meant he never showed up for work."

The other notations were dates of birth and death for Halle and his wife, Elizabeth Balcombe Halle. No other dependents were listed. If they had a child, the clerk supposed, the records would be kept with the parish priest of the Anglican Church in India.

Shipping lines and merchantmen kept excellent records, he was assured by an oily orderly in the Office of the Navy. They kept all bills of lading, passenger lists, and customs receipts. The British Navy insisted upon that. Unfortunately, all such documents would be kept in warehouses near the docks, which, as everyone knew, were subject to frequent fires.

Damn, it would take weeks to scour the wharves for the records he wanted, if they still existed. Kenyon thought about hiring Bow Street to help — or a secretary.

Lady Anstruther-Jones sent a note saying that her assistant had unearthed the letter from Elizabeth Halle, and there was something they might find of interest. Could they call on the morrow? So Kenyon canceled the trip to Bath, again, and had their bags unpacked. He sent the embezzler to the shipping offices, Ned to find a gift for Lady Anstruther-Jones, and another check to the hotel's owners. The monkey, it seemed, could unknot its dog collar. Dinner would be delayed until a new chef could be hired.

Aurora was so upset, so remorse ridden, that Kenyon just had to think of some way to please her. Here she was in London for the first time in her life, and cooped in a second-rate hotel that could not even keep a decent chef. Windham had been thinking of spending the evening at his clubs, but he'd have to listen to congratulations and the usual ribald teasing on the nuptials, which was not a topic in which he could find much humor. He decided to escort his problematical partner to the theater. They could sit in relative privacy in his box, insulated from chitchat, although unavoidably on view. Let the *ton* see her, he decided. The announcement notices were out; they were already sunk. When the truth came to light, they'd just have to move to the Colonies. Aurora might as well enjoy herself until then, and he might as well enjoy having such a pretty woman on his arm. They'd have a pleasant evening out, not thinking of the muddle they were in. That was how Lord Windham planned it, at any rate. He did not, however, plan on one of his ex-mistresses being in the cast that evening.

The night began well enough. Aurora was stunning in a new creation from one of Ned's struggling seamstress friends. The modiste's days of obscure stitching were over, unless Kenyon missed his guess, as soon as Society discovered who had the dressing of Lady Windham. And the *enciente* maid Judith knew her craft, too, for instead of the usual braided bun, Aurora's hair was all tumbled curls, threaded through with ribbons and pink silk roses to match the gown. She was stunning. How could he have thought her passably pretty at first glance? And how was he going to keep his hands off her? Dash it, when she was his wife and he had all the time in the world, he burned like a callow youth. Now that he did not have her, could not have her, *must* not have her, the fire was a conflagration. He didn't need the hot bricks at his feet in the carriage. He needed another cold bath.

She was entranced by the spectacle of the theater, the ornate architecture, the myriad lights, the haughty majesty of those in the tiered boxes, the raucous jollity of those in the pit. And Kenyon was entranced with her. He could look his fill, too, for once, for opera glasses were nearly universal here, and his were specially ground lenses. One lens brought the stage closer; the other let him read the program — or the tiny freckles on Aurora's nearly bare shoulders. Tearing his eyes away before he was tempted to tear the pink silk and lace gown away altogether, Kenyon noted that nearly every other pair of opera glasses in the place was also trained on his wife. He didn't doubt they'd be overrun with curious callers during the intervals, so he made sure Needles, in his own new finery, was stationed by the door of the box to deny them to visitors. Kenyon didn't want any questions, and he didn't want any interruption of what time they had left.

The first act was a blur for both of them. Kenyon was swinging his opera glasses between the actors and Aurora so frequently that he could hardly get his eyes to focus together anymore. And Aurora was all too conscious of the attention she was drawing from the other theatergoers, making her feel like one of Uncle Ptolemy's specimens, stuffed and put on display at the Bath Amateur Naturalists Society meetings. Kenyon was staring also, she knew, although he tried to hide his bad manners behind the binoculars. She wanted to pat her hair back into place, or pull up the neckline of her gown — or go home and finish what they'd begun on their wedding night.

Ned must have turned away thirty callers between acts, proudly declaring that his lord and lady were not wishing to be disturbed. During the second act, however, he entered the box carrying a screwed paper. "One of the stage hands brung this. Said it was important-like."

Kenyon untwisted the page, then turned it over, then upside down. "Bad light in here, don't you know," he said, reaching for his reliable quizzing glass on its ribbon.

"Oh, just let me have it, you clunch. I swear you are as vain as a swan." She took the page and held it closer to the one candle left burning in its sconce at the rear of the box. "It's written lightly in pencil; that's why you had a problem."

He had a problem because he couldn't see a blasted thing. "But what does it say, my dear?"

"It says, 'Things are desperate. Come to the Green Room after the performance. It's a matter of death or death. Lola.' "

"Lola's in the cast? She must be the only soul in London who hasn't read about the marriage." Kenyon fixed his opera glasses on the stage, scanning the actresses. "Yes, she's the one in —"

"She's the one in blue who has been gazing forlornly up at this box for two acts," Aurora noted dryly. "The one who is waving to you, now that she has your attention."

He moved the fingers of his right hand in return. "It's not what it seems. We had dinner a few times, that was all."

Aurora was smoothing the paper across

her lap. "I may be green as cabbage, my lord, but I am not as stupid as one. Nor is it any of my business what you did before I met you, much less married you. What are you going to do about Miss, ah, Lola?"

Kenyon thought for a minute, thinking that he wouldn't be needing any cold baths, not with the icicles dripping off her words, but he did not have a great many options. If one of his own footmen were in attendance, he could send the chap in his stead, but Needles was only a boy. And he could not simply ignore Lola's plea for help. "I'll have to go see what the difficulty is."

"Of course you do. She's counting on you."

"Likely she's between protectors and needs a loan to tide her over. Or needs a place to stay for a few days. I'll drive you home, return here in time for the last act, hand Lola a few pounds, and still be back at the hotel for our late dinner before the cat can lick its ear."

"If you drop me at the hotel, I shall ask the first gentleman I see to escort me to the dining room. I hope it's that tobacco merchant."

"What, the dirty dish who tried to look down your décolletage as we were leaving? I almost called him out then and there! Besides, supper with that shabster would destroy whatever reputation you might ever hope to have."

"So would my husband's visiting his former mistress in public view not three days after our wedding. We are still married in the eyes of the church, the law, and these thousand people. Unless and until you prove that I am not Aurora Halle, I am Lady Windham, your wife. You did swear to honor me at that ceremony, didn't you? Well, there is no honor in shaming me before all of London."

She had a point, Kenyon conceded. She also had a green streak a mile wide, which secretly delighted him. "Very well, we will go together, but you will stand in the corner and not speak to anyone. Is that clear?"

It was clear that the man accosting Lola was not going to abide by any rules of gentlemanly conduct. He had a firm grasp on the front of her gown and was pulling her from the room when Kenyon and Aurora and Ned got there. No one seemed inclined to stop him, since the man was as tall as the door frame and nearly as wide. He made the earl look puny.

Kenyon groaned.

"I paid for you tonight, and I'm gettin'

you tonight, you cheatin' doxy. No one diddles Nick Chubb."

"But I thought you were giving me a gift, is all. I sold the bracelet to buy coal, like I told you. You never said I had to pay you back in any way."

"Every gift has its price, duckie, and you're about to pay the piper."

Kenyon stepped forward and cleared his throat. "I'll be happy to pay the lady's debts, Mr. Chubb, is it? Lola seems reluctant to share your company."

Chubb swung around. "Who the devil are you to be sticking your long nose into Nick Chubb's business? I want what I paid for, and no dandified toff is going to do me out of it. 'Sides," he said, looking back at the corner, "you got your own dollymop. Go plow your own field, like a gentleman farmer, iffen you know how. Unless of course you want to trade?"

So Kenyon hit him. It was a flush hit to the jaw, one Gentleman Jackson would have approved, and nearly broke the earl's knuckles. Chubb did not even let go of Lola's dress. He simply picked Kenyon up with his other hand and tossed him against the door, headfirst. Lola screamed. Aurora screamed. Three other actresses screamed, and one fainted. Two actors fled, one stage-

141

door beau hid under the table, a reviewer from the newspaper started writing furiously, and the manager called for the constable. Kenyon dragged himself up, shook his head to clear it, and landed Chubb another facer, this one to the nose. Chubb shoved him into a tea cart, which toppled.

"I am beginning to get annoyed, boy-o," the behemoth bellowed when Kenyon came at him again, this time with a blow to the breadbasket. Chubb grabbed him again and held him off the ground, at which Aurora decided it was time to act. She could feel her stomach lurching and refused to let her husband be vanquished while she vomited. So she picked up the nearest thing to hand, the stage pistol that had been used in the last act, and began beating Chubb about the knees, since she could not reach his brain box, which was too small a target anyway. The pistol went off in a harmless cloud of smoke and dust, but creating more panic in the onlookers. Aurora almost swooned herself, thinking she'd shot her husband. But Kenyon roared, landing a solid clout on Chubb's ear, which caused the giant to drop both the earl, who banged his head against the table, and Lola, who fainted dead away. Aurora kept clubbing at Chubb with the gun. He raised his fist to brush her aside, but Ned leaped onto his back, placing his hands over the bully's eyes. "Kick 'im in the privates, m'lady!" the boy shouted, so she did. While Chubb was doubled over, Windham coshed him over the head with a wooden chair, just in time for the Charleys to come haul him off.

"I thought I told you to stay in the corner," was all the earl could say as he watched the reporter tear out of the Green Room with his pad and pencil still flying.

"That was the bravest thing I have ever seen," Aurora marveled as she wrapped her handkerchief around Kenyon's battered hand, once they were finally in the carriage.

His heart swelled, almost as large as the lump on his head. And it did not matter that he couldn't see her in the coach lamp's dim light, or that he couldn't see out of one eye at all; he could hear the warmth in her voice, the pride, the admiration.

"Why, we all might have been killed if Ned hadn't jumped on Chubb that way." She patted his bruised cheek. "And you did well too, my lord."

Chapter Twelve

For twenty-odd years, almost no one but his lordship's valet knew that the Earl of Windham wore spectacles. It was not vanity, Kenyon always told himself. It was a matter of strength, power, authority. And he looked foolish in glasses.

Now everyone would know unless, of course, they assumed he'd donned the peepers to hide the magnificent black eye he sported, which was only half true. He'd mostly chosen to wear his spectacles on his daily call at the War Office in hopes that no one would recognize him. He'd rather be known as the four-eyed earl than the bridegroom of a ballock-basher. Every scandal sheet, every broadside, held a cartoon of last night's events: Aurora as Boadicia, rosebuds in her hair, defending the family jewels. Aurora as David, aiming her slingshot at Goliath, and himself, not Ned, on the giant's back, yelling, "Aim lower, my dear." The reason Kenyon was so sure it was his caricature was that the dashed swell was looking through a quizzing glass. Bloody hell.

For a man who despised having his name simmering in scandal broth, Windham was not doing a good job of keeping his affairs out of the public eye. His marriage to Genevieve and her French leave, then Brianne's elopement and nonmarriage, were nothing to the continual catastrophe that was Aurora. He could only imagine how many trees would be cut down for pulp when news of her false identity was aired, and another Warriner marriage was dissolved.

The earl intercepted a few winks at the War Office, a few fingers held alongside noses. Damn, a fellow saw too much when he wore his glasses. And glaring at the insolent curs through thick lenses was not nearly so effective in depressing pretensions as peering through his looking glass. He shouldn't have listened to Aurora about wearing the spectacles. Zeus, he shouldn't have listened to her about going to the Green Room. He shouldn't have married the confounded chit.

The War Office had no news for him. The McPhee solicitor had no information for him, either, only copies of Aurora Halle's adoption papers — and titters. Gads, who would employ such a twittering toad? But the man appeared honest, and unaware of any possible legal legerdemain.

Could his wife really be the child of Elizabeth and Avisson Halle? Lud, that would leave Kenyon with a flea-wit who fell into one disaster after another, but not a fraud. That would mean, however, that Lady Anstruther-Jones was wrong, and England's Empress of the East was never wrong.

"You did just as you should, child," Hortense was telling Aurora as they entered her presence that afternoon.

So the old crone was not infallible after all, Kenyon thought, seating himself on his pillow as if paying homage to a fairy queen instead of a dab of a dowager.

"I am more and more impressed with you, missy. Might even leave you something in my will."

Lord, not the weapons collection, Kenyon prayed. Heaven alone knew what mayhem Aurora could create with an arsenal.

Fearfully eyeing the stuffed black leopard who was not at Lady Anstruther-Jones's side but was lapping at the ornamental fountain, Aurora hastily disclaimed any need for such a bequest. "Sweety is more than enough, my lady. We are quite enjoying his antics, aren't we, Kenyon?"

"Oh, quite, my dear. I can't recall when I've been half so amused." Waking up to find Sweety on his chest, with his shaving razor in one hairy paw, had been absolutely hilarious. Much more such jollity and he'd laugh himself to death.

"Hah! You've got no time for watching a monkey's antics, from what I hear. Up to your own, everyone says. Well, Windham, the gel is a goer, but I am not impressed with you, sirrah, not at all."

Aurora leaped to his defense. She stayed on the pillow, of course, but she hotly protested Lady Anstruther-Jones's criticism of the earl. "But Chubb was enormous. The biggest man I've ever seen. That's why no one else would help poor Lola. Windham was magnificent, like a knight on a charger, not hesitating an instant to assist the lady. And he would have won the day, I am sure. Eventually."

"I'm not talking about any brawl, missy. Win or lose, Windham had no business taking his bride to meet his *cheri-amour*." She thumped her cane on the floor for emphasis, which sent a flock of tiny, colorful birds winging from the trees. Aurora wished she had Aunt Thisbe's books with her to identify the species.

"She was not my *cheri-amour*," Kenyon protested, when it seemed that his wife's defense had taken a detour.

"Oh, she was perhaps a patroness of Almack's whom I hadn't heard about previously? Or a lady-in-waiting at court? The woman was someone you should have been introducing your bride to, I'm sure, to see her established in the beau monde, yes?"

There was, of course, no answer. Kenyon sighed, almost wishing Sweety had gone ahead and slit his throat.

"Furthermore, young man, you were not forthcoming with me on your previous visit. Didn't mention your bride's full name, as a matter of fact. I had to read it myself, or have one of my secretaries do it, which is one and the same. Aurora *Halle* McPhee, the *on dits* columns say, which you forgot to mention."

"I did say we were looking for information about her relations, Elizabeth and Avisson Halle. I saw no reason to be more specific."

"Like saying they were her parents. But were they?"

"That is the question, ma'am. You are the one who said the Halle daughter was dead. Is she, or did you discover other information?"

Lady Anstruther-Jones fussed with her pipe, then wound the butterfly music box while Kenyon waited on tenterhooks, or on a sore posterior from landing so hard last night. "Ma'am?"

"I think I am not in the mood to answer any more questions."

It was a dismissal, after she'd dragged him here, and out of his boots, and kept him from Bath where he might have found some answers, by George. Kenyon was ready to tell the wizened old viscountess what he thought of her and her homicidal ape. His wife had other ideas.

"Rather than answer questions, my lady, perhaps you'd rather open the gift we brought. We are enjoying the monkey so much we wished to repay you for the pleasure."

Kenyon had forgotten the wicker basket she'd carried in the curricle. Too concerned with his own doubts, he'd neglected to ask about the gift Needles had procured. Jupiter, let it be something exotic and expensive. Otherwise, they'd be out on the street, and so would the uncertainties concerning Aurora's birth.

Aurora brought the basket over to Lady Anstruther-Jones and raised its hinged lid. "Hold your hands out, my lady," she said.

"Eh? Feels like a pricker bush or something. You haven't brought me a cactus, have you, missy?"

"No, my lady. It's *Erinaceus europaeus*, a hedgehog Ned found at the market. Some boys were selling it, for stew if you can imagine such a thing! If you give it some seeds or an apple slice, it will uncurl and walk around your lap."

"Why yes, I believe it's licking me! You mean to say that someone was going to eat this charming little creature?"

"I'm afraid so. But now I am more afraid the leopard might. I hadn't thought of that at the time, only how happy the little fellow might be in your indoor garden."

"Oh, Baku is so ancient he has hardly any teeth left. That's why I never sent the old boy back to his jungle after the emir brought him to me. He wouldn't have survived a week. Baku, that is, not the emir. I don't suppose you two would want —"

Two voices answered as one. "No!"

The old woman shrugged her thin shoulders and kept running her fingers over the hedgehog's spines. "And you say that boy Ned rescued this darling from a cook pot? What an intrepid lad he is, to be sure. I don't suppose I could hire him away from you, could I? With a sharp boy like that, there's no telling what I could do."

"Oh, no, I could never part with our Ned, especially not after last night. But I do know of a one-eyed veteran who is in need of a position. He's willing to do anything."

"If the rest of him's intact," she said with a cackle, "send him over. I've never turned down a willing man yet. Which reminds me, I have a gift for you, too — a wedding gift."

At her gesture, one of the maids brought out a parcel wrapped in a square of silk, tied with a gold cord.

"But you should not have, my lady. Truly, Sweety was generous enough."

"Nonsense. Besides, I can't enjoy the thing since my eyes went bad anyway."

Aurora was carefully unfolding the fabric, which was beautiful on its own, all hand-painted flowers and birds, to reveal a book with carved wooden covers. When she reverently turned the first page, she saw that the richly colored illustrations and the chapter capitals were limned in gold, like a cloister's book of days. "It is exquisite, ma'am. I will treasure it forever. I only wish I could read the text."

"Well, it's Sanskrit, so I'm not surprised you can't. No matter, there are pictures enough."

Aurora was turning the pages. "So there

are, and lovely ones at that. Look, Kenyon, people play leapfrog in India, too."

Kenyon had been watching her as she opened the gift, studying the innocent delight, the gentle curve of her mouth in an *oh* of appreciation. Deuce take it, he still hadn't bought her a bridal gift, nothing but some additions to her wardrobe that were his rightful expense anyway. He wanted to bring that pleasure to her, and more. Blast the old besom for putting the seeds of doubt in his mind in the first place. And . . . leap frog? He grabbed the book, eliciting a squawk of protest, and gave it a quick glance — his spectacles were good for something — then slammed the covers shut. "My word, ma'am," he said, "you have given my wife a pillow book!"

"And what has you in a fidge over that, Windham? It ain't as if she's some milk-and-water maiden. The gel's a married woman now. And you'll be happy she has it. English gels aren't taught how to please a man, or to be pleased. That's why so many men stray from their wives' beds. You won't have to."

"Good grief, you meddlesome old —"

"Thank you, Lady Anstruther-Jones. It was lovely of you to worry about the success of our marriage. Perhaps if you told us what you discovered in my mother's letter, we would have a better chance."

"Aye, I can see where making love to a dead woman could dampen your husband's enthusiasm."

She couldn't see anything, the harpy, but, with or without his spectacles, Kenyon could see her scrawny neck under all those necklaces. He wanted to wring it. No man wanted a practiced courtesan for a wife, by all that was holy, and if he did, he wanted to be the one to teach her, not some book! Hell, the monkey was a better gift. At least the monkey didn't think he needed instructions on pleasing his wife. He would have left then and there, but Aurora was finally getting the septuagenarian strumpet to speak.

"As I told you, I had my assistant find your mother's letter. Elizabeth Halle's letter, that is, that she wrote to me after I expressed my sympathy for the loss of her daughter. She was everything polite, but one sentence struck me as odd. That's why I invited you back."

"And we do appreciate it, my lady," Aurora said, poking Kenyon in one of his sore ribs until he murmured his agreement.

"Hmpf. Well, the odd thing was, I had offered to pay for a marker for the child's grave. Everyone knew the Halles didn't have a shilling to spare. Elizabeth wrote back that a headstone wouldn't be necessary, thank you. Not that she already had one, or that the infant was cremated, or they were sending her back to England for burial, just that one was not needed."

"Because the infant was not dead!" Aurora crowed in triumph. "I knew it!"

"I'm sorry, child, but I know there was a funeral."

"But you can't know if the casket was empty. I believe my mother wanted to send me back to England before she died herself, and her husband would not agree."

Kenyon noted that she no longer referred to the scapegrace Halle as her father, only as her mother's husband. He couldn't blame her. If he were related to such a loose screw, he'd try to distance himself, too. "What do you think, ma'am? Could Mrs. Halle have feigned the child's death and smuggled her out of the country?"

"I think I love a mystery more than anything!"

Kenyon was polishing his spectacles with the silk from the book wrapping. "Well, I am sure we are glad to brighten your day, ma'am, but you can understand how the uncertainty of the situation is upsetting, to say the least."

"You always were a restive sort of boy, Windham. It's a wonder you ever sat still long enough to learn to read and write. I comprehend your problem — I ain't the chowder-head you seem to think — but I'll have to think on it some more."

Aurora was frowning at him, but speaking to Lady Anstruther-Jones. "We are grateful for any scrap of information you might remember. In the meantime, do you recall Lord Phelan Ramsey? He was the younger brother of the Earl of Ratchford, and I believe Lord Phelan was in India at the same time all of this was transpiring. In fact, according to what I have been told my whole life, it was Lord Phelan who arranged for nursemaids and such for my journey to my new home."

"Yes, he was in India, although I could not have been so specific as to the time. His brother offered to buy him a place in the Company, I remember, since George's marriage and son had cut Phelan from the succession. Phelan was a lazy ne'er-do-well who came out to look us over, stayed one month, and decided he hated the heat, the insects, and the thought of work. He'd rather be Ratchford's pensioner, it seemed. No one thought anything of his calling on the Halles, since he'd lived near Elizabeth's family most of his life. He spent his month or so in India drinking with Halle, since Elizabeth was beginning to ail and the child took most of her time. I suppose Lord Phelan was a good enough friend to Mrs. Halle to aid her in the deception. I can't imagine why, else. Have you asked him about it?"

"As soon as we find him," Kenyon replied. "I thought he'd be back in London by now from a certain errand he had, but no such luck. We'll come upon him soon, I am certain."

"And I'll keep thinking. We'll figure it out — see if we don't."

The more Kenyon thought about it during the ride home, the more Aurora's theory seemed possible. Either that or he was wanting it to be true so their marriage was legal and unchallengeable. Of course that still left Podell and his scurvy schemes. "What do you think, my dear?"

Aurora looked up from her book. "I think I couldn't stand on my head like that."

Chapter Thirteen

The answers had to lie in Bath. Or tell the truth, in Bath.

Windham's brother, unfortunately, was lying in France, and his sister was in a decline in Derby.

Christopher was finally ready to be transported home, although the prison doctors were not encouraging about his condition. With defeat staring the French in the face, they'd been more willing to negotiate, for a higher price, of course. Windham did not trust any army transport ship to bring Christopher home, though, nor any private fishing boat — not after Andrew's passage. The earl wanted to fetch Kit back in his own yacht, with his own doctors aboard. He'd made a last promise to their mother to look after Kit, and by Jupiter, he meant to do it. He hadn't been able to keep the clunch out of the army, not with patriotic zeal and a craving for adventure coursing through Christopher's young blood. Damn, Kenyon would have gone, too, if he hadn't been responsible for the title and properties and investments and dependents. Kit had been safe enough in the command post position Kenyon had purchased for him, but what had the cabbage-head gone and done? He'd gone exploring on his own, looking for the lost Windham legacy, the jewels Genevieve had taken. He was captured, of course. It was a marvel he was not shot instantly as a spy.

As for his sister in Derby, Windham's aunt had written that when they received his message saying Podell was not only alive but was about to marry another young woman in Bath, Brianne had shut herself in her bedroom and had not come out since. Aunt Ellenette and Frederick feared for Bri's sanity.

"Coming from Aunt Ellenette," he explained to Aurora as he paced the confines of the hotel sitting room, "who has nothing but feathers in her own cockloft, it's a grave concern. Oh yes, Aunt Ellenette. I have any number of relations I have not mentioned, not wanting to frighten you off altogether. Aunt Ellenette is . . . odd, but she's always been at Windrush, so we have grown accustomed. She has a pug dog. Frederick is fat, mean, and droolly."

"There's nothing terribly odd about that.

Lady Anstruther-Jones has a pet leopard," Aurora reminded him from her place at the writing desk, where she was trying to compose a thank-you for Lady Anstruther-Jones. Since Kenyon had confiscated the book, Aurora felt awkward enthusing over the gift, especially knowing the note would be read by the viscountess's secretary. She was glad for the interruption.

"Yes, but she talks to Frederick."

"Many people talk to their pets. Most, in fact, I believe."

He sighed. "Frederick talks back. Aunt Ellenette believes the mutt is the reembodiment of her dead husband, Charles, my father's younger brother, who was also fat and mean. I do not recall if he drooled. He, or Frederick, has opinions on everything concerning the family."

"Your aunt and Lady Anstruther-Jones would be great friends if they met."

"Heaven forfend. Either way, if Frederick says Brianne is in a decline, then my sister is in queer stirrups indeed." His sister never had been a comfortable sort of girl, but Kenyon saw no reason to drag all the family linen out for viewing at once. Brianne was headstrong, hoydenish, and hard to handle — on her good days. The earl loved her, of course, but he'd been secretly delighted that

159

Harland Podell had wooed her away from Windrush. Now she was back, permanently, cutting up his peace.

"The poor thing must be having a hard time of it. To be widowed is bad enough, I'd imagine, but to have her marriage dissolved as if it never happened must be devastating. Where does that leave her?"

"On my hands forever, as damaged goods." He ran his fingers through his hair in frustration. "Deuce take it, I cannot see my way to managing everything at once."

"Of course not. The trip to Bath can certainly wait. No one will question our wedding lines for now; if the marriage has to be annulled or dissolved like your sister's, I'll be no more ruined next month than I will be next week. You must take your yacht to France, naturally."

He faced her, leaning over the desk and putting his hands on the wood to either side of her. "You cannot go along, so don't even think it. I mean to carry physicians and medical supplies, and bring home as many of Christopher's men as we can carry on the yacht. I could have had the noble jobbernowl home six months ago if he'd agreed to leave his men. There will be no room, and no place for a lady."

"I was not suggesting I go with you, my

lord. I thought I might travel to Derby in your stead, to ease your sister's mind. At least I would be company who understands her plight."

Kenyon took both her hands in his. "You'd do that — you'd help my sister? I thought you might go to Bath by yourself, with outriders, of course."

"Your sister needs me more."

"Gads, I haven't been much of a husband, yet you'd sacrifice your own plans for a woman you don't even know, because she is my sister." He kissed first one hand, then the other.

Blushing, Aurora pulled her fingers away. "I never had a sister," was all she said. "I always wanted one."

"You haven't met Brianne yet," he muttered, but he was vastly relieved, she could tell. So was she. Aurora thought they'd do better apart, she and her halfway husband. She had her principles, but, as he'd proved, she also had passion. Whenever he touched her, or brushed by her, or smiled at her, as now, Aurora's stomach fluttered in a way that had nothing to do with nausea. She was Kenyon's worry; she wanted, quite desperately, to be his wife. Until the doubts — his doubts — about their vows were resolved, 'twould be better for both of them to put distance between. The English Channel was a bit more distance than she thought absolutely necessary, but with all the problems he had, she could not add to his burden.

Aurora had problems of her own. She'd be going off with Sweety and a street urchin to face the dotty aunt and the dieaway sister — and the boy who might be Kenyon's son but who was definitely Aurora's son. She wondered if the resident Warriner ladies would resent her, if they would hand over the keys, if they would find her a worthy bride for the Earl of Windham. Of course they would not. They were unbalanced and unhappy, not deaf, dumb, and blind.

Aurora wanted someone bigger than Ned in her corner for this battle of acceptance, so she wrote to her aunt and uncle, inviting them to visit her in Derby. She missed them terribly, she wrote, and was sure they'd enjoy exploring a new venue with her. She added the request that her aunt search through the attics and bring along any letters she might have from Aurora's mother.

Aurora put the pen down, hoping that a lord as grand as Windham would have a stagnant pond or two. And that Kenyon wouldn't mind she had invited another pair of eccentrics to his estate. How could he mind Uncle Ptolemy's turtles, when he wouldn't be there?

The trip to Windrush took longer than expected. Aurora's maid, Judith, growing larger by the moment, grew uncomfortable sitting for long stretches, and the constant motion of the carriage roiled her stomach. The sounds of her retching made Aurora ill, so they took to stopping frequently. Every time they did pull over at a grassy area or an inn, Ned went off exploring. Never having been out of the City before, he kept getting lost. The urchin who could find his way about London's netherworld in the dark on a foggy night, could not tell a bush from a brier patch. So the one-eyed soldier, having decided that the duties at Lady Anstruther-Jones's house were not to his liking, had to ride after him on Magpie, the old cart horse who had no hurry left in him. By the time they found Ned, Sweety needed to be exercised, Magpie needed to be rested, and Judith was hungry again. The driver was nervous around the monkey, the groom was nervous around a pregnant woman, and Aurora was so nervous about her reception at Windrush that she did not even mind the extra days of travel.

Things were worse there than she'd imagined. Mrs. Podell, who was now reclaiming her maiden title, Lady Brianne, would not come out of her room to greet her new sister-in-law. Aunt Ellenette would not permit the monkey in the house, because Frederick did not like him. The bailiff refused to hire a handicapped man or find a home for a fallen woman, and the local vicar, on their first Sunday service in Windrush's private chapel, lectured on loose women, looking at Judith, then Aurora. Lady Brianne did not attend. None of the neighboring gentry called with congratulations; all of the tenant farmers called with complaints.

Whereas Aurora had feared the Warriner ladies would not relinquish the reins of Windrush Manor, she found them practically thrown at her. Declaring she was at wits' end — not a far journey, it seemed — Aunt Ellenette handed over the keys to the household, the unbalanced account books, and a loose ceiling tile that had fallen on her bed, almost flattening Frederick. Then she retired to the shabby sofa with a novel and a box of bonbons.

Lord Windham, it appeared, had been away a bit too long. If he'd been nearby, Aurora would have tossed the tile at him. But he was gone, and she was Lady Windham, and she was going to prove she could make him a proper countess, or die trying.

She set Mr. Dawson, the former East India Company employee who was not an embezzler, in charge of the ledgers. She sent Ned to explore the rundown house to see what needed to be repaired first. The place was enormous, but she didn't think he could get lost. And she set the bailiff straight as to who was in charge. Lord Windham had given her a blank check, his signet ring, and a hurriedly scrawled note stating, "Lady Windham speaks for me." She also spoke to the vicar about Christian charity, and about who held the purse strings of his living.

Aurora rode around the estate, introducing herself to the tenants' wives, the ones who really knew what needed to be done. They needed a school and a doctor, and that marshy area drained so the insects couldn't breed. They needed a lower price at the flour mill and a higher price for their spun wool. Windrush was overrun with rabbits and deer, eating their kitchen gardens, while the parish poorhouse went hungry, they told her.

In the village the shopkeepers couldn't wait to pour their complaints into her ears as soon as their outstanding bills were paid.

The roads were in poor condition, so little traffic passed through, which meant less business. The tosspot of a sheriff, appointed by the magistrate, had fallen off his horse, so now they had no one enforcing the law or keeping the pub from getting boisterous on a Saturday night. The earl, of course, was magistrate, and in charge of maintaining the section of highway.

Aurora made lists, and then more lists. She cashed her blank check, and more checks. She sent to London for supplies and fabric swatches and more of the unemployed soldiers. The road was regraded, the tenants' roofs were rethatched, and a reasonable rate was established at the grist mill. Aurora had to agree to hire the miller's untrained daughter as her maid to replace Judith, in exchange, but the girl was learning. The vicar's nephew was hired fresh out of university to teach at the refurbished school, to Ned's sorrow. He was finally getting to know his way around the countryside, and now he'd be in a classroom. No doctor answered her advertisements, but Aurora knew Windham was intending to bring one with him, to care for Christopher.

Once the Windham dependents' needs were met, Aurora turned her attention to the house. She had the indolent staff working harder than they had since Windham's mother's time, cleaning and polishing and mending. Aurora ransacked the attics, ordered from Ackerman's, and appointed Mr. Dawson, who was not an embezzler, as factotum, now that he had the accounts up to date. The bailiff quit in protest before Mr. Dawson could discuss the discrepancies he'd found. Aurora hired one of the tenant farmers to oversee the lands, pending Lord Windham's approval, of course.

She found an empty cottage for Judith and helped clean that, too. Judith would move in as soon as the house was ready and Aurora's new maid could sew a nearly invisible seam. The injured veteran was going to move in, too, as soon as the banns were read. He didn't mind standing father to another man's babe, he said, for with one stone he wasn't likely to sire a son of his own. He became the new gamekeeper, charged with keeping game on the poorhouse table and out of the tenants' gardens. He was also named the new sheriff, pending Windham's approval, of course. Aurora saw no reason he couldn't do two jobs.

She fell into bed every night exhausted, but she was taking care of everything she could except for the swamp, leaving that for Aunt Thisbe and Uncle Ptolemy when they arrived, pending Windham's approval, of course. Now Lady Windham was ready to see about her new relations.

Chapter Fourteen

"Meals will not be served in the bedchambers henceforth, except for breakfast." Aurora made the announcement in the little chapel after the Sunday service. Everyone in the household was present, except Aunt Ellenette, who never rose before noon, and Lady Brianne. "My aunt and uncle are arriving shortly, as are his lordship and Captain Warriner. The staff will have enough extra work."

"But my lady is ailing," claimed the former Mrs. Podell's maid, a gray-haired woman of more starch than sense. "My lady cannot be disturbed."

"Your lady," Aurora declared, "is disturbing the entire household. The footmen have better things to do than carry trays all day, and the kitchens cannot be expected to prepare meals at all hours. They certainly should not have to cook Lady Brianne's favorites when the rest of the family is eating something else." She thought she heard an "Amen" from the rear, where Cook was sitting. "If she is too ill to come downstairs, Cook can send up some beef broth or calf's foot jelly — invalid food."

"That's right, Lady Windham, you tell 'er." That also came from the back. The servants had given over resenting Aurora's demands when she had seen their quarterly wages paid on time, and increased, besides. Loyalty to the family was one thing; new uniforms, new mattresses, and new coins were another. Besides, the new Lady Windham was family now, wasn't she?

Lady Brianne's maid crossed her arms over her bony chest and stuck her chin out. "We'll see who rules this roost soon enough."

Since the woman's belligerent pose merely reminded her of Frederick, the pug, Aurora just smiled. She'd routed the mutt; she could best the maid. Unchecked by his mistress, Frederick had snapped at Judith, growled at Ned, and shredded Aurora's favorite slippers. So she brought Sweety inside from the stables. "If your pet can reside indoors," she'd announced to Aunt Ellenette, "so can mine." She had a portion of the conservatory turned over to the monkey, and the boot boy assigned to playing with Sweety when Ned was at school. And she brought the monkey into the parlor on occasion, on a leash. Frederick never bothered her again after Sweety swung him overhead by his curly little tail. In fact, Frederick hardly came out from under the sofa. If he spoke about it to Aunt Ellenette, Aurora did not know, for that highly affronted lady was not speaking to her. Now Aurora did not have to hear how Windham's mother had managed the estate.

"Until his lordship returns," she told the maid, the same as she had told Aunt Ellenette and the other servants, "I am in charge. If I declare supper be served in the wine cellar, I expect Lady Brianne to be there. And do not think to cross me in this, to carry trays or fix meals yourself, for I write your pay check, not Mrs. Podell."

Head high, Aurora left the chapel, praying none of the servants could tell how she was trembling within. Never in her life had she threatened a servant or delivered ultimatums to a lady who was older than she was, and better born. But she'd promised to comfort Windham's sister, and the woman was going to be comforted, willy-nilly.

Aurora had yet to get a glimpse of her new sister-in-law. She had noticed curtains twitched aside when she was coming or going from the carriage drive, and she'd heard doors quietly cracked open when she passed in the hall. Lady Brianne was curious, at any rate. Soon she would be hungry.

She must have had a reserve cache of food, or Aunt Ellenette was bringing her bonbons, for Lady Brianne did not appear at the luncheon table, the dinner table, or in the drawing room for late tea that evening. The next day's luncheon also passed quietly without her presence. Aurora was thinking about the price of wool, and Aunt Ellenette was still not speaking, except to Frederick, who was not permitted in the morning room since he had attacked one of the footmen over a plate of meat pasties.

That evening Aurora had Judith and her new maid, Maisy, take extra care with her toilette. She wore her prettiest new gown and her mother's pearls, thinking how pitifully equipped she was to impress the one-time heiress, the one-time Incomparable, the one-time Toast of London. One more day of Aunt Ellenette's sullen silence and she'd bring Sweety to the dinner table.

Lady Brianne had certainly not gone to any pains to impress Aurora. She came down to the drawing room before dinner supported by her maid on one side and a sturdy footman on the other. She wore a black crepe gown that was finely crafted but ill-fitting, as though she had gained a few pounds from such prolonged inactivity. Her complexion, which should have been the peaches and cream of an auburn-haired beauty, looked pasty from lack of sunlight, and her hair hung limply down her back, under its scrap of black lace. She was, however, wearing diamonds — the Windham diamonds if Aurora was not mistaken from Kenyon's description, jewels which should by rights go to the new Lady Windham. The heavy necklace and matching ear bobs would have commanded attention at the opera or Carlton House. They looked absurd at a family dinner for three women. The challenge was issued, though, the insult egregious. Aurora decided not to rise to that bait, however. She'd let Aunt Thisbe and Uncle Ptolemy drain Grendel's fen; the earl could defang the dragon himself.

Aurora made a polite welcome, inquiring into her sister-in-law's health and expressing pleasure that she could join them.

Lady Brianne sniffed. "As though I had a choice." She gave the barest nod to acknowledge Aurora's greeting before taking a seat next to her aunt.

"Where is dearest Frederick, Aunt Ellenette?" she cooed. "I was hoping for some intelligent conversation during dinner."

Aurora grimaced to see Brianne peering into the corners of the room and under the furniture, looking for the pug dog. Another Warriner too proud to admit a defect in the noble line — just what she needed.

"Shall I send a servant to fetch your spectacles, my lady?" she asked, all solicitous courtesy. "Squinting causes frown lines, I always thought."

Lady Brianne hurriedly removed an elegant gold lorgnette from her gown's pocket. "That will not be necessary." She then proceeded to inspect the redecorated room, addressing her remarks to Aunt Ellenette exclusively. The sofa was too close to the fireplace, the new draperies were too garish in color, the china dogs on the mantel were too mawkish for a gentleman's residence.

Aunt Ellenette tried to hush her niece. Not speaking was one thing, but to be so blatantly offensive was another. Besides, Aunt Ellenette adored the Staffordshire dogs. She also appreciated how comfortably cozy the sofa was, how the whole room seemed brighter with the new hangings, and how her bedroom ceiling no longer sagged. Further, no one was bothering her with menus or mending or tradesmen's bills.

Aunt Ellenette might even enjoy having the new Lady Windham around, if Frederick approved. Since he hadn't come out from under the bed since that dreadful ape incident, she did not know. She did know proper behavior, though. "But the room is much tidier, dear. You know how we used to sneeze from the dust."

Brianne did not listen to her aunt's gentle hint. She likely never listened to anyone, Aurora thought, recognizing Lady Brianne's spitefulness from the spoiled beauties she had seen in Bath on occasion. The erstwhile widow was not in a decline; she was in a petulant pother. The well-padded female was not vaporish, just viperish, and Aurora was done listening to her venom. The diamonds and the fault finding were petty aggravations, more a reflection of the woman's bad manners and bad temper than anything else. But for Lady Brianne to criticize the fire screen Aunt Thisbe had embroidered as a wedding gift was the outside of enough.

"*Lumbricus terrestris* is an invaluable creature and deserves to be immortalized, Lady Brianne. More important, the screen was a gift from my beloved aunt, who is due to arrive any day. If this is the way you intend to go on when my relatives come, perhaps you would do better in your rooms after all." It was not quite a threat, for they both knew Aurora could not lock the earl's sister in her chambers.

"Earthworms?" Brianne raised her eyebrow, peering at Aurora through her lorgnette as though her sister-in-law had also crawled out from under a rock.

"I expected better of Lord Windham's sister." Aurora spoke quietly, not permitting herself to be goaded into behavior equally as unladylike.

"Oh? I expected exactly what I got, an encroaching mushroom."

Aurora knew a great deal about mushrooms. She wished she had some *Amanita phalloides,* or death caps, right now. She wished the butler would announce dinner. She wished the Earl of Windham to Jericho.

Lady Brianne was going on, spewing weeks' worth of rancor. "You are nothing but a climber, heady with power and new-found wealth. I hear you are spreading my brother's blunt in the parish, currying favor. As if that would get the neighbors to accept an obscure Bath miss whose family is barely connected to the aristocracy by the thinnest thread. Furthermore, your taste is abominable. I'd be ashamed to invite relatives of *mine* here."

Since Lady Brianne's relative was at that moment frantically fanning herself with her handkerchief, Aurora spoke up. "You could have helped, you know. I sent word I was inspecting fabric samples and such. For that matter, you could have refurbished this room any time in the past ten years. Heaven knows the house looked as if it hadn't been cleaned in a decade. The rest of the property was in equally as deplorable a state."

"Why should I concern myself with Windrush? It's your house."

"But you live here. The people depend on you. The earl depended on you to look after the place while he was abroad or in London."

Lady Brianne sipped her sherry. "How *bourgeoisie* you sound. And Genevieve was chatelaine here before me, for all she cared. Blame her for the neglect. Besides, she took everything of value with her when she left."

Aurora gazed pointedly at the diamonds at Lady Brianne's throat. "Perhaps not everything."

"Genevieve couldn't wait to be out of here, and I cannot blame her." Brianne held a scrap of black lace to her brow, remembering her role as betrayed woman. "I'll likely end my days here."

Not if Aurora could help it. "Nonsense.

177

By next spring everyone will have forgotten the circumstances of your marriage." They'd be too busy digesting Aurora's. "You can go to London and set up an establishment of your own."

"On what? I have no income but the pittance my brother doles out to me. No, I'll spend what's left of my sorrowful existence in this very house with no friends, no future, and a fortune hunter for family."

Even Aunt Ellenette gasped at the insult. Not even Frederick had dared suggest such a thing.

Aurora was clenching the stem of her wineglass so hard she feared it would break — or that she'd toss the contents in Lady Brianne's spoiled, spiteful, squinty face. "Is that what you think, that I married your brother for his wealth?"

"I think you are nothing but an opportunist, Miss Aurora McPhee that was. You tempted Harland and then saw a better chance with Kenyon, so you threw yourself at him like a Covent Garden familiar."

Luckily, Aurora did not know what a Covent Garden familiar was. "What, you are blaming me for falling into Podell's clutches? Isn't that the pot calling the kettle black?"

"He might have come back to me,"

Brianne insisted, "if you hadn't put out lures."

"He'd had himself declared dead, for goodness sake. And he'd spent your fortune. He wasn't coming back, you ninny." This last was from Aunt Ellenette.

Aurora was more shocked that Lady Brianne would *want* the dastard back. "You do know he had another wife, a previous one?"

"Of course I know. Everyone knows. I was never really married, and now I never will be! I am the laughingstock of London."

"Gammon. You are the widow of a hero who died fighting for his country. That's all anyone needs to know. Kenyon made sure everything else was kept quiet in Town."

"Quiet, when he had to ride ventre à terre to stop another wedding?"

"We are giving out the story that, learning of your husband's death, a despicable cad took Podell's name, since his own was known to the law. Your brother got wind of an engagement and, suspicious of the similar names, investigated. He saved the day and Podell's reputation. He is also saying that we knew each other for years. You can, of course, deny the whole tissue of lies, which, yes, would make you the fool who is still wearing the willow for the man who ruined her. Since you also ran off with the dirty dish to disoblige your family, no one will doubt your idiocy."

Brianne fingered her black crepe gown. "Perhaps it is time I put off mourning."

"We could go to the village in the morning."

"Faugh, there is nothing worth buying so far out in the country."

"There is now." Aurora had sent for Marie the milliner and one of the modiste sisters when she saw how the local women had no fashionable choices. She had set them up in a shop together, and they'd already repaid half her loan.

Brianne's ears perked up at the word of a new shop, then her shoulders drooped like a weary swan. "But I have no money. I've already spent this quarter's allowance."

"Kenyon left me enough for both of us. All of us," she amended, sending Aunt Ellenette into a happy twitter.

"There's nowhere to go, so there's no need for fancy togs."

"Nonsense. There must be assemblies somewhere nearby, but we can call on the neighbors for a start."

"They'll never be home to us."

Aurora might have lived a sheltered life in Bath, but she knew something of human nature. "What, a countess and an earl's sister? Besides, the local gentry will be scrambling to entertain us once they hear of the ball I am planning to celebrate your younger brother's return." Aurora didn't know how long Christopher's recovery would take, nor did she have any idea whom she'd invite, but she was going to have a party with every available gentleman she could scrape up. One of them, pray God, would be nodcock enough to fall for Mrs. Podell.

"A ball?" Brianne was saying. "I'm sure you'll make it a skimble-skamble affair without my help. What could an upstart like you know about entertaining nobility? You'd hire three field hands with fiddles instead of a respectable London orchestra — and serve bread and butter. Lobster patties, that's what we need. And the monkey must not be permitted in sight. Nor that nasty little boy who follows you around like a puppy. We'll have to order champagne and additional flowers and —"

"Dinner is served, my lady," the butler announced, a week too late, it felt to Aurora.

"Do you know, I don't believe I feel quite the thing. I am afraid you two ladies will have to excuse me," she said, but they were so busy planning her ball that neither of the Warriner women noticed when she left.

"Shall I have a tray sent up to your room, my lady?" the butler asked. "I realize you said meals were to be taken in the dining room, but —"

"No," she said, dashing for the stairs. "I don't think that will be necessary."

Chapter Fifteen

Some letters are read once, some twice. Some had to be read with crossed lines, and some had to be read between the lines. Kenyon's letter to Aurora, his first ever, was definitely in the last category.

My lady wife, Windham's note began, giving her heart a caress, *we have arrived in London at last but are delayed here until Christopher's health improves, on doctors' advice.* He did not have to say that the journey was a nightmare and his brother's condition was precarious; she understood. He did not say he missed her, but Aurora decided he was too concerned with his brother to think about any other emotions. And he must be exhausted. Perhaps he was simply not the type to express the more tender sentiments. On the other hand, perhaps he simply did not miss her.

The earl wrote that he would continue his investigations at the East India Company and the shipping offices, and would send his solicitor, Juckett himself, to Bath to question Phelan Ramsey. That meant he was still not resigned to their marriage, Aurora interpreted, her spirits plummeting. Kenyon was looking to disprove her identity, no matter what he said about seeking Podell's motives. He wanted an easy end to their marriage.

Lord Windham went on to say that his banker had transferred additional funds for her use. Oh dear, he was politely telling her that she was up River Tick. What if his pockets weren't as deep as she thought? Lud, she knew she was spending money as if it were water, but there were so many good uses for it. And he had told her to freshen up Windrush for his brother's arrival.

Aunt Ellenette had written to him, it seemed. *I understand it is a difficult situation, one you were not prepared for, but please try to ease the turmoil in the house.* He obviously agreed with his sister that Aurora was not equipped to manage a great estate. Well, she was at least trying, unlike his last countess. And she would not give Frederick his own chair at the dinner table, no matter how upset Aunt Ellenette said he was. And no matter how many tattletale letters she wrote.

Kenyon's next paragraph was even more damning. He asked her, no, it sounded more like a warning, to be circumspect among the neighbors because he wanted no more scandal attached to his family name. He didn't trust her; that was plain as pudding. What, did he think she was going to run off with the vicar or something? Or did he think that she enjoyed being the center of gossip? No wonder Kenyon did not miss her if he believed she was like the deceitful Genevieve.

Aurora was upset. All her exhausting efforts had gone to make his home more comfortable, to lift some of the burdens of responsibility from his shoulders, to share his concerns. And he thought she was a spendthrift, a troublemaker, an adventuress, uncultured, unreliable, and unlovable. Her eyes were filling, making it hard to read the last lines: *When in doubt, consult my sister.*

She should take that hobbledehoy harpy as a model of how to go on? *Hah!* That spoiled damsel was running Aurora ragged with her demands and derision. Half the bills Kenyon was receiving were for Lady Brianne's new wardrobe, and there was a continual battle to keep the purchases to merely expensive, Brianne's taste running to the extravagant. One would think the lady was planning a second London come-out, instead of putting off her blacks at a few country entertainments. One would also think Brianne was an heiress, instead of a dependent. She still made no effort to help Aurora with the household, but was constantly informing her of how efficient her mother had been, or how beautiful Genevieve had been, and all Kenyon's other mistresses. She'd even hinted that he was in London right now, amusing himself with the likes of Lola. Worst of all, she was barely civil to Aunt Thisbe and Uncle Ptolemy when they arrived.

Aurora's relations, at least, brought her comfort, in the few hours she got to spend with them. They brought their familiar collecting jars and nets and magnifying glasses, their notebooks and identification guides, and disappeared. And they brought her mother's trunks. When Aurora had five minutes to herself, sometime next year, she hoped, she'd be able to look through them. The McPhees were delighted with Derby, and the lower acreage that never drained was a naturalist's nirvana, with spring so close. They commandeered another section of the conservatory for their studies, retreating there for hours when they were not out conducting field research. They were happy to share the succession houses with the monkey, who Uncle Ptolemy was positive he could teach to talk. If Frederick could speak, Uncle said with a wink, the monkey could. Aurora swore Sweety had more sense than Kenyon's sister. Consult Brianne? When cactus grew in that swamp.

Aurora ripped her husband's letter into quarters, then crumpled the pieces in her hand, and threw them into the fire, thinking of her mother's neatly saved letters. She'd be hanged if she saved such a patronizing, pompous piece of poppycock, which was barely legible, meaning his lordship was too proud to wear his glasses in Town. She sat back at the desk, idly straightening piles of correspondence Mr. Dawson had not yet answered or filed away pending his lordship's return. The topmost letter had a name that caught her eye: Harland Podell.

The letter was from the earl's solicitor, addressed to Lord Windham. Mr. Juckett did know she was handling the estate matters, however, and could have marked the letter personal or private if he had not wanted it read by other than the earl's myopic eyes. He had undoubtedly reported its contents to Windham when he returned to London, anyway. Besides, Kenyon already believed her guilty of worse crimes and worse manners. He, moreover, was in

London with the Lolas of the world, while she was here with his querulous kin. She liked Lola better, too. Aurora read the letter.

Harland had yet another wife. Another heiress, Miss Nialla Benton was the only child of a wealthy mine owner in Lancashire, the perfect target for a fortune hunter. As Juckett's men had discovered, Miss Benton was seventeen when Podell met her at a local assembly two years ago, a year before he married Brianne, claiming a baronetcy and a promotion in the works.

Mr. Benton was not impressed, deeming his fortune worth a son-in-law with a barony, at least, but Nialla was taken with the lieutenant's looks and address. She was also taken out to the balcony at a different party and discovered in Podell's arms.

How many times had Podell performed his compromising ploy? Aurora bitterly wondered. Enough to be well practiced, for certain. The engagement was announced, then the hurried wedding, then he left to rejoin his regiment. Or search out another bride, Aurora guessed.

Mr. Benton was too downy a bird to hand over a king's ransom to Podell in one huge lump. He'd grown wealthy by not trusting anyone, certainly not a nob, and saw no reason to start now. So he tied Nialla's dowry in trusts, with the interest payable quarterly. He himself kept control of the capital.

Podell could not die a hero's death for this bride, since he had to return to Lancashire every three months to express his devotion to his young wife, and to collect his blunt. He lived like a lord at his father-in-law's expense for a fortnight, then left for another few months. There were, blessedly, no children. The Jamaican Podells seemed to be the legitimate offspring, so the dastard had no bastards.

At the earl's request, Mr. Juckett had written to Mr. Benton, who was naturally outraged on his daughter's behalf. He swore to make her a widow, one way or t'other. Since no one knew where Podell was at the time, before Aurora's mock wedding, Benton declared that he had died in battle like so many other brave boys. His little girl did not have to know the truth, or the shame of her sham marriage. She was blameless, and her fortune was nearly intact, if her maidenhead was not. Her loving father would make sure that Nialla suffered no further at Podell's hands. And he'd send his minions to join the earl's in tracking the cur down. Benton was grateful, the solicitor wrote, and extended his appreciation to Windham for investigating the vermin and bringing Podell's misdemeanors to his attention.

Mr. Juckett concluded his letter to Lord Windham by saying that he would write to Mr. Benton, announcing Podell's departure from England's shores. If the coal merchant wanted to send someone to see that Nialla became a widow in deed as well as in name, the world would not mourn the loss.

Aurora placed the letter back on the pile. They were going to let some poor woman believe that her hero-husband had perished, that he had passed on? He'd passed on to Brianne and Aurora, that's what he'd done, and Lord knew how many others. Miss Benton's whole life would be blighted. She might never come out of mourning. No, Aurora believed that a woman deserved the truth, no matter how painful. And she deserved to hear it from another Mrs. Harland Podell.

"What, call on a Cit?" Lady Brianne bristled when Aurora suggested the visit. "You might count coal heavers as desirable acquaintances — Lud knows your aunt and uncle dote on dung beetles — I do not."

"We need to show her that she is not alone. That she should not regret the loss of such a slimy scoundrel."

"But she is a coal miner's daughter, Aurora."

"Does that mean she has no feelings? All women can be hurt, or have you forgotten your own pain?"

"So send her a letter." Brianne turned back to the fashion magazine she was studying. "You can sign my name if you wish."

"She needs to be told in person, and you need to see that I did not steal Harland's affections from you, once and for all. The man was a pernicious polygamist." Aurora was tired of her sister-in-law's sniping and sour disposition. She was also tired of arguing about money. "Besides, I shall not leave you here to bankrupt your brother's estate. In fact, I have already instructed Mr. Dawson to deny you any more funds, and I have informed the dressmakers and other merchants that I will not honor any more of your bills."

Brianne threw the magazine to the floor and shouted, "How dare you."

Aunt Ellenette put down her novel and picked up her pug, then sidled out of the room before Brianne threw herself into a full-fledged tantrum.

"Why, you're no better than a tradesman's daughter yourself, and your father didn't even manage to make his fortune in India. You cannot tell me what to do, what to wear, where to go."

"It's my money," Aurora said quietly.

"Or your brother's. He will always provide for you, naturally, but he does not have to go into debt for you. He is already complaining of the outlandish expenditures, and not half the dressmakers' bills have arrived. You may discuss your financial situation with him when he returns. Till then, I hold the purse strings, and I say when they will be loosened."

"But I cannot leave now, while planning for the ball is in such a crucial stage. I have been thinking about rewording the invitations."

"Plans for the ball will have to wait until we hear from your brothers. We were too optimistic, I fear, concerning Captain Warriner's condition."

"Nonsense, Kit always loved a good party."

"And he will love this one, when he is ready to dance and enjoy the company. I am afraid you will have to make do with whist parties and charades with the vicar in the meantime. You could always try putting your hand to hemming the new draperies."

Brianne waved her manicured hand in the

air. "Oh, I suppose I cannot let you go to Lancashire alone. Kenyon wouldn't like it above half. He asked me to keep an eye on you, you know."

"And you've been so good about watching me sew the curtains. But you have been complaining about the wall coverings in your bedroom" — and everything else — "so this would be a good opportunity to have the work done without suffering the mess and bother. I expect we shall be gone for two days at least."

"That Chinese silk with the gold bamboo? It's hardly worth doing, else."

And that was extortion, plain and simple, but Aurora agreed. She'd have no peace otherwise, for one thing, and Brianne would be less likely to notice the improvements she was making on the nursery floor and report them to Windham, for another. The school-room and one of the bedrooms were being overhauled for Andrew, for the time when Aurora convinced her husband to bring their son home. The nursery itself, with its dusty crib, could wait — another decade, it was seeming. "Shall we leave as soon as the rolls of paper arrive?"

Brianne nodded. "But I will not travel with that guttersnipe page of yours, nor the ape."

Aurora saw no reason to take Ned out of school, and she saw no reason to travel with a monkey again, ever. "Very well, but I will not travel with Frederick, either. He slavered all over my skirts the last time your aunt insisted he come along."

"And I'll want my own maid along, not one of your charity cases. And a room of my own when we put up at inns. And I get to ride facing forward."

Aurora simply made note of her sister-in-law's demands and stipulations. She was happy enough getting the lazy creature out of the house. With any luck, Aurora might even convince Lady Brianne to think of Miss Benton's welfare instead of her own, for once. Now if she could only convince her to leave the diamonds home.

Chapter Sixteen

As Uncle Ptolemy always said, what cannot be cured must be endured. He was speaking of gnats, though, not nags. Short of putting a gag in her mouth, Aurora saw no way of putting a stop to Brianne's complaints. The carriage was too crowded, the road was too bumpy, her throat was parched, and her eyes were tearing from the dust. Perhaps Aurora should have taken the monkey, after all.

Aunt Ellenette had stayed home, on Frederick's recommendation. Of course he'd tell her not to go if he couldn't; the servants would strangle him in her absence. And Brianne's maid, wise woman, developed a cough, rather than share a coach with her lady. They took Maisy instead, who sat up front between the driver and the guard. Maisy was thrilled to be jaunting about the countryside, and delighted to be squeezed next to Richard, the guard.

Aurora squeezed her eyes shut, hoping Brianne would take the hint and be still. She hoped in vain. Heavens, had no one ever taught the woman manners? Granted Lady Brianne had lost her mother at an early age, and had a father who thought the sun rose and fell with his baby girl, but she'd had governesses and gone away to school. The previous Lord Windham should have asked for his tuition fees back.

At least now Aurora understood why the current earl stayed away from Windrush so much, letting it fall into disrepair, and why no one had chased after Lady Brianne when she eloped with Podell. The only wonder was how Podell had lasted the entire way to Gretna Green without leaping out of the coach. Brianne's dowry must have been large, indeed. Aurora was developing a headache already, and they had barely left the carriage drive.

They did arrive at Mr. Noah Benton's home eventually, and Aurora would have been happy if it was a coal miner's cottage, so long as they'd reached their destination. Benton's residence was no humble thatch-roofed house, though; it was a mansion to put Windrush to shame. Palladian columns fronted the sprawling building, and wings reached back in both directions. The vast lawns were as smooth as a billiards table, and the flower beds rivaled Bath's Sydney Gardens. The windows shone, the brass gleamed, and swarms of servants hurried out the door to meet them and see to their needs.

Lady Brianne fingered the diamonds at her throat with a smirk. "I told you we needed to show the Cits our superiority."

As it turned out, no one was impressed except the servants, who rarely got to offer refreshments to two ladyships. Mr. Benton was at one of his mines, they said, not expected back until suppertime, and Mrs. Podell was away, visiting her old nanny. Aurora accepted the offer of tea, rather than face the carriage again so soon. Trying to decide if they should stay in the neighborhood overnight, Aurora complimented the housekeeper on the excellent strawberry tarts, then asked after Mrs. Podell's welfare.

"We are thinking that she must be related to my sister-in-law's dear departed husband, who was also a Podell. While we were in the neighborhood, we decided it was only proper to make our condolences for your Mrs. Podell's own recent loss."

Brianne almost choked on the tart she was eating, her third, Aurora noted. Aurora pushed the plate away, lest she have to purchase another, larger, new wardrobe. The housekeeper also coughed, then cleared her throat. "I'll be that happy to pass your sympathies along, my lady, but there's no saying when Miss Nialla, Mrs. Podell, that is, will return. Sometimes she stays overnight with Nanny Dunn, and sometimes for . . . for days."

"She must be very fond of her nurse-maid," Aurora said, to which the house-keeper bobbed her head so vehemently in agreement her mobcap nearly flew off. "I suppose we could stop by Nanny Dunn's to pay our respects."

"Oh, no, my lady, you wouldn't want to do that. Why, Nanny lives up in the hills. Carriages can't get there, no, not a'tall. You'd have to walk." When Brianne gasped at the idea, the older woman nodded again. "That's right. Two or three miles, it is. And . . . and Nanny doesn't like strangers."

That seemed to be the end of it. Aurora got up to go, saying, "I suppose I could send a letter after all."

As Brianne stuffed a strawberry tart in her pocket and another in her mouth, she mumbled her agreement. "The chit is living in the lap of luxury, wanting for nothing. Why would you want to meddle? She'll get over Podell, and her father will buy her another husband. A wealthy, titled one this time, you can wager on it."

Maisy reported otherwise. One of the servants there made friends with her. Well, he made advances, but Maisy saw no need to tell her mistress that she'd been flirting with a footman behind the bushes. It was Jeb who warned her the ladies wouldn't be staying, that they wouldn't be seeing Mrs. Podell, not today nor any day. When she told him that her mistress was that determined to have a coze with the young widow, Jeb snorted. It wasn't likely that anyone in the house would be giving out Miss Nialla's direction, he said, not if they wanted to keep their jobs. Jeb was taking a post in London next month, so he did not care.

While Lady Brianne was washing her hands in a spare guest chamber, Maisy was trading kisses for information. Contrary to what he'd told the earl's solicitor, Mr. Benton had not calmly accepted his daughter's dissolved marriage, nor had he told her that Podell was dead. Instead of offering solace, in fact, he'd tossed her out of the house, like a soiled dove. By selling her jewels and clothes, Nialla had managed to purchase a cottage in a nearby village, where she was stigmatized as a fallen woman. Heaven knew what she'd do when her blunt ran out — likely become the whore her father named her.

"I do not approve of servants' gossip,

Maisy," Aurora firmly chided. "What's the direction?"

Nialla's house was a hovel at the end of a rutted road that was more of a cow path. The grass was overgrown, the shutters were hanging, and the roof had collapsed over one corner. Brianne refused to step out of the coach. Aurora was getting down when the door to the cottage opened and a petite, pretty redhead came out. The girl's freckled face was alight until she saw that the luxurious coach was not her father's, come to take her home. Her eyes filled with tears, and she clutched an already damp handkerchief. They had obviously found the latest Mrs. Podell.

"If you are looking for the village," she told Aurora with a sniffle, "you have missed the turn. It's back that way." She waved a reddened hand in the right direction, almost as if she were waving to her former life.

Before the woebegone young woman could back through her doorway, Aurora introduced herself as Lady Windham, to which appellation she was becoming accustomed. Nialla curtseyed, but without recognition of the name. Then Lady Brianne stepped out of the carriage. While she was making the introduction, Mrs. Harland

Podell to Lady Brianne who was also Mrs. Harland Podell, Aurora noted that Brianne had removed her necklace, thank goodness. At least her sister-in-law had some drops of human kindness in her blue blood, not flaunting the diamonds in front of the downtrodden.

Once Aurora explained who they were, and that they had come to inquire into her welfare, Nialla almost kissed her hand, then threw herself into Brianne's arms, weeping. Still acting uncharacteristically unselfishly, Brianne held her hand out, for Aurora's handkerchief for the girl.

"I . . . I have felt so alone, you see," Nialla apologized, stepping back and wiping her eyes, "with no one to talk to except my cat. And to know that someone cares at last, strangers, at that, is overwhelming. But we are not truly strangers, are we?"

"We are practically in-laws," Brianne said dryly, straightening her hat.

"But why did you pick this location if you have no friends here?" Aurora wanted to know, horrified that this delicate creature was on her own in this isolated spot.

"I had friends, or so I thought. They were all afraid of my father, though. Everyone for miles around depends on him for their live-lihoods, you see. No one would take me in, or hire me, or even tell me what my jewels were worth, but I . . . I stayed nearby hoping my father would relent. And I had nowhere else to go."

"That cad!" Brianne swore, inspecting the outside of the dilapidated cottage through her lorgnette.

"My father said he was ashamed, after boasting to all his cronies of the fine connections I was making. My presence only reminded him of the humiliation."

"I didn't mean your father, although Mr. Benton has a great deal to answer for. Our pigs live better than this. I meant Podell, that serpent, for taking such cruel advantage of such a sweet little lamb as yourself."

Aurora couldn't help thinking that she was no older than Nialla, yet Brianne had never expressed the least sympathy toward her.

"You are so good, Lady Brianne, a true angel of mercy," Nialla said, starting to weep again. "And you too, Lady Windham, for bringing her."

Brianne preened, as though coming here were entirely her idea, but she did give Aurora some credit. "Oh, she was in Podell's sights, too, for some reason."

Nialla said, "Most likely because she is so beautiful."

Her remark had Aurora preening a bit herself. "Why, thank you."

Brianne tapped her foot in the mud. "Hmph. Aurora made a lucky escape, though, and landed in clover, whilst the two of us suffer and scrape by."

Some scrapings were more luxurious than others, Aurora reflected as she followed Brianne and Nialla into the two-room cottage. Brianne would never want for anything, while this Mrs. Podell did not have enough wood for a fire. The interior was somewhat better than the outside of the cottage in that it was clean, but it was bare and cold. Brianne took the only comfortable chair, of course, leaving Aurora to sit on a wobbly wooden seat at the table. Nialla offered them refreshments, hard toast, thin jam, weak tea, which neither Aurora nor Brianne had trouble declining after the lavish repast at Mr. Benton's. They both understood the food might be Nialla's only meal that day. Enjoying her role as Lady Bountiful, Brianne even unwrapped the strawberry tart from her pocket and placed it on the tray, saying, "You might enjoy this later."

Nialla took one look at the pastry and started crying again, her lip trembling. "It's . . . it's one of Mrs. O'Shea's, isn't it?"

If Mrs. O'Shea was the cook at Mr. Benton's house, it was. While Brianne awkwardly patted the other girl's back, Aurora was worrying. What were they supposed to do with this weepy little widgeon? She desperately wished her husband were here, for Kenyon would know what was best to do. He'd rescued her, and Lola, so she had every confidence he would not leave this damsel in such unconscionable distress. "There's nothing for it," she declared. "You'll have to come with us."

While Nialla sobbed, Brianne said, "Excuse us a moment, please," then grabbed Aurora's hand and dragged her outside. "Are your attics totally to let? We can't take her home with us like some lost puppy! Her presence will stir up the very scandal Kenyon has been trying to stifle."

"No, it won't, not when we tell the same story we gave out at her father's, that her dead Podell was a cousin to your dead Podell."

"What, and they were both named Harland? That bird won't fly."

Aurora thought she was doing remarkably well for a woman who had never made up a single fib in her life before meeting Windham. "It could be a family name. Or her departed spouse could have been

Harley. No matter, we shall not leave that poor girl here like this."

"Of course not," Brianne surprisingly agreed. "But you could write her a check, for heaven's sake; you don't have to adopt her."

"And when the check is gone? Here she has no chance for employment — if the little peagoose is capable of anything — or for marriage. What other options are there for her? With us, she can start anew."

"But she has freckles and her people are in trade!" To Brianne, either condition was like being infected with the pox. One might sympathize, but one did not invite such an unfortunate into one's home.

"Derby society is not like London. No one will question her ancestors if she is our guest."

"She is *your* guest. Remember that when you try to explain her presence to Kenyon. He will be furious."

He'd be more furious when he discovered how Aurora managed to redeem Nialla's gems from the slimy, unscrupulous jeweler who had not paid her a fraction of their worth. Brianne knowledgeably declared that Nialla ought to have been able to live comfortably off their sale for years. Luckily, the chit had not sold them outright and still had a week left in which to reclaim them at the price she'd received, plus interest, of course. And of course Aurora did not have that much cash in her reticule. She did have a check, though, which the shopkeeper was reluctant to accept.

"Why should I? How do I rightly know you're who you says you are?" He jerked one hairy, dirty thumb in Nialla's direction. "Word is, she ain't no Mrs. Podell, even. You mightn't be no countess, and that one" — with another jerk toward Brianne, who huffed — "mightn't be no lady a'tall."

"Do you see that coach outside, sirrah?" she asked. "It has a crest that even I can see without my looking glass. And my sister-in-law has the Windham signet ring."

She also had the Windham diamonds. Aurora left them as collateral, over Brianne's hysterical clamor. "Oh, hush, it's only for two days until Mr. Dawson can return to exchange them for the money."

"Dawson? Dawson? You're entrusting my diamonds to an —"

"He is not," Aurora declared, shoving Brianne into the carriage. "And they are my diamonds anyway."

Brianne howled the entire first leg of the journey home, but not so loudly as the cat in its basket.

Chapter Seventeen

Some expressions sound better between the pages of a novel than in real life. "Stand and deliver" was one such phrase. Hearing the words, and the gunshot that followed, was not thrilling, the way it was when one was at home, reading by the bedside candle. It was terrifying. Nialla started to scream. The shot, or her screams, frightened the horses, who tried to bolt. The driver cursed and shouted, fighting for control of the cattle. The guard would have fired back, or would have helped with the reins, but Maisy had thrown herself into his arms at the first sight of a pistol-waving, masked horseman in their path.

Brianne was leaning out the window, shouting encouragement to the driver. "Outrun the dastard, Oliver. Mow him down. Shoot him, for heaven's sake!"

Since it was obvious that the driver, Oliver, could barely keep the horses from galloping off the road, Brianne was in danger not only from the highwayman but from falling out of the careening carriage altogether. Aurora tugged on Brianne's skirts until her sister-in-law sat back down, clutching the overhead strap to keep from being tossed around the interior of the coach. "The bandit is going to overtake us in a minute," she reported. "His horse is an enormous gray."

All they could do was sit and wait, holding on to each other and Nialla, who was clutching her cat's basket as if it were a life ring, and sobbing, of course.

"Well, at least he won't get the Windham diamonds," Brianne crowed.

"No, but what about the Benton jewels?"

Nialla sobbed louder.

Aurora was feeling around behind the cushions and under the seat, looking for somewhere to stash the velvet pouch they had rescued from the moneylender. A determined high toby man would search, she knew, but she could not tamely hand over Nialla's fortune. Her searching fingers touched something hard, something deadly.

"A pistol? Excellent! Now we can give the muckworm a taste of his own medicine. Hand it over, Aurora."

"What, give you the gun? You could barely see the highwayman's horse!"

"But I wouldn't be sitting with the thing

on my lap, waiting to be ravished and robbed!"

"Ravished?" cried Nialla, falling off the carriage seat in a dead faint.

Aurora grabbed for the cat basket before Puss landed on her head. Moving as quickly as possible, she raised the basket's lid and stuffed the velvet jewel pouch inside with the frantic cat, who clawed furrows in Aurora's new gloves. Aurora moved even faster, shutting the lid. Then she tucked the pistol in her pocket, hoping the skirts of her carriage dress would hide the bulge.

"Is it loaded?" Brianne asked.

Aurora hadn't thought to look. For that matter, she didn't know how to look, or where. She'd never handled a pistol before in life. She just nodded. There was no reason to frighten Brianne more than necessary.

As the carriage was coming to a halt, they could hear the highwayman shouting to Richard, the guard, to throw down his weapon, or be killed. They heard the thud and Maisy's cries. Then the would-be robber yelled, "You inside. Come out with your hands raised or I shoot your driver."

Aurora nodded to Brianne, who opened the door and slowly stepped down. Aurora followed, her hands elevated, and stood close beside Brianne, so the pistol's outline wouldn't show. "Our friend has fainted," she told the man who faced her, his gun now pointing straight at her chest. "But she has nothing for you anyway."

The man was tall, but not so tall as Windham, nor so broad in the shoulders. Between the mask over his eyes and the hat pulled low over his forehead, Aurora could not discern his coloring, but what showed of his complexion seemed fair and smooth-shaven. His clothes were dusty but well tailored, and his top boots were in the highest kick of fashion. Either he was truly one of the gentlemen of the road, or he was a very successful bandit, Aurora decided.

"My, my, my. This is my lucky day. Two beautiful young ladies out for a drive. I wish I could just steal kisses, my lovelies, but I do have to eat. It's your reticules I'll be having first, then."

"Here, you varlet." Brianne tossed hers at his feet. "Much good it will do you, being as empty as your brain box if you think you can get away with this. My brother is — *ooph.*"

Aurora had shoved Brianne from behind, before the gudgeon could reveal their identities and have them held for ransom. Not seeing the tree branch in her way, Brianne stumbled and would have fallen, except the highwayman caught her and held her against his own chest to steady her. Brianne raised her fist and struck him in the jaw. No ladylike slap, the blow sent his head reeling. "How dare you, sirrah! It's bad enough that you accost innocent wayfarers during the daylight hours, but to prey on defenseless women is beneath contempt. I am sick unto death of men who take advantage of women and then leave them broken and bruised."

"I only wanted to put some food in my belly, miss. And I had no way of knowing you were three females."

Hearing laughter in his voice, Brianne was not mollified. First Podell, then Nialla's heartless father, now a masked man trying to steal their last shillings, was all too much. "Shoot him, Aurora! Shoot the dastard before he bothers another female."

The highwayman finally took his eyes off the magnificent auburn-haired beauty who was so bravely, so buffle-headedly raging at him. He looked up, into the muzzle of Aurora's pistol.

"I wouldn't do that, my lady. My own weapon is aimed right at this beauty's heart, you see." He held Brianne's arm in his free hand so she could not escape, though she did continue with her curses until he said, "What a tongue you have, my lady. You should put it to better use." He pulled her closer and kissed her quickly, ending her harangue with a gasp. Then he told Aurora, "Yes, it would be a great waste to shoot your friend."

"She is no friend of mine," Aurora told him, thinking of what a public service he'd be doing to rid the world of Lady Brianne. "She's my sister-in-law. And I think you are too much the gentleman to shoot a woman."

"But I think you are too much the gentlewoman to shoot a man. Have you ever fired a pistol before?"

"Many times — with great accuracy."

"Ah, those would be the times you released the safety catch, I suppose," he said, laughing.

Now Brianne started raging again — at Aurora. "First you drag me off on your errand of mercy and lose my diamonds, and now you turn craven about shooting a criminal! You might as well hand him Nialla's —"

"That will be enough, Brianne, or I swear I will let him shoot you!"

The highwayman was laughing again, enjoying himself enormously, it seemed, at their expense. "Nialla's . . . what, my ladies?"

"Her cat," Aurora promptly answered.

"Our friend in the coach is fond of her cat. You wouldn't be. It scratches." She held up her gloved hand to show.

"Ah, but I think I might have to see this cat for myself."

Aurora glared at Brianne, who promptly brought her free hand to her forehead and declared, "I think I am going to swoon." Which she did, collapsing right into the highwayman's strong arms. Which gave Oliver, the driver, the opportunity to bash the man over the head with a rock, which then caused a great deal of blood, which caused Brianne to faint in truth.

Which left Aurora with two unconscious females, one concussed criminal, one cater-wauling maid, one less than competent guard, and Oliver, who was all for leaving every last one of them behind for agitating his precious horses.

Aurora couldn't do it; the earl might notice his sister gone missing. Much as she might wish otherwise, she held a vinaigrette under Brianne's nose while Oliver bound the highwayman with a rope from the fellow's own horse, then went to help Richard soothe the nervous cattle. Aurora revived Nialla, too, and threatened to have Maisy bound and gagged unless she cease her shrieking. Aurora then turned to bandage the bandit, using his own neckcloth, which she noted was of fine fabric and freshly laundered.

Brianne watched from over her shoulder, now that most of the bleeding had stopped. "What shall I do with this?" she asked, holding out the highwayman's pistol.

"I suppose we should take it, and him, with us to the constable or sheriff in the next village." Aurora was not pleased with the idea of taking a criminal up in her carriage, but she could not leave him bleeding by the roadside, or free to hold up the next coach.

"He did not actually rob us, you know."

"Not for lack of intention, though. If not for Oliver's cleverness, I hate to think what might have happened."

"And Lady Brianne's quick thinking," Nialla added, which had Brianne puffing out her chest.

The highwayman groaned as Aurora untied his mask, so she gently laid his head back on the grass where they'd dragged him, in case another carriage came by.

"He's quite attractive, don't you think," Brianne said, studying him through her lorgnette, "in a common sort of way."

There was nothing common about the fellow that Aurora could see. He had pale gold hair, almost white, a square jaw, a slightly crooked nose, and laugh lines. He looked to be in his middle twenties. "No, he doesn't resemble any gallow's bait I ever imagined. I do not think he is a baseborn ruffian at all."

"Thank you, my lady," the highwayman said with another moan, opening his blue eyes. He had the audacity to wink up at Brianne, who blushed. He sat up, with Aurora's help, since his hands and feet were tied. "Wesley Royce, at your service, my ladies." He tried a bow, but only succeeded in rattling his aching head worse. "Well, more at your mercy, it would seem. Do you think I might have a sip from the flask in my saddlebag? Then I'd beseech you to listen to my tale."

"Here, hold this," Brianne told Aurora, thrusting the gun into her hands. "I'll get the flask."

His tones were cultured, and he seemed the gentleman, but Aurora still kept the gun trained on this Wesley Royce, ropes or not. He might be a lord out on a lark, but he'd frightened them half to death. Nialla was still trembling, so Aurora told her to sit in the coach and console her cat.

Brianne returned and took Aurora's place by the highwayman's side, holding the flask to his mouth. After he drank, he smiled at her and said, "I never would have shot anyone as pretty as you, you know."

Brianne smiled back, until Aurora hissed at her. "The dastard tried to rob our coach, you ninny, and he took liberties with your person."

"That's right, he did."

Brianne's dreamy voice scared Aurora more than the robbery. Lud, what if the addlepate decided to take to the high toby with this handsome rogue? Kenyon would have her liver and lights. "Let us hear your sad story, sirrah, and no more fustian."

The highwayman, if Aurora could believe him, was the Honourable Wesley Royce, younger son to a baron, whose stepbrother had cheated him of his inheritance. Their father's will was forged, he swore, or coerced from the old man on his deathbed. Baron Royce had been fond of his second wife's boy, Wesley told them, despite his devil-may-care ways. According to the new baron, however, their father had disowned him as a profligate and a wastrel. Wesley had been cut off without a groat. Not wishing to take the king's shilling and die as cannon fodder, Wesley had taken to gambling. He'd managed to support himself in a degree of style for the past months, but luck was a fickle friend, and he wished for a more reliable income.

"So you took to a life of crime?" Aurora asked in disbelief. "Risking your life seemed better than risking your brass in a game of cards?"

Brianne was hanging on the highwayman's every word. She glared at Aurora. "It's much more exciting."

Wesley winked at Brianne again, but addressed Aurora. "This was to be my first and last foray into felony. In fact, it was to be more in the nature of a loan. I fully intended to repay you for whatever I'd taken, my lady. I only wished to borrow a stake, you see, so I might establish myself as a gentleman in London. Bath or Brighton if the takings were not so high."

Wesley did not notice the thunderclouds forming on the ladies' brows, but he heard the ice in Brianne's voice when she asked, "And what then, sir, once you had set yourself up as a man of means?"

"Why, nothing that hasn't been done a thousand times before. In the age-old fashion of dispossessed dependents and under-the-hatches heirs, I would find me a wealthy widow or a rich man's daughter to wed. I could not afford to be fussy, naturally."

Brianne stood up from where she'd been

kneeling at Wesley's side. "You . . . you swine! You pig! You blot-on-the-earth bastard! You're just like every other lily-livered libertine who thinks to repair his own fortunes off some poor female's affections. How dare you hold up our coach, so you can then rob some woman of her dowry, her dignity, and her dreams?" In the midst of her tirade, Brianne began kicking at Wesley's legs. "You miserable, mangy cur! You —"

"That's enough, Brianne," Aurora said, fearing her sister-in-law was about to start kicking the poor, bewildered man in the head. But Brianne was in a rant, and intent on trampling this latest traducer of women into the ground. Aurora tried to take her arm but, enraged, Brianne struck out at her, slapping Aurora's hand away . . . the hand holding the pistol.

Chapter Eighteen

"I've shot a man."

The horses reared in their traces, Oliver and Richard ran to their heads, Maisy started screeching again, Nialla passed out onto the carriage floor, and Brianne and Aurora looked at each other in horror. "I've shot a defenseless man," Aurora repeated, "while he was on the ground, tied hand and foot."

"He deserved it," Brianne told her, trying to lessen Aurora's guilt. "He was nothing but a wicked highwayman anyway. And not even a very good highwayman at that, getting captured on his first attempt." She dashed away the tears in her eyes. "We just saved the sheriff the price of hanging him, that's all. And now some poor woman is safe from his foul designs. He would have made a dreadful husband."

"I . . . would have made . . . a good husband. Meant . . . to try, by George."

He wasn't dead, not yet at any rate! Aurora rolled him over and saw the bloodstain spreading from his shoulder. "His shoulder! I didn't kill him!" She tore open his coat and his shirt, to Brianne's exclamations of shock, or interest. The wretch had her lorgnette out. "Tear up your petticoats, Brianne. Hurry. We have to stop the bleeding."

"My petticoats? They're new — and silk." She helped rip Maisy's petticoats instead.

When Wesley was bandaged, the horses calm enough for Oliver to trust them to Richard, Nialla stepped groggily out of the coach, crying that all their misfortunes were her fault, that if they hadn't been trying to help her, they'd never have found themselves in this position. The silly goose was weeping again, or still, but Aurora had no dry handkerchief to lend her, so she handed her Mr. Royce's flask, after swallowing a mouthful for her own nerves.

"Here, take a sip. It will make you feel more the thing. And if anyone is at fault, it is I, for not being more careful with the pistol."

Brianne didn't take any responsibility, but she did take the flask and drain it.

Wesley stared longingly at Lady Brianne, or the flask, and said, "I am the only one at blame. I deserve to die, as Heaven is my witness, for bringing such grief to such kind young ladies." He was holding his hand out. Since the flask was empty, he must be seeking forgiveness, so Brianne took it.

"You are not going to die until they hang you. I refuse to believe otherwise," Brianne insisted.

As usual, it looked as if Brianne was going to get her way, for the bleeding had stopped, and the wound looked to be a clean one, having passed straight through the man's shoulder. Aurora thought a surgeon should look at it, though. "Brianne, hold the horses while Oliver and Richard put him in the carriage. I . . . I will be back in a moment."

She fled behind the coach. Nialla, holding the highwayman's head, looked toward Brianne, who shrugged. "She's just going to shoot the cat."

The cat now? Nialla fainted again.

Once they were under way, Aurora decided to press for Windrush. She simply could not hand Mr. Royce over to some local law enforcer, not after shooting him. Kenyon would be home soon. He'd know what to do. He was a magistrate himself, after all. And Oliver assured her that the head groom could doctor the prisoner better than any sawbones. If his condition worsened, they could always fetch a surgeon from the next town.

Still holding Brianne's hand — for whose comfort? Aurora wished to know — Wesley begged a favor. "Please . . . I cannot just go off . . . leave Lucy and the babies to starve."

Brianne dropped his hand so fast it bounced off the window of the coach. "You are already married?"

"Not . . . wed . . . yet."

But there were babies? "Shoot him again, Aurora," Brianne said, "or I swear I will do it myself."

Following Wesley's hoarsely whispered directions, the coach, with his horse tied behind, made its way up a narrow path to an old woodsman's shack. Aurora and Richard, rifle finally in his hands, rapped on the door. Still muttering dire imprecations, Brianne held Wesley's own pistol on the half-conscious highwayman. Of course it was empty, but Aurora deemed it safer for all of them not to tell her sister-in-law that. The battered brigand had the audacity to smile at her, though.

No one answered her knock, so Aurora opened the door and called, "Lucy?" before stepping into the rude shelter. "You're Lucy?"

Lucy turned out to be a shaggy black-and-white mutt, with four tiny pups.

Kenyon would know what to do with those, too.

Heavens, Aurora thought as they made their crowded way home, she was expecting a great deal of the husband who didn't want to be. Here she'd been going to show him what an exemplary wife she'd make, not causing any gossip, not squandering his fortune, not abandoning his sister to the melancholy. Well, one out of three was something. Brianne certainly did not mourn Podell any longer. But instead of making his life easier and his house more comfortable, Aurora was burdening Kenyon with more problems, more potential scandals. Why, his new wife might even be charged with shooting a defenseless man. She could not think he would appreciate that, or that he'd come visit her in jail. He'd most likely use it as an excuse to divorce her if he couldn't get the marriage annulled.

Aurora did not want her marriage dissolved. Every day that passed by reinforced her belief that she could be very content with Kenyon, indeed. When she decided to bring Nialla home, it was because she knew he would be kind and capable. With Wesley, he'd be fair. She just knew he could not be cold and callous and uncaring. He was a good man. Moreover, he attracted her like no other, not even Podell. Why, looking at Wesley's handsome visage made her think that auburn hair was far more attractive than blond, and while Brianne almost swooned at the sight of the highwayman's bare chest, Aurora couldn't help comparing it to Kenyon's, with its soft downy covering. She missed him! Aurora couldn't imagine how that was possible after so short a time, but she did. She missed Kenyon's strength, and she missed his smile. She wondered if he'd ever smile at her again, after she brought her houseguests home.

What had the woman done to his house? Granted, it looked cleaner, smelling of lemon oil and beeswax, with flowers on all the tables. And the carriage path and the highway had been smooth, thankfully, for Christopher could not have taken much more jostling. The shrubs were pruned, the windows were washed, and the brass was polished, but Kenyon didn't recognize half the furnishings and less of the servants. And his wife was not there!

Dawson came to the hall and instantly took charge, deploying the multitudes of military-type footmen to settle Christopher in the room prepared for him, to escort the surgeon to his own apartment, to help the earl's valet with the trunks. And saying, "I shall notify the kitchens of Captain Warriner's arrival," he disappeared before Kenyon could ask where she was, his wife. Hell and thunderation, she'd gone away and left the management of his household in the hands of an embezzler. Kenyon touched the new vase on the hall table. Meissen, unless he missed his guess, so it didn't matter that his majordomo was an embezzler. There wouldn't be enough funds left to be worth stealing.

One of the new footmen directed him to the parlor, where Aunt Ellenette babbled about headstrong misses — Aurora or Brianne, he couldn't tell — and Frederick predicting trouble in the coach, which almost had Kenyon rushing for the stables. Then he reminded himself that Frederick was always foretelling doom, from spoiled food to the end of the world, so the earl decided to ignore Aunt Ellenette's prattling, but not her complaints that they never had fresh oranges anymore. He went on to the conservatory, with its fountains and forcing houses and flora from around the globe. His mother's pride and joy, it was maintained in her memory.

His mother would not have recognized the place. It was overrun with creatures with fins or flippers or fur or feathers — in basins and buckets and his copper bathtub, with a splinted-wing swan in the ornamental fountain. Any number of oddities swam in jars, and one he'd hoped never to see again was swinging from the branches of an orange tree, explaining the lack of fruit. He removed his spectacles, for some sights were better not to see. Oddest of all, perhaps, were his new aunt and uncle by marriage. They had no idea where Aurora had gone, or why, just that it had something to do with Mrs. Podell. They were not the least concerned.

"Oh, our Aurora can do anything she sets her mind to." And no, they had not heard from Lord Phelan since he'd left Bath, but they had brought Aurora's mother's letters, peculiar as the request had been. Mr. McPhee did offer to gather leeches in case Christopher needed purifying, but the poor lad had lost so much blood it was a miracle he was still alive, so Kenyon politely declined. Mrs. McPhee offered some mold she'd been growing. He declined that also, with another shudder, so the two turned their backs on him as if he were a servant and resumed their rapt study of some new larva they were hatching out — in what looked very much like his shaving mug.

He could do without his monogrammed mug, but there had better be another bathtub upstairs, Kenyon seethed. After the long, dusty journey, traveling slowly so as not to reopen Kit's wound, the earl wanted a bath and he wanted his wife, blast her! He hadn't thought of much else these weeks of worrying, or the long nights staying up by Kit's bedside. The worst was over, although Kit had lost his arm and still had bouts of fever and delirium, but the doctors were confident he would recover. They could go home. The closer Kenyon got to Aurora, the more he wanted to be close to her, despite his scruples, despite his good intentions, despite the uncertainties. He wanted his wife, by Jupiter.

Everyone else thought they were married. Damn, they might as well be, and the hell with his doubts. He was just suspicious after Genevieve, that was all, Kenyon told himself. He'd learn to trust again, and Aurora would learn to accept his attentions. They would be husband and wife in truth, he decided — as soon as she came home.

Unless she'd left him already. Thunderation, she could not have run off, could she? But she wouldn't have left her relatives here, nor the boy, Ned. Hell, she wouldn't have taken Brianne with her if she were making an elopement or an escape.

The devil take it, he shouldn't have left her. If he couldn't take her with him to fetch his brother — and no woman should see what he'd seen — he should have found someone in London to guide her, to protect her, his innocent bride. Or he should have insisted she return to her own family in Bath, eccentric as they were. They loved her and had her best interests at heart. Instead, he had sent her to Derby, where he himself could never bear to stay above a week at a time. How could he suppose Aurora would handle Aunt Ellenette's flights or Brianne's fits and starts? Why, he wouldn't be surprised if his sister was dragging his countess off to join a band of Gypsies — or a traveling circus.

Lud, he was tired. All Kenyon wanted to do was to rest his eyes on his wife's angel's face. Instead, he saw Brianne's hatchet-faced maid, arms crossed over her bony chest. She was the one who, sniffing in disapproval, informed him that the two most bacon-brained females he knew were out hunting for a third. He'd disown both of them, he swore. He'd have to get into the carriage again and go looking, for who knew what trouble two wantwits would get into. Ned raced in from the stable yard, nearly mowing Kenyon down on the stairs to his bedroom. The boy claimed to know just where the ladies had gone, and was anxious to go find them, too.

"It ain't . . . It isn't right m'lady went off without me. Who knows what can happen to two gentry morts on their own?"

Who knew, indeed? Ned didn't mention he wanted a day off from school, and Kenyon didn't mention Gypsies or traveling circuses. They'd go tomorrow, though.

First he wanted a bath and a meal and a rest. He opened the master's chamber and grabbed for his quizzing glass just before he would have tripped over a new footstool. Damn, she'd rearranged his bedroom! Was there no end to her interference?

But his man, Tarlow, was beaming. "No more carrying buckets of hot water, my lord. We have plumbing."

Soaking in the new porcelain tub in the new bathing room, Kenyon decided he'd forgive his wife anything — except leaving him.

After a fine dinner he sent compliments to the cook. They had a new stove, also, it seemed. He looked in on Christopher, who was weak and wan but happy to be home, except that Aunt Ellenette had spilled his soup down his nightshirt, trying to feed him, and Frederick had jumped on the bed to lick it up, jarring his wound. No, Kit didn't want one of the maids to come, to shower him with pity or to shrink back at the sight of his scars. The maids would get used to him, Kenyon told his brother, and the scars would heal. He only hoped the invisible scars would also diminish.

Kenyon fed his brother, only spilling a little, wishing again that Aurora were here. She would know how to mend Kit's inner wounds. As bighearted as she'd proven to be, his wife would never cringe. She might lose her supper afterward, but Christopher would never suspect. Or was he pinning too much hope on such a slip of a girl? Kenyon did not know, and wouldn't till the infuriating female came home.

Soon, he hoped. Let it be soon.

Chapter Nineteen

Manners pave the rocky paths of social interaction. They also throw up roadblocks. Out of politeness, the earl agreed to a hand of whist with his McPhee guests and Aunt Ellenette, although he would rather be in bed, with his wife or not. Aurora's relatives had asked, out of politeness, thinking they should not abandon their new nephew for their laboratory, not on his first night back. And Aunt Ellenette agreed, out of politeness, although she had no head for cards.

Or anything else, her partner, the earl, recalled after two hands, during which she consulted over every discard with the fattest dog he'd ever seen, and the worst cardplayer. As host, he could not desert his guests; as winners, the McPhees could not withdraw; as he was comfortable on his mistress's lap, Frederick growled when anyone made a move to leave. At last the tea tray arrived, which interested Frederick more than the cards, so they could all take refreshment then, feigning yawns, seek their own beds or bugs or boxes of bonbons.

Lord Windham checked on his brother one more time, relieved to find Christopher sound asleep and cool to the touch. One of the footmen was sitting by the bedside, ready to fetch the earl or the physician if need be. Kenyon could finally retire to his cold, lonely, empty bed. He pounded his pillows; he threw off the top blanket. He rolled onto his stomach, then curled on his side, then lay flat on his back, arms and legs spread-eagled, staring at the ceiling. *Bah!* He got up and paced.

One of his routes took him past the door that connected to the countess's chamber. He cracked the door, thinking he might as well see what changes Aurora had made there, but the room was in darkness, and cold besides. With no Lady Windham at home, the servants had not lit the fire, so the earl did, just in case. Soon he could see that his wife had made her mark here also, with pastel colors instead of the maroons and golds Genevieve had preferred, less furniture, and fewer knickknacks on every surface. A man wouldn't have to fear breaking something fragile every time he stretched, or left his spectacles behind. One of the few decorations was a miniature portrait on the dressing table. Her parents, perhaps? A similarity to her mother ought to quiet some of his qualms. Podell? The fire needed more kindling; the bounder's picture would do nicely. The portrait, he was touched to see, was of himself, the miniature his mother used to have on her nightstand. Lord, he'd been young. He wondered where Aurora had found it, and why she'd placed it in her bedroom. Since there were no pins stuck in it, he chose to see the portrait as a hopeful sign.

He wandered around, touching this pillow and that book, imagining he could smell the lilac scent she usually wore. Feeling foolish, he even opened the doors to her clothespress, just to make sure she'd left most of her things behind, he told himself. He was not spying. Besides, a husband had the right, if not the duty, to oversee his wife's activities. Then he saw the large portmanteau on the wardrobe floor, filled with stacks and stacks of letters. They had to be Elizabeth Halle's, the ones that the McPhees had brought. Kenyon dragged them over to the chair by the fire without a moment's hesitation. Hell, she had to have read his mail to go haring off to Lancashire and Mr. Benton. Why, she was likely wining and dining at the wealthy mine owner's house this very minute, if his sister had not convinced her to detour to an inn nearer the shops. The promise of spending more of Kenyon's blunt would have been the only enticement for Brianne to enter a trades-man's home.

Dash it, who knew what kind of low com-pany they'd be introduced to at Benton's place? For that matter, they could have been set upon on the road. Two well-dressed women in a crested carriage were an easy mark for thieves — or those roving bands of bitter, unemployed veterans. And there had been labor unrest near Manchester just re-cently. Kenyon had to laugh at himself; he'd be envisioning white slave traders next. They were safe, and he was going to read the letters. Lud, Elizabeth Halle must never have thrown away anything.

He was asleep in the chair in Aurora's room when he heard the commotion. Fearing that his brother must be having a relapse and no one knew where to find him, Kenyon dashed out into the hall. The noise was coming from below, though, from the entry hall. His wife was home! Pausing only to tighten the sash of his dressing gown, the earl started down the stairs. He paused midway, his mouth hanging open.

A man was hanging on his wife's arm — a handsome young man, foxed by the look of him and the way he leaned on Aurora. Brianne was on the sot's other side, and a carrot-topped waif trailed behind, clasping a large basket in her arms. A skinny dog was whining beside a box a maid was carrying in. Kenyon didn't even want to think of what might be in the box, or the basket, or in his wife's brain, bringing this motley group home in the middle of the night.

It was a miracle he didn't fall the rest of the way down the stairs, because he hadn't taken his eyes, or his spectacles, off his wife and the clodpole who was cuddling her in her husband's own home. The dastard would be dead by morning. Thinking that he must look like a trout tossed on the riverbank, Kenyon snapped his mouth shut and started across the entry hall, seeing red. No, he was seeing blood. Dear Lord, they were all muddied and rumpled and bloodstained. The redhead was weeping, and the maid's skirts were torn, and his wife — hell, there was blood on his wife.

Kenyon shouted for the butler, his valet, the housekeeper, and Kit's doctor, and anyone else who was neither deaf nor deceased. Servants in all states of undress came running, and men raced in from the stables, too, some with pitchforks in case the house was under attack, and some with buckets of water, in case of fire. The dog was barking, something was screeching from the basket, and the redhead was still weeping in Mrs. McPhee's arms. Two footmen tried to assist the young man, with Brianne screaming at them to be careful, by Jupiter, and his wife — His wife was looking at him as if she'd caught her first glimpse of land after the Flood.

Kenyon waded through the mess, issuing orders as he went for spare bedrooms, for the surgeon, for the dog to be taken to the stables in Ned's charge, for hot water and tea and fires, and for everyone else to go back to bed. Then he grabbed Aurora's arm and dragged her into the nearest room.

He meant to shout at her for worrying him so, and getting into so much trouble. He meant to inspect every inch of her for injury. He meant a lot of things, but all he did was open his arms, and she flew into them. He hugged and rocked and comforted her, then realized she was hugging and rocking and comforting him, too. Zeus, it felt so right.

Aurora felt safe, protected, cherished. Kenyon cared. She never wanted to leave the sanctity of his arms. Now she was home.

Actually, she was in the broom closet, but who cared? When a mop handle poked him in the back, Kenyon did. "Come, my love, you'll be more comfortable upstairs. You can tell me your adventures there." And he could better tell her on the bed how much he'd been missing her.

First she needed a bath.

While his wife was washing, Kenyon thought he'd get a start on unraveling this latest mare's nest. Hurriedly dressing in shirt and pants, he quickly checked to make sure his brother had not been disturbed, but the footman whispered that all was well.

Well? With who knew what being welcomed at Windrush? Horse whiskers.

The surgeon, stepping out of the handsome stranger's room, confirmed having stitched a gunshot wound, as Kenyon had surmised. The doctor had administered laudanum, he reported, so there was no questioning of the man this night. The young lady in the next room had also been dosed, for agitation of the nerves, as well as Lady Windham's maid.

Moving down the hall, Kenyon tried Brianne's door, which was firmly locked. She shouted, "Go away, I am sleeping," when he called to her. The excursion had not improved his sister's personality any, then. It was a wonder Brianne hadn't been the one shot.

Downstairs, Aunt Ellenette was frantically inspecting Frederick for fleas. That's what came of mingling with the lower orders, she declared, demanding he evict the woman who was obviously no better than she ought to be, the unknown invalid, their various four-footed companions, and his countess while he was at it. "The place has not been the same since she got here!"

"No, it hasn't, thank goodness." He left his aunt sputtering and went out to the stables, still hoping to find someone who could provide some information. Oliver, the coachman, was all too happy to see his employer, needing to make sure the earl did not blame him for any of argle-bargle.

The red-eyed and red-haired female, as Kenyon had guessed, was another Mrs. Podell, although this one claimed her dead husband's name was Harley. The story Oliver told of her circumstances made him wish once more he hadn't been so lenient with Podell, whatever he was called. He'd have to make do, Kenyon decided, with taking his horsewhip to the poor chit's father. If the deep-pocketed poltroon had guarded his chick better in the first place, she'd not have strayed from the nest.

As for the highwayman, Kenyon would hand him over for trial in the morning.

"Happens your ladies might have

somethin' to say about that."

"No."

Oliver shrugged. "The bloke's a gentleman, right enough — and handsome as the devil, smooth-tongued, too. The countess believed his story 'bout gettin' choused out of an inheritance."

"No." Not no, he wouldn't pardon the bastard for almost shooting Aurora, but no, he would not be cuckolded again, not by a criminal. A French nobleman was bad enough, but a disinherited knight of the road was too much!

"Lady Brianne won't take kindly to hangin' the rascal. Taken with him, she was."

"My sister? With a common thief?"

Oliver spit his tobacco juice between his teeth and out the stable door. "Ain't common. Son of a baron."

"The son of a bitch could have overturned the carriage, killing all of you."

"Speakin' of bitches, young Ned took the dog to his own bed. The cat'll need an earth box."

"The cat?"

Oliver nodded. "Big, mean 'un. But your lady's pluck to the backbone, my lord. She'll have it straightened out in two shakes."

Two shakes might have awakened Aurora when he returned to her room, but Kenyon was reluctant to disturb her. She'd been through a lot, poor puss. No matter that he needed to hold her, touch her, be with her, be one with her, more than he needed to breathe, Kenyon softly kissed her forehead and turned to leave.

She smiled drowsily and reached for his hand. "Thank you, my lord."

"It was nothing, the merest kiss. I did not mean to wake you."

"No, I mean for seeing to everyone and managing so well." She sighed. "I just knew you'd get everything squared away."

He had not done anything yet; the servants had done all the work. Still, his heart glowed, for the confidence she had in him. He brushed a curl off her face. "We'll talk about it in the morning."

She yawned and rolled over, burrowing deeper under the covers. "Good. Remind me to send Dawson back for the diamonds then, too."

Oliver had not mentioned any diamonds. "What, did you finally select the wedding present I've been promising you? I'm surprised you had time for visiting the shops, with all your adventures." He was venturing closer to the bed, thinking he might just slip under the covers while she was so sleepy and sweet and smelling of roses from her bath.

"No, silly, the Windham diamonds."

He jumped back. "What? You drag home a dog, a cat, a watering pot, and a well-born knave, but you lose the Windham diamonds?"

"Don't forget Lucy's babies."

"Lucy? Who the devil is Lucy?"

"She's the dog. She has four of the sweetest puppies."

And he supposed she expected him to provide for them, too. "Well, I pray one of the pups can talk like Frederick. Maybe it'll tell me what I did to deserve this."

Chapter Twenty

Nialla was up early. One tended not to sleep well in a strange household, with one's life in turmoil, and a hungry cat sharing the bedroom. She was dressed and on her way in search of breakfast or someone who could direct her to the kitchens when she heard swear words, some of the same ones her father had used when he threw her out of the house. There was no way on this earth she was going to go near anyone that angry again if she could help it, so she crept down the hall, hugging the wall. The cursing was growing more plaintive, though, and weaker, so she peeped into the partly opened door as she passed. A gentleman was tangled in his bedclothes, struggling with one arm to reach something on the far side of the nightstand.

This had to be Captain Warriner, Lady Brianne's injured brother. He could not order her from the house, she didn't think. Nialla hesitated but, understanding hopelessness, she stepped inside the room and asked, "May I help you, sir?"

"Deuce take it, girl, yes. The footman left to fetch breakfast, and I've knocked my spectacles to the floor, so can't see which of these blasted bottles has the fever pills I'm supposed to take."

Nialla forgave his curses, for he was a soldier, and his rudeness, for the poor man must be in pain. She located the glasses and put them in his hand, not daring the familiarity of placing the spectacles on his nose. Then she started reading labels on the scores of bottles on the table.

"What are you doing?" Christopher looked up, expecting to see one of the maids, who probably could not read. "I can — Well, hello, Sunshine." This was no maid, but an adorable little redhead with freckles.

Nialla blushed, but found the appropriate bottle and poured out a cup of lemonade for him from the pitcher by his bed. He swallowed, then apologized. "I am sorry, ma'am, for mistaking you for a servant. You must be the Mrs. Podell my brother told me about last night. Welcome to Windrush."

She stared at the floor. "Thank you, everyone has been so . . . so kind."

"You ain't going to cry, are you? I'd rather face the French cannon again, rather than that." Nialla sniffled but shook her head, so he went on. "And don't go thinking that anyone here will be holding what happened against you. My brother told enough for me to wish I could call that cad Podell out myself."

"He told you? I wish he had not. I am so ashamed."

"Fustian. No one thinks any the less of you, ma'am. Your father is another story. But you do not have to worry about that kind of thing anymore. My brother will take care of everything. He always does. Great gun, the earl."

"That's what Lady Windham said, too, but I cannot help worrying. The earl and the countess and Lady Brianne have been so good to me, going to such effort, for no reason. I am no connection, no responsibility of theirs. And I feel odd, accepting their charity."

Christopher pushed the cup of lemonade aside, spilling a little, which had him blue-deviled again. "You don't have to tell me about accepting charity. Confound it, I'll be a yoke around their necks for the rest of my life."

"Surely not." She put her hand to his forehead without thinking. "Why, your fever is almost gone. You'll be recovering faster now."

"And then what?" he asked bitterly. "I cannot go back to the army. It was bad enough that my poor eyesight kept me from a field command. Dash it, if Kenyon hadn't twisted some arms, I'd never have been allowed my colors at all. But now? I would not even be fit for a desk position. Besides, the war is almost over, everyone says so. But the military was the only career I've ever known."

"You'll find something else, I'm sure. Some way you can support yourself so you won't feel so dependent on your family."

He lightly touched her hand. "And so will you. You'll come about, I'm certain."

"How? I have even fewer skills than you."

Kit did not have the answer, but he smiled, for the first time in months, it seemed. "I know — you'll feel better about accepting Windham's generosity if you make yourself useful around here."

She had to laugh. "You obviously don't know how many servants Lady Windham has tripping over each other. According to your sister, the countess turns no one away."

"But those are servants, Sunshine. You could be doing Windham and his bride a great favor if you help me, so they don't feel obliged to. You cannot imagine how frustrating it is not to be able to turn the pages of a newspaper, or shuffle a deck of cards."

"Truly? You're not just being kind, trying to make me feel less indebted, are you?"

"Word of a Warriner. I have spent so much time looking at walls, I'd welcome Old Harry himself if he'd play chess."

"I'm not very good at it."

"Even better! I hate to lose."

"And it would be proper? No one would think it wrong for me to sit with you in your bedroom?"

He laughed again. "You are the least likeliest-looking matron I've ever seen, Sunshine, but you are a respectable widow, for all anyone knows. And we'll leave the door open. Besides, my condition is not quite conducive to an affair. Not yet, at any rate."

So Nialla sat by the bed, reading the morning newspaper to Captain Warriner, discussing the day's events and sharing his breakfast when it came. He augmented the war news, and she talked about the latest styles, neither feeling the least awkwardness at her cutting his food, or him spilling the occasional forkful. They decided which plays were worth seeing, what *on dit* could not possibly be true, and that Windham should speak up in Parliament about the plight of returning soldiers. So intent was

Nialla, in fact, that she forgot about feeding the cat.

The cat had long since decided to find its own meal, pushing open Nialla's bedroom door and following its scarred nose down the stairs.

Brianne was up early, unusually so for one who seldom stirred before noon, but she had too much on her mind to waste the day in bed. She had to speak to her brother before he made any decisions concerning the Honorable — or not — Wesley Royce. Her high-handed brother was *not* going to hand Brianne's highwayman over to the authorities. She'd help him escape herself first.

Why this was so, why she was ready to forsake her principles for the sake of a handsome rogue, she was not sure. Not because he had laughing eyes, she told herself, and not because he'd kissed her. How dare he take such liberties! And perhaps he would again if she helped him steal out of the house. "Steal" was perhaps the wrong word to use, she pondered as she scrambled into her gown and pulled a comb through her hair. But she knew what it meant to be trapped, confined by conventions. At least Mr. Royce had taken control of his own fate. He deserved another chance.

Not that she believed her highwayman should walk off, scot-free, she thought as she went down the hall, not noticing the cat sniffing past her. Her brother had too fine a sense of justice, for one thing. But there was no reason Wesley could not work off his misdeeds, like those boys who'd broken the church window last year. Yes, she decided, that was it. Kenyon would find Mr. Royce a position, proving that he did not have to resort to a risky life of crime.

Mr. Royce disagreed. "What, let your brother frank me, after trying to rob his womenfolk? What kind of man do you think me, woman?"

"A prize fool, but I'd see your neck out of a noose anyway."

"You don't understand about a man's honor. I could not accept favors from Windham, and he would not offer. I consider myself lucky not to be facing transportation. His man was by this morning and said he didn't think the earl was that angry, but I am not going to press my luck or abuse his hospitality a moment longer than I have to. I'll be on my way as soon as you leave me to get dressed."

So she picked up his freshly laundered breeches, his carefully mended coat, and the clean shirt of Kenyon's that the valet had brought, and shredded them, using the knife on his breakfast tray. "You are staying."

Wesley threw his head back and laughed. "If a woman feels that strongly about keeping a fellow in bed, he'd be no gentleman to deny her. Come give us a kiss, my impetuous darling, and we'll talk about it."

The earl was up early. Despite the short hours of sleep, his mind was too restless for him to stay abed. Kenyon needed to reassure himself that his wife had not taken any ill-effects from her brush with Benton or the bandit. He pulled on his robe and opened the connecting door.

Aurora was still asleep, looking warm and rosy, and so damn appealing Kenyon wanted, quite desperately, in fact, to crawl into bed beside her. But she needed her rest, and he needed to make sure that his brother was still on the mend. Leaving him in the hands of servants was worrisome.

He need not have troubled himself at all, for his brother was eating and drinking and, yes, laughing with little Mrs. Podell. She wasn't even weeping, bless her skitter-witted soul.

They never noticed him in the doorway,

or when he left. He never noticed the cat creeping down the stairs. He was too busy marveling that his sister was also up and dressed before luncheon, and visiting with the highwayman. Oliver must be right, then. Lud, a highwayman for a brother-in-law! Of course it was better than a bigamist. And if Royce made Brianne happy — and out of Kenyon's hair — he'd send his solicitor to see about the man's inheritance this very morning. Hell, he'd pay it himself.

The rest of the guests, Aurora's aunt and uncle, were already out collecting whatever it was they collected, according to the footman in the hall. Kenyon expected to see tadpoles in his teacup next, but if they were content, he was content not playing the polite host every moment. Aunt Ellenette was in the breakfast room, the footman informed him, but Frederick was with her, so she already had someone to talk to. She'd take exception to his undress anyway, so he went back up the stairs to his wife's bedroom.

Aurora woke up late. She'd intended to get the household in order so his lordship would not be put to the least bother. Her husband had been so understanding, so reassuring, so — So she sat in bed, dreaming over her chocolate. She smiled at him when he came into the room, almost as if she had conjured him out of sweet reveries. He certainly looked like a maiden's dream this morning, with his hair still tousled from sleep and a slight shadow on his jawline. "Good morning, my lord."

"And to you, my lady." He placed the rose that he'd filched from the hall table on the pillow beside her.

"I'm glad you came. We need to talk."

He sat beside her on the bed, smoothing the hair away from her cheeks. She did not shy away, so he touched her lips with his fingers, butterfly soft. "Sh. Not yet. Everyone is well and accounted for. In fact, I don't know how you planned it, but your latest venture has wrought miracles." And her body, under its thin silk covering, was making magic of its own. He kissed her, tasting the chocolate on her lips. "Hmm. You know, I have been thinking, my dear, that we know each other a lot better than we did. We really ought to have our wedding night one of these days."

"Hmm." Her whole body was *hmm-ing* in response. "But what of your doubts?"

Windham was relieved that she hadn't mentioned *her* doubts. His bride was not going to stand on her scruples any longer, thank goodness. He couldn't have stood another day. "I read some of your mother's letters," he told her. "The ones she wrote to your aunt. She begs forgiveness for what she is about to do, without specifics, in the same letter sending her daughter away. You must be right. Elizabeth planned to claim her child's death to get you away from your lawful father."

"So there is no more question about the legality of our marriage?"

"I still wonder about Podell, but I am growing more and more understanding of his need to make you his. Lud, I burn for you, Aurora."

He loved her blushes, though not as much as he loved her bare skin. He took off his robe and started to untie the ribbons of her nightgown.

"My lord! It is daytime!"

"Yes, I noticed. So?"

"The servants!"

"Know better than to interrupt a gentleman and his wife on their honeymoon. I'll lock the door if it will make you feel better."

"Are you sure?" She was not just asking about the door, but about his feelings, their future, everything.

He was sure he'd embarrass himself like a schoolboy if he had to wait much longer. "Positive." He slipped beneath the covers beside her, stretching his length against hers. She pressed nearer, craving the closeness as much as he did. "Everything is going to be fine. In fact, it's going to be heaven, my love. You'll see."

That's when the cat found something to eat: Frederick.

Chapter Twenty-one

The Meissen vase was the first of many fatalities. The seven-piece Wedgewood tea set was now the seventy-piece set. The Sheraton chair was now a footstool. The first footman on the scene was still on the floor. As the chase moved toward the kitchens, the staff started cheering for the cat instead of trying to separate Puss and the pug. Odds were being shouted out and wagers placed until Windham arrived, glaring at all of them.

Since none of his well-paid servants seemed to think halting the havoc was part of his or her duties, the earl tossed a pot of water on the combatants, which caused Cook to set up an even louder ruckus. That was her soup stock.

Trying to get out of the way, two scullery maids slipped on the water, knocking over a table piled with chopped vegetables for the soup. The earl had to reach in and pull the furry mass apart, getting bitten, scratched, and sopping wet. Aurora had the presence of mind to grab a large towel — for the cat.

When the beast was wrapped in the fabric, she gave him a pat — the earl. She gave the dog one of the soup bones and the cat the plate of kippers that were going to be his lordship's breakfast.

Aunt Ellenette needed the services of Christopher's physician. So did Frederick, though he complained with every stitch — the doctor, not the dog. Not knowing how to dose an overweight, overwrought pug with laudanum, they gave him some brandy. It was the first time in anyone's memory that the pug wagged his tail.

The cat was banished back to Nialla's room, with a better latch on the door. Nialla was in tears at the scope of the destruction. She'd begun to hope, to have dreams again, but now she recalled she was nothing but a displaced, disgraced chit, even deeper in debt to these people whose beautiful home Puss had tried to destroy. Reading to their brother could never be recompense for this mess.

And Christopher remembered he was nothing but a disabled soldier who could not comfort the poor little peagoose. He couldn't get out of bed when she rushed past sobbing, couldn't take her in his arms, even if she didn't have the Fiend's own feline in hers. Damn, he'd never get to hold another woman; worse, he'd never get to hold this one. Kit swept his arm across the bedside table with all the bottles. None of them were going to give him back his arm or his life, so what was the use?

Brianne and Wesley had an argument almost as loud as the dog and cat when he tried to get up to help Aurora.

"Lady Windham this and Lady Windham that. Aurora's all you care about," shouted Brianne, consumed with jealousy. "I saw you making sheep eyes at her in the carriage, and you've been singing her praises all morning. And she's most likely begging my brother to spare your life just because you smiled at her, the noddy. Well, you are nothing but a here-and-thereian, and she is as fickle as Kenyon's first wife."

On her way back to her room, Aurora gasped. Kenyon, at her side, would have stormed into the guest chamber and committed mayhem of his own, had not Wesley's quiet voice reached them in the hall. "You shame your brother with your accusations, and you shame your sister-in-law, who has never been aught but a perfect lady. You shame me, to think that I would repay them thus for my very life. If you think so ill of me, my lady, perhaps I should leave after all."

When Kenyon ordered his sister to apologize, Brianne threw a tantrum that likely gave the highwayman a permanent disgust of her, to the earl's deep regret. But she did beg everyone's pardon before retiring to her room, back in mourning. Before Kenyon could assure his wife that Brianne would recover and no, he did not suspect her of dallying with the highwayman, not for more than a minute or two, anyway, a maid rushed in. The monkey was loose outside on the grounds.

"Oh, dear, he'll catch cold. And I promised Lady Anstruther-Jones I'd take good care of him. What if he gets stolen?"

"Who the devil would want a bothersome beast like that?"

Trying to chase after Sweety, Ned climbed aboard Magpie, the retired cart horse that acted as a lawn sculpture these days. City child that he was, however, Ned fell right off, and had the wind knocked out of him. Windham thought he might have broken a rib. Ned was delighted that he wouldn't have to go to school for a few days, but that still left the monkey up the tree, and Lord Windham's wife looking at him expectantly. This was not what he had counted on seeing in her eyes this morning.

No, Aurora did not think the monkey

would come down when he was ready.

Damn, Kenyon thought as he unbelted his silk dressing gown, leaving his legs et cetera bare beneath his nightshirt. Instead of mounting his beautiful bride, Lord Windham was mounting a blasted oak tree, which the infernal monkey climbed higher, of course, as soon as the earl was close. Kenyon had no choice but to follow, with half the shire looking up, he was certain, at his et cetera.

Aurora's aunt and uncle meandered past, their arms full of nets and jars. They suggested a bowl of fruit, which reminded Kenyon that he never did have breakfast. What, were all his hungers to go unfulfilled this morning? "No, thank you, I never eat while I am up a tree. I'll find something later. Oh, for the monkey."

Aurora sent a footman off to kitchens — and giggled at him.

"Funny? You think this is funny, madam?"

She must have, for she nearly bit her lip, trying not to laugh out loud.

The fruit did not work, nor the bread, nor the chicken — the rest of lunch, in other words. Finally, Aurora herself hauled the inebriated pug outside to a blanket, despite Aunt Ellenette's screeching, and the monkey flew down the tree, almost dislodging the earl, eager to have a game of tail-pull. Aurora caught Sweety before he could reach the dog and, since it worked with the cat, wrapped the monkey tightly — in Kenyon's robe. She told one of the gardeners to bring a ladder around for the earl as she left.

How could a day that had started out so promising turn so perverse? The early sunshine had fled behind the clouds by the time Kenyon was down and dressed, and the day grew as dim as his chances of getting his wife alone this morning. Looking at her as she ministered to the boy, Ned, Kenyon became uncomfortable in his unmentionables. Dash it, a man ought not lust after his own wife. He ought to be able to satisfy his needs; that was supposed to be the advantage to a man in marriage, wasn't it? It was the only one, as far as he could see. Too bad he was not getting to savor the rewards, only suffer the rest.

Then the post came, and the day went from bad to worse.

Lord Phelan Ramsey was spotted in London, Windham's man there reported, but was playing least in sight. Creditors were lined up outside his lodgings, and gambling partners were calling in his vowels. Word had gone out, it seemed, that an expected windfall had not materialized. The windfall was to have landed in Ramsey's lap remarkably close to the time of Aurora's failed marriage to Podell.

"Too shady by half," Windham muttered, and Aurora had to agree. Her aunt and uncle had no idea where Lord Phelan might have come into an inheritance or a coup from investments. As far as they knew, his lordship lived on a small family annuity and his wagering winnings. In their infrequent dealings with him, he'd never mentioned another source of income.

Windham told himself it did not matter. He did not need any more confirmation of his marriage, nor discussion of its legality. In fact, he just might owe Podell a favor. Nor did he need another fortune if one did, indeed, exist. Thanks to Aurora's escapades, money might be flying out of the Windham coffers as fast as the monkey flew through the orange trees, but Kenyon could stand the nonsense. Still, that niggling doubt remained at the back of his mind.

Aurora was more than curious; she was all for finding the missing lord and the feasible fortune. "I can think of a thousand ways to spend a few extra pounds and pence. Then I wouldn't have to be constantly counting the cost of every little thing."

If Aurora thought she was being economical, Kenyon dreaded to think what she might consider extravagant — elephants in the apple orchard, perhaps, or a home for unemployed orange-sellers. But he did enjoy his hot water, Kenyon reminded himself, and he did like seeing his wife smile, when she was not laughing at his expense. "I'll ask my man to hire a Runner to look for Ramsey. It's better to know what he was up to, than wonder for the rest of our days."

Ned was all for going himself. "Ain't — isn't — no one in London I can't find."

Aurora frowned. "I thought you were too sore to go to school for a week."

The boy ignored her. "If your bloke's punting on Tick, guv, I know all the sponging houses an' diving kens he'd try. No Runner can get near half the places me an' my friends can go."

"He has a point."

"He has lessons, if he's to grow up to be a Runner." Both males were looking at her so pleadingly — Ned to be allowed to return to London and show off for his chums there, and the earl, for her to get rid of the lad so they could have some privacy — that she said she'd think about it. Ned went to pack.

The next letter was going to give

261

Windham all the privacy he wanted, in Paris. Peace was about to be declared, the secretary wrote him, and the earl was needed to help draft terms of surrender. According to Whitehall, his experience in the diplomatic corps, his fluency in the language, and his influential connections made Windham a prime candidate for the committee.

"Damn and blast! I'll have to go back to France."

"Why can't you simply tell him no?" Aurora thought her husband had spent little enough time with her since their wedding as is. Besides, he'd just returned with his brother. Surely the Warriners had done enough for king and country.

"You don't understand, my love. This isn't any secretary asking, this is the Home Secretary, writing on Prinny's behalf. To refuse would be close to treason, I'm afraid. *Noblesse oblige,* and all that."

It was deuced unobliging to expect a new bridegroom to leave his wife. Windham crumpled the letter in his fist. "I might be able to take you with me, though. What do you think?"

Aurora chewed on her lip. She thought she'd like nothing better than spending time alone with this appealing man she'd married. "I'd love to go with you, but what about everyone here? I cannot just abandon poor Nialla one day after inviting her, and Brianne needs a more watchful chaperone than Aunt Ellenette, with Mr. Royce in the house. I'm afraid I should stay behind."

At least she did not sound relieved to be spared his company. "I would feel better leaving you to look after Kit, too, thunderation."

"Do not curse, you'll be part of history. Besides, you can travel faster and get home that much more quickly. When do you think you'll have to leave?"

"As soon as Tarlow can pack."

"Today? Thunderation!"

With all the farewells and all the instructions, half of which Kenyon knew his wife would ignore, they barely had time for a good-bye kiss, in view of almost the whole household. Even Brianne left her bed to wave a handkerchief as his coach rolled down the carriage drive. Without a word, she pressed it into Aurora's hand when the carriage was out of sight.

Trailing back to the house, Aurora wiped her eyes and firmed her backbone. Her husband was counting on her to manage in his absence, to oversee the welfare of his family and dependents and property — to be Lady

Windham, in other words. It was a big responsibility, but she could do it, for him.

Aurora started by opening the rest of the mail that Kenyon had not gotten to. She put the bills in a pile for Mr. Dawson, the invitations in a pile for Brianne, and read the remaining letters herself. One she read twice. Then she sat staring at nothing while she tried to decide what her husband would want her to do. Ignore it, most likely, but that was not Aurora's way. No, she would have to do precisely what he would least wish her to do, and right after promising to stay out of trouble.

Trouble? This was going to be worse than losing the Windham diamonds, worse than introducing a highwayman to his hare-brained sister, worse even than the monkey. Aurora was going to bring the Earl of Windham's son home.

Chapter Twenty-two

Bells were pealing everywhere — church bells, fire bells, even cow bells.

"Why are they all ringing?" the boy asked when he stepped down from the coach.

Unable to wait in the parlor like a properly sedate matron, Aurora had raced down the stairs when she heard Andrew's carriage. She barely restrained herself from hugging him, her son. From being the only child in a household of scholarly adults, she now had a brother and a sister, and a little boy to love! One look at the anxious face that reminded her of his father, and she adored him already.

"Why, the bells are ringing to welcome the Windham heir home, of course," she told Andrew, half laughing.

"Truly?" Andrew was not quite sure he believed her, playful teasing not having come his way in the past.

"Truly. Oh, I suppose they might be celebrating the end of war, too, but your homecoming is certainly the first cause for joy at Windrush."

He was following her into the enormous entry hall, staring around, stepping carefully around anything that looked remotely fragile or valuable. "I am glad it is over. My mother died in that war, you know."

"Yes, I do know, and I am very sorry. My mother died when I was a baby also. I lost my father, too."

He shrugged as if fathers were of no account. "Who took you?"

"My aunt and uncle, who are now your great-aunt and great-uncle. Ah, do you like lizards?"

He stepped back, as though she were dicked in the nob. Aurora knew she was babbling, but she so wanted him to be happy here. "You have an aunt and uncle of your own, of course. Brianne and Christopher are anxious for your company." They were anxious to be out of the country before Windham got wind of what she'd done. She'd had no choice, Aurora had told them. The school was stricken with the mumps, and all the boys were sent home, but the family Andrew stayed with between terms was off on holiday, not expecting him. Was she supposed to tell the school to deposit the boy at an inn, like some unwanted parcel? No, she'd had no choice. Windham would understand. "And you are lucky,

Andrew; you still have your father."

That ended that avenue of conversation. Andrew stood in the center of the library she'd led him to, not touching anything, just staring at the carpet. Andrew was small for his age, shy, and obviously terrified of his father.

"He'll be sorry he wasn't here to greet you, I'm certain." Aurora was trying to reassure both of them.

Andrew shook his head. "No, he won't. He'll hate me. I'm stupid. Everyone says so. And the family I stay with doesn't want me back, either. They say he doesn't pay them enough."

"Gammon. I know he pays them very well. And you are not stupid, I am sure."

"It's true. This isn't my first school, you know. The other one said they couldn't teach a dunce cap like me to read, so they sent me away. I cannot do arithmetic, and my penmanship is dreadful, and I hate that dumb place! The instructors are mean, and I don't care if they won't take me back!"

He and Ned would be excellent friends, Aurora thought. She also thought Andrew and Brianne had a lot in common, which was not as pleasant a prospect. Hoping to head off a display of temper, she asked, "If not reading or writing or arithmetic, what subjects are you good at? Globes? History?"

"French is the only thing I can do, on account of getting the accent right. But then the other boys call me a Frog."

"My uncle adores frogs — the croaking kind. Perhaps he'll let you hold one."

Andrew scuffed at the carpet. "I won't be here long enough. *He* will be back, now that the truce is declared. He won't let me stay. He'll just find another mean old place to send me."

"Fustian, once Lord Windham gets to know you, he'll regret not having you home more often."

Andrew gave her the look children reserved for adults making particularly childish remarks. "I am dumb at schoolwork, not queer in the attic. He won't like me. I never do anything right. I always bump into things and can't ever hit the ball at cricket. The masters say I am slower than molasses, and the other boys laugh at me all the time."

Aurora would not believe that Andrew was anyone else's boy, and she could not believe that a child of Windham's might be dim-witted. Stubborn, yes. She found one of Windham's ubiquitous looking glasses in the desk drawer and held it and a book out to the boy.

He turned scarlet. "I can't —"

"Try."

"I can! I can read it! I say, what a marvelous device."

"Has no one thought to have you fitted for spectacles?"

"Criminy, no. The other boys would have laughed."

"Your father wears glasses" — when she nagged at him — "and your uncle, who is a genuine hero, with medals and all. If he can wear spectacles, so can you. We shall send for a pair this afternoon. Meanwhile, here." She looped the ribbon over his head, and, unable to help herself, she kissed the top of his head. He had brown hair, not the auburn of the other Warriners, but this was Kenyon's son, she'd bet her life on it. She already had, most likely.

"All the finest gentlemen carry quizzing glasses, don't you know. And . . . and I shall try not to embarrass you again with such demonstrations of affection."

Blushing, he forgave her. "Do you remember your mother?"

"Not much. Half of what I do remember might be from my aunt's stories anyway. Do you recall yours?"

"Not much. She was very pretty, they tell me."

"She was beautiful. You can ask Brianne and your Aunt Ellenette." Who were forever reminding Aurora that she did not measure up. "There is a portrait of your mother in the attics. We could bring it down for your room if you like. You have her coloring and chin and handsome brown eyes. But I recognize some of your father's and aunt's characteristics."

Andrew took that as a compliment. "You're pretty, too."

"Why, thank you. I can see we are going to get along famously. Do you like animals?" His tepid reaction to the mention of frogs was worrisome, for this household.

"I don't ride, if that's what you mean. They said I was too small and too paper-skulled to bother with lessons."

The boy was Windham's heir, for heaven's sake. He had to ride! "I bet you just couldn't see where to go."

Once Andrew got settled, Brianne and Wesley were delegated to give him riding lessons, on old Magpie for a start. Archery and cricket classes were added when his new spectacles arrived. Nialla and Christopher had him reading the newspapers with them, discussing the day's events. They were also teaching him chess, card games, and spillikins, which Kit could manage one-handed. When Aurora unearthed a box of tin soldiers in the old nursery, the boy and his uncle enacted endless battles on Christopher's bed.

Aunt Thisbe and Uncle Ptolemy took him collecting with them, teaching him the wonders of scaly, slimy creatures, and that getting one's clothes dirty was not a crime. They let him help in the laboratory, too, by keeping Sweety busy. But Andrew's very favorite activity was playing with Lucy and her pups. Wesley said he could have one for his very own, but he couldn't choose, so spent hours with them in the stables. Eventually, Aurora had Lucy and the babes installed in the nursery, so that she might get to have some time with her son, too.

With Lucy in the house, Frederick discovered love. He followed the bitch around, panting, and did not bother anyone else, for once. He even let her puppies climb over him and chew on his ears.

Speaking of love, Brianne and Wesley did not argue half so much, not in front of the boy, at any rate. Windham's solicitor was looking into getting copies of Wesley's father's will, to see if there were grounds for a challenge. Ned was also snooping around while he was in London, for hints of skullduggery. If someone forged the will, and if that someone was a professional, Ned would sniff him out. Meanwhile, Wesley's wound was mending, and he was helping put food on the table with hunting and fishing, at which Brianne constantly tried to outdo him. She never wore her black gowns, and she never asked for the diamonds, once they were back. She never left Aurora alone with Wesley if she could help it, but she never let her jealousy override her manners again, either.

Christopher was recovering more slowly, but he felt stronger daily. He decided he might even try to ride again soon. Perhaps then his brother would let him manage one of the lesser properties, so he could support himself . . . and a wife. He could learn, couldn't he? Dash it, if that's what he had to do to provide for Nialla so he could offer for her in good conscience, he'd do it. And she thought she'd like nothing better than to be a farmer's wife, raising roses and little Warriners. Christopher had Andrew fetch him books on agriculture from Windham's library, and made him read parts with him, for the estate was to be his someday and he had to know as much as his father and uncle did.

That was Aurora's job, taking Andrew around in her gig, introducing him to the tenants and explaining how they depended on his family for their livelihoods, so he had to watch out for them. She made sure to show him the land that he was to be caretaker of, and his son after, the fields and forests, the streams and the spinneys. She didn't think a son of Windham's could turn out to be a conscienceless care-for-naught, not with Kenyon's sense of honor, but she was going to make sure her son — the only son she'd have if Windham stayed gone — knew what was owed his name and his title.

And then, while everything was going so well, of course, Andrew got sick with the mumps, which was, of course, just when Windham decided to come home.

He was not angry. Angry was for the diplomatic corps, which was anything but diplomatic, for the rulers who could not see beyond their own greed and ambition to the people who were suffering. Angry was for incompetence and idiocy. Now Windham was incensed. Smoke should be pouring from his ears. Lava should be bubbling out of his mouth. Lightning bolts should be flying from his clenched fists.

Aurora should be fearing for her life, but she knew Kenyon would never hurt her, no matter what, just as she knew he would get over having his wishes thwarted. He'd get used to having the boy at home and come to love Andrew as she did.

"Love him? I do not want to look at him, madam, as I believe I made perfectly clear. I may have to acknowledge the child as my heir, by all that's holy, but I do not have to accept him as my son. From all reports, the brat is thoroughly unlovable, besides being dunder-headed and doltish. No son of mine would be tossed out of three schools before he reached his ninth birthday."

"Perhaps you should blame the schools, not the boy. Andrew is not the least bit slow. He can already defeat Aunt Ellenette at piquet."

Kenyon raised one eyebrow. "The monkey could outplay Aunt Ellenette."

"He only beat Christopher at chess once, so far, but Andrew is invincible with marbles. Uncle Ptolemy is impressed with his ability to draw the insects and such they are studying, and Nialla says he has an aptitude for music."

Kenyon made a rude noise. "It sounds as if you've done a fine job of getting him used to life at Windrush. But you have done the boy a disservice, madam wife, for he is leaving here as soon as the school reopens."

"No, we shall find a better school, closer to home."

"You can send him to Baluchistan, but he is not coming back here."

Aurora thought she had a better chance of persuading Kenyon if he met Andrew. "He is anxious to see you, too, my lord." Andrew was petrified, besides being puffy, peevish, and as hard to please as any sick little boy. This was not the time she would have chosen to bring the two together, but this might be Aurora's only chance. "He cannot leave the nursery, naturally. You'll have to go up."

"No. No, I will not meet him, and no, I will not change my mind. I do not want him in my house. Can you not understand that, woman?"

"No, and I cannot understand a man who would turn his back on a sick child, especially his own son." She crossed her arms over her chest, showing that she could be just as stubborn. "I do not wish to be married to a brute like that."

"Your wishes do not matter, Lady Windham. We are wed, remember?"

"Then we can live apart. It is done all the time in the *ton,* I understand."

Although that was what he'd intended at the time of their wedding, he refused to accept such an arrangement now. "I will not permit you to leave, Aurora, I swear it."

She sniffed at his high-handedness. "And I will not permit such a cold, cruel man to be father to my children, by heaven, to reject them if he is out of sorts."

His eyes narrowed, seeing her bedroom door slammed in his face. "Meaning?"

"Meaning I cannot love a cruel man."

"Love again? That claptrap had nothing to do with our bargain."

"Well, it matters now, you moron, and if you are too blind to see that, no spectacles can help you!"

Chapter Twenty-three

Did she love him? Was that what she'd been saying? Kenyon rolled the thought around in his mind. He considered the way Aurora rushed out to greet him, forgetting the servants watching, and how she seemed to glow with an inner smile when he was near. Could she love such a hard-hearted man, he asked himself, so wounded in his pride that he would not trust another woman? And did it matter? They could have a fashionable marriage like most of his friends, without the tender emotions, but the earl was suddenly finding that idea dismal, so, yes, it mattered. More than he could have imagined, Kenyon desired his wife — and no other. He had not even been tempted by the courtesans flocking to the powerful at the peace talks. But he craved more than Aurora's exquisite body. He wished her to share his house and his thoughts and his worries as much as his bed. And he wanted her to want that, too. He wanted her to like him. Kenyon was beginning to think that without her affection, her respect, her love, he would never be a whole man again. Damn, he must be in love with the plaguey chit. What a coil!

Could she truly love the impossible man — despite his arrogance and pigheadedness? Well, yes, Aurora very much feared that she did. Her heart was as silly as the rest of her, the parts that tingled at his touch and warmed at his glance of approval, refusing to listen to her head. Logic and limiting one's involvement had nothing to do with love, she was finding. But everything was going to be all right, for he loved her, too. He would have strangled her otherwise.

Too weary from his journey to argue more that night, Lord Windham went to his own bed. Tomorrow he'd make her see reason, he swore. But tomorrow came and he never saw his wife at all. He met with Dawson and the new bailiff, watched his brother try to exercise some strength back in his muscles, listened to his sister sing her highwayman's praises, and looked for Aurora. He was not going to the nursery.

At dinner, she wore a pale green silk gown and her mother's pearls. Deuce take it, Kenyon thought, he still had to purchase something for her, something just from him, not out of the vault. He knew the Windham diamonds were returned, if Dawson hadn't switched paste for the real ones, for he'd seen them in the safe when he put some government documents there this morning. He would not think about the jewels, nor how Dawson had opened the blasted safe to put them away.

Aurora had purplish shadows under her eyes that he could see from the opposite end of the table, most likely from catering to the brat, as if there weren't a hundred servants better suited to be nursemaid. He could not say anything — not that she'd listen — not when the others were so studiously making polite conversation. No one mentioned the boy.

She was not in the parlor with the other ladies when he led the men back after dinner and a smoke. Brianne and Wesley got up a game of piquet, the McPhees adjourned to their laboratory, and Nialla excused herself to bring Christopher the book he'd asked for. No one expected her back.

They were all avoiding him, Kenyon knew, as he intercepted yet another reproachful look, from the footman this time. Even Aunt Ellenette picked up Frederick and her novel and retired early. The earl waited, but Aurora did not come down for tea, either.

He decided that a gentleman could make some concessions in the interest of domestic harmony. He would meet the boy, if that's what it took to show his wife that he liked children and was kind to animals. He'd rather meet Uncle Ptolemy's pet toad, but how bad could nodding at the brat be? And if he did not wear his spectacles, he would not have to search for family resemblances.

Aurora was not in her room when the earl went to tell her his decision. He did not really expect her to be this early, but he waited. She never came.

He had not intended to meet the boy tonight, or in the nursery. A formal audience in the library seemed more fitting, Kenyon thought. But his feet were headed up the stairs to the nursery, to fetch his wife back, the earl assured himself, before she took ill herself from tending to the whelp. Besides, with any luck the boy would be asleep.

Aurora was sitting by his bedside, mending by the meager light from one shaded candle. A nursemaid was fast asleep on a cot in the corner. "This is absurd," Kenyon started, whispering. "If the girl cannot stay awake to watch him, then hire another."

Aurora looked up, but did not smile at

him. "Andrew needs his family, not a servant, when the fever makes him fretful. He's been having nightmares, the poor dear."

"Then light another candle, for heaven's sake."

"That's how much you know. The light is bad for his eyes, the doctor says."

"Well, sitting here in the dark isn't doing you a lot of good that I can see. You are looking worn to the bone."

"I am tired," she admitted. "Brianne and Nialla both offered to take turns sitting up with Andrew, but I was too worried. He seems to be doing better, don't you think?"

Better than the half-drowned rat who'd arrived from France? Kenyon shrugged. "He appears to be sleeping soundly."

"Does he seem warm to you?"

In the dim light, without his spectacles, Kenyon thought the boy looked like a white mouse in a nest of blankets. He was pale and small and fragile-looking. "No, not at all."

"How can you tell? You didn't touch him."

She never said anything about touching him. Kenyon was here to meet the boy. The child was asleep. He'd done his duty and could leave. "I don't want to awaken him."

Aurora nodded, then yawned. "Pardon me."

"No, dash it, I will not. You are about to collapse. What good will you be to him in the morning, then?"

"Yes, but —"

"Yes, but nothing. You go to sleep. I will stay here with the boy."

"You?"

"Yes, madam, even I can sit still in a chair and watch a sleeping infant. You said yourself he is resting comfortably. If he worsens, I can send for you."

"You'd do that for him?"

He couldn't lie. "No, but I would do a great deal for you, my lady."

Aurora stood on her toes and kissed his cheek, then hurried from the room before Kenyon could change his mind. It was a start.

The chair was not particularly comfortable. No chance of him falling asleep on the job, Kenyon realized. He shifted his position, then again, when his leg started to grow numb. His foot bumped the bed. The boy's eyes opened. Kenyon held his breath, hoping the lad would go back to sleep. Lud, what would he do if not? He'd roust up the maid, that's what. Just when he thought he could exhale, the child whispered, "Are you my father?"

Trust the brat to get to the heart of the

matter at first sight. Kenyon knew this had been a wretched idea, but he answered the only way he could. "Yes."

"Am I dead?"

"Good grief, no."

"I heard Aunt Brianne say you'd see me in Hell before you came to visit."

"Aunt Brianne's manners are not always all they should be. And you should not have been listening to adult conversation."

"Even when she was in my room? She thought I was asleep."

"I see. Well, a gentleman would not repeat what he was not supposed to hear. And he would not say Hell."

"Oh." The boy sighed. "There are a great many things a gentleman has to know, aren't there?"

"Hell, yes."

"Mama says that's why you never came to visit at school, on account of your being too busy being a gentleman and an earl and a friend of the Prince. And lots of other important things."

"Mama?" For a moment Windham worried that the boy was taking a page from Aunt Ellenette and Frederick's book, talking to his dead mother.

"Lady Windham," Andrew said with a hint of impatience that he had to explain.

"You know, your wife. She says I'm her only child for now."

At this rate he'd be her only child till the cows came home. "Aren't you sleepy?"

"No, sir."

His lordship looked around until he spotted a jug and a cup. "Do you want some barley water for your throat?"

"No, thank you, sir."

The earl watched the boy as he lay rigid, staring at the ceiling. The whelp did not appear to be drowsy, dash it, and Kenyon was all out of polite conversation. He had nothing to say to the lad, no burning questions the child could answer. Windham might have shouted, "Are you my son?" But now this child was his, for better or for worse, just like his wife.

The silence was worse. Blast, he'd been right all along. What did he know about children? Nothing, and he'd never been bothered at the lack. He did not belong in any nursery, and the child did not belong here. The lad should be with a competent family, somewhere else, somewhere far from Windrush.

"Are you feverish?" he asked in desperation. "Should I fetch a cool cloth for your head?"

"No, thank you, sir."

"I am not one of your instructors, Andrew. You do not have to stand at attention — or lie at attention — and 'sir' me to death."

"No, sir, my lord."

"Deuce take it, you're not a servant. Why don't we try 'Father' for now? I am not quite ready for 'Papa.' " Kenyon doubted he'd ever be ready for that.

"That's all right, sir . . . Father."

No one had ever called him that before, and now it came out hoarse, choked. "You are not going to cry, are you?" Kenyon was halfway out of his seat, ready to shout for Aurora.

"No, sir."

Kenyon leaned closer, eyeing the boy suspiciously. He was tense and unhappy, almost as if he were afraid of his own father, dammit. But he was not crying. "Good lad." The earl sat back. He'd stay and let Aurora get her rest.

Silence filled the corners of the room, like bone-chilling fog or throat-scratching smoke. Kenyon checked his pocket watch by the single candle. Not a quarter of an hour had gone past. Lud, this night was going to last forever. Then he noticed a stack of books on the floor. "Would you like me to read to you? I could hold the candle closer to me so it won't bother your eyes."

"Thank you, sir. I would enjoy that."

Kenyon went through the pile of books, only to discover they were all learned discourses on crop rotation, manure composting, and milch cows. "What is this dry-as-dust stuff doing up here?"

"Uncle Kit was studying it, and Mama says I'll have to know it too, for when I'm Earl of Windham."

What, was Aurora wishing to be rid of him so soon? Nettled, he said, "I am not in my dotage yet. You have a few years yet to stay a boy." Meanwhile, he was peering at the titles on the spines of the books on the nursery shelves. "Ah, I knew this would be here. *Sir Timothy and the Terrible Dragon.* It used to be one of my favorites when I was your age. Kit and I used to play at knights and dragons all the time. Brianne was always the maiden we had to rescue, though sometimes we left her tied up for the dragon to get, on purpose. Surely you'd rather hear of a fearless warrior and his trusted destrier than a dissertation on mangel-wurzels."

Andrew was already reaching for something on the nightstand. "You can borrow my quizzing glass if you like."

Kenyon recognized the piece as one of his. "No, thank you. I have my spectacles with me." He took them out of his pocket and put them on, seeing no other choice if he wanted to see the pages, and began reading about the noble knight and his steed, Victory. " 'Even his sword had a name,' " he read, " 'and that was Serpent-Slayer.' Don't tell Uncle Ptolemy."

Kenyon thought he'd read a chapter and the boy would fall asleep, but he was halfway through, however, and Andrew was sitting up in bed, clutching the sheets, cheering on Sir Timothy. The earl doubted Aurora would consider such behavior conducive to rest and recuperation. "Perhaps we ought to stop here and save the rest for tomorrow night."

"You'll come back?"

Lud, had he just promised to return? "I couldn't leave poor Victory wandering in that cave, could I?" And he could not leave the boy looking so uncertain, so fearful. "I'll come back. Go to sleep now." He put his spectacles back in his pocket so the boy would not think he was going to cheat and finish the tale on his own.

"Were you very clumsy as a boy?" Andrew asked, hiding a yawn behind his hand.

"Very. Are you?"

"Not anymore, now that I have my spectacles."

"Good. Go to sleep."

"Did you like school?"

"Some of it." Kenyon realized that the boy was trying his damnedest to stay awake, and not for the pleasure of his father's company, he'd wager. "Now shut your eyes. I'll stay here to make sure you don't have nightmares."

Relieved, Andrew lay back on the pillows. "Mama says it's the fever, not that I am a coward or anything."

"Of course not. Even Sir Timothy must have had nightmares now and again, facing a dragon as big as the sky."

A few moments went by, but this time the quiet was companionable, peaceful. The earl was congratulating himself that he had survived the encounter, perhaps even alleviated some of the sprout's anxieties, when Andrew whispered, "Good night, Father."

"Good night . . . son."

So Kenyon came back the next night, and the next. If he didn't sit up with the boy, Aurora would, he knew. He told himself he was protecting her health. And he told himself she would be pleased. Hell, he even told himself he wanted to know how *Sir Timothy and the Terrible Dragon* turned out. He did not admit that he liked spending time with the lad, or that he was worried Andrew was not strong, or that he knew his wife's door would be closed to him anyway.

During the day, Kenyon was busy about the estate; he should not have left it in a hireling's hands for so long. With so much to do, he seldom saw his wife, who was in the nursery more often than not when he returned to Windrush. So was the rest of the household, he realized, even Kit, now that he was mobile. They were all taking luncheon and tea in Andrew's room, playing games, singing songs, admiring Lucy's pups.

No one asked Kenyon to take part in the nursery gatherings. No one asked him if he wanted company through his long, nightly vigils. And no one asked him if he'd ever had the mumps.

Chapter Twenty-four

He was puffy, peevish, and as hard to please as any sick little boy. In his fevered dreams, Kenyon thought his wife had left him. She had, but not the wife who mattered. "Aurora!" he cried out.

"Yes, dearest, I am here." And she always was, sitting by his bedside or stretched out beside him, ready to stir at his slightest movement.

"You won't run off?"

Having answered the question infinite times in the past few days, Aurora told him, "Not till you're well."

Soothed, Kenyon went back to sleep, only to dream that they'd stolen his son, his baby. "Andrew!"

"He's fine, Kenyon. Almost entirely recovered."

He squeezed her hand, pulling her closer so he could see if she was telling the truth. "He's not gone?"

"He never was as sick as all that, my dear. The doctor says he can resume riding lessons next week. Shall I bring him in to visit? I know he's worried about you, too."

Kenyon moved his head up and down, nearly groaning at the pain. With his privates so swollen, he might never father another child. He prayed the good Lord's rod and His staff to comfort him, for his own sure as Hades did not.

So Andrew came and climbed aboard the huge four-poster bed that had belonged to five generations of Windham earls. He fixed his glasses more firmly on his nose and started reading.

"That's 'chivalry,' cub, not 'shivery.' "

Aurora tiptoed out of the room, free to tend to the rest of her household for an hour or so. Andrew already believed his father hung the stars, for while he was recuperating, it was: Father says this, and did you know that Father once did that? The boy had slept most of the days away, waiting for his father's nightly visits. Aurora would have been jealous, but she was so pleased for both of them. Andrew would watch over the earl for her, and keep him from fretting.

Before she left, Aurora turned and fixed the image in her mind of Kenyon and his son, snuggled together on the big bed. He was such an admirable man, her husband. He was unshaven and ornery and unwilling to admit he'd been wrong about the boy, but Aurora thought she'd never seen such a handsome, heart-pleasing sight. She shook her head, to think the clunch had tried to deny himself such love. Her so estimable spouse could be a jackass, but Andrew did not seem to mind, and neither did she.

For the next few days, Kenyon kept Andrew with him whenever he could. He did not want any highwayman teaching his son to ride, nor his soldier-brother instructing him on land management. He did not want his spoiled sister near the boy at all, with her moods and megrims and bad manners. He didn't even want to share the brat with Aurora's aunt and uncle. What if Andrew contracted another chill out on their gathering expeditions? No, the boy was better off right here where Kenyon could watch him.

The others had other thoughts on the matter. Soon the whole menage was gathered in the master bedroom most of the days, laughing, playing games, re-enacting battles with the toy soldiers, chasing Lucy's puppies. Frederick was chasing Lucy, but only Aunt Ellenette cared. Nialla and Kit were seldom more than a foot apart, and Brianne and the highwayman were still trying to best each other at every activity.

Kenyon did care about both situations, neither match being what he would have chosen for his siblings. He could do nothing while so incapacitated, though, except keep them here, like the boy, where he could watch them. He did not want any sneak thief stealing his sister's reputation, and he did not want any air-headed adventuress taking advantage of his brother's vulnerability. There was safety in numbers, at least, even if Kenyon's room was so crowded he could not sleep.

At night things were looking up; the swelling was going down. And he had Aurora to himself. Unfortunately he could barely keep his eyes open by then, but he tried, drinking in the sight of her trying on a sari from her mother's trunk or sitting by the fireside, reading more of her mother's letters. Most were letters from school friends, telling of their lives, their marriages, and children, not adding one whit to what Aurora and Kenyon knew about Elizabeth's circumstances. She'd saved the letters, though, as a reminder of the home she'd never see again. That told them something.

At the bottom of the satchelful of letters, Aurora found a thin bundle tied in a frayed ribbon, as if these letters had seen frequent rereading. They were addressed to "My

Dearest Elizabeth," and signed, "Yours forever, George."

They had to be from Lord Ratchford, Lord Phelan's brother, the one Lady Anstruther-Jones had thought Elizabeth would marry. They'd been childhood friends, Aunt Thisbe had told her, and would have announced an engagement but for mourning his father. Then something happened — an argument, Aurora's aunt thought — and he went off to inspect his new properties without leaving an itinerary or an indication of his return. Before he did come home, Elizabeth had married Avisson Halle and sailed off to India. The last letter in the pile was a message of desperation. Furious that she had not waited for him, George called Elizabeth heartless and inconstant, cruel and craven, not to tell him to his face that she loved another. George vowed to be faithful to Elizabeth in his heart until his last breath, but he would marry the first woman he met in London to assure the succession, now that he had no hopes of marrying for love.

"How sad," Aurora murmured, wiping her eyes. "To think of such a great passion coming to naught. It's just like a novel."

"A bad novel. I prefer dragons, myself."

Aurora ignored his callous remarks. "I

wonder what they argued about. I doubt it would be another woman, the way he swears his loyalty to her."

"Who can tell with a female? If she loved him all that much in return, she should have waited . . . unless she could not. Do you have your mother's marriage lines?"

"Yes, in her Bible. Why?"

"And do you have your birth certificate?"

"Of course. It's signed by the British consulate in India. You're thinking . . . ?"

"Quite. What if Elizabeth found herself in an awkward situation, with no way to reach her lover? She might have taken the only chance to avoid a scandal and give her child a name, albeit the name of a ne'er-do-well who would have found her small dowry worth his freedom. Go compare the dates, Aurora. I think we are getting closer to solving the mystery."

She returned with the papers, pale and chewing on her lip. "Not many seventh-month infants survive, do they?"

"I'm afraid not."

"Then I am a bastard?" Oh, Lord, she thought, how could the Earl of Windham be married to a female born on the wrong side of the blanket? He'd be shamed in front of the beau monde, and he'd hate her for that. Perhaps the marriage could still be annulled, if his condition precluded the much-delayed consummation. He'd hate her for that even more, since it was her idea to bring Andrew home. "Oh, I am so sorry."

"Why? Your parents were dutifully married, and your father, your mother's husband, acknowledged you as his."

"But in truth I am baseborn."

"So what? Half the births in the *ton* come early. No one suspected for all these years that Halle was not your true father, so why should they question it now, when all the participants have passed on? Besides, you should be happy that scoundrel wasn't your real sire."

"And you don't mind?"

"What, that my wife has the blood of one of England's finest families in her veins? You're the same person you were ten minutes ago, aren't you? The same managing female with the same generous heart."

He patted the space beside him on the bed, and Aurora joined him there. Sheltered in his arms, she realized it really did not matter who her actual father was. "But, you know, I wouldn't be surprised if George found out about the child. He must have sent Lord Phelan to India to verify the rumors."

"What he must have done was planned to

settle money on Elizabeth's and his daughter. Ratchford was always warm in the pocket."

"But I bet Lord Phelan convinced my mother to say I was dead. She was already ailing and needed a way to keep me safe from Halle. She couldn't send me to George, of course, for he was married by then, but her sister and Uncle Ptolemy would never question my parentage. They could change my name, and Halle would be none the wiser."

"Unfortunately, neither would George. I'd wager Phelan never told him the truth, perhaps out of spite. Remember that Lady Anstruther-Jones thought both brothers were in love with your mother. Or else perhaps Phelan was simply trying to keep the money out of Halle's hands."

"So he let George die thinking my mother and I were both lost to him?"

"And the money would stay in the family coffers. Ratchford's heir was not terribly robust, if I recall, so Phelan might have been hoping to succeed to the title and estate himself."

"Yes, but once he'd notified George of the child's supposed death, what further interest could Lord Phelan have in me?"

Kenyon thought a moment. "What if

George left an inheritance and never changed his will? By keeping the secret, Phelan made sure the money was never paid out. There would be no benefit to him — and embarrassment to the Ramsey family name — in bringing you to the court's attention. Neither you nor your relatives would have thought to look into Ratchford's will, of course, so he was safe. But then you grew up."

"To a marriageable age."

"Exactly, and Phelan realized he could share the bounty if he found the right swine to marry you."

"Harland Podell."

"Right. I'd be surprised if Podell ever makes it to Jamaica, knowing as much as he does about Phelan's plans."

"What, you think Lord Phelan is dangerous?" Extortion and criminal connivance were one thing; murder was quite another.

He pulled her tighter to his side, wincing at the discomfort. "Not to you, my dear, for Ramsey lost all chance of sharing in the inheritance when we wed. Your demise would only make me a richer man, if I pursued the matter."

"I suppose that's why he is hiding out now, so we cannot ask questions about

Harland, or about George and his will. No one would have thought to make inquiries if you hadn't been so suspicious."

"Well, this is all conjecture on our part. We'll know more when my solicitor communicates with Ratchford's man of affairs, or Ned finds Phelan for us."

Aurora was thinking of what she would do with an unexpected inheritance. She'd be advertising her mother's sins, for one thing, and wreaking havoc in the new Lord Ratchford's life. He was her half brother. His children were her nieces and nephews. It seemed her family was growing by the day, and they would all be affected by stirring up the scandalbroth. "I need to think about this."

"Of course you do, but not tonight. Tonight you should be thinking of your husband, and how much he is longing to hold you."

"But you are holding me, silly." And his hand was stroking up and down her arm, making her feel as if she were the one with the fever.

"Now who is being silly? This is snuggling. I mean holding, bare skin to bare skin, body to body. I mean I want to see every beautiful inch of you, touch you, taste you. Let your hair flow through my fingers to spread across the pillow. Hold you when you cry out my name, and when your body sings with the pleasure I am aching to give you."

"Oh, my." She snatched the cool towel off his head to place on her suddenly overheated brow. "Do you think you are up for such . . . such strenuous activity?"

The way he felt, he might never be up again. "Hell, no, or we wouldn't be talking, sweetheart. But soon."

Chapter Twenty-five

Soon. Aurora hummed to herself as she cut flowers for Kenyon's room. Soon. Andrew was already up and about, almost entirely recovered, so his father should be on the mend shortly. Lucy and her pups had been restored to the stables, having grown too rambunctious and too untrained for the nursery — and poor Frederick having become too much an embarrassment to the ladies with Lucy nearby — so Andrew was out with them when he was not keeping his father company. This pleased Aurora, since now she did not have to feel guilty giving so much of her time to Kenyon.

Soon he'd need less. Kenyon was less fevered, less prone to waking all wild-eyed and wet. He hardly stirred at night, so she was able to sleep on the bed next to him, but not touching, with his soft, regular snoring a welcome sound to her now. Aurora could stop it by putting another pillow under his head, but then she'd awaken, heart pounding and stomach in knots, thinking he'd stopped breathing. A little snoring was a small price to pay for the reassurance and for not having to keep waking him, to be sure.

With his cheeks much less swollen, the earl had begun to let his valet shave him, so he looked more gentleman than rogue, but no less dashing. Aurora had stroked the bristle on his unshaven chin when she bathed his face with cool water; now she had to pretend to feel for fever as an excuse to touch the smooth planes of his jaw and cheeks. In a few more days she could touch him all she wanted. Now where had that immodest thought come from? she wondered. Unnerved, Aurora almost cut her finger instead of the rose.

Surely, she was the luckiest woman on earth, she thought. Or she would be, soon.

Soon, dash it. Kenyon was nearly recovered, except for a lingering weakness and a bit of swelling. But before too many more days had passed, he'd be able to make love to his wife. He ached, but this time inside, to show Aurora how much she had come to mean to him, how she had made his home into a place of warmth and laughter. And she had given him his son. All the words he'd never spoken to a woman and did not know how to say . . . he would show her. Soon.

Before the end of the week he intended to settle some other unfinished household business, too. He'd see about getting Wesley Royce's inheritance restored, even if he had to shake it out of the snake who'd stolen it. And he'd visit Noah Benton and beat some decency back into the dastard, if that's what it took to get Nialla reinstated. Turn his back on his own daughter, would he? Not once the Earl of Windham was recovered, he swore. Ignoring his own former lapses in familial feelings, Kenyon planned on shaming the Cit into providing a decent dowry for the chit, and for Christopher.

Thinking that he'd never regain his strength by lying on his back, Kenyon decided to start exercising. He'd begin with a short walk, say to and from the stables, to see how exhausted that made him. And he'd do it now, while Aurora was busy elsewhere, so she would not tell him it was too far, too soon. He was a man, and it was time for him to step out from under petticoat rule, even if he fell on his face.

The grooms had all the carriages out in the stable yard for washing on this sunny spring afternoon, so the earl waved to them as he passed, hoping none of his servants could see how his knees trembled with the effort. He leaned on the door when he was inside the large building, catching his breath while letting his eyes adjust to the dimmer light. He couldn't see Andrew, even with his glasses firmly in place, so he started down the long aisle, greeting his cattle as he passed each stall. Not until he reached the last few stalls did he get a hint of Andrew's location. The dogs were yelping; the boy could not be far away.

Kenyon's legs almost gave out altogether — and his heart, too — when he reached the farthest box, the one that housed Wesley Royce's great gray brute of a stallion. There was Andrew, trying to catch a puppy that had wandered into the stall. He was darting practically under the steel-shod hooves while the stallion blew through his nostrils and flattened his ears. Another moment and boy and dog would be ground into the straw under the huge horse's feet.

Kenyon couldn't shout, not with his heart in his throat. Besides, he might rattle the stallion even worse. "Andrew," he whispered, "back up to the wall and edge yourself out of there, now."

"But I have to get my dog."

The earl's blood was pounding in his ears. "Now, Andrew."

But the boy made a last dive for the little mutt. The stallion snorted and reared up. Drawing strength from his soul, for he had none in his legs, Kenyon leaped into the stall, scooped up boy in one arm and dog in the other and heaved them both over the door before facing a mountain of maddened muscle.

"Father!" Andrew shrieked, which redirected the stallion's attention enough that Kenyon could follow his own advice, flattening himself against the side of the stall and inching toward the exit. He spoke to the horse meantime, trying to calm him with his voice. Of course, if the stallion had understood Kenyon's words about turning him into a gelding, or goldfish food, he might not have been so amenable. The earl slammed the gate behind him and collapsed onto the dirt floor of the stable. The pup came to lick his face. Kenyon shoved it aside, gasping, "That's the one you chose? The stupidest mutt of the litter?"

Andrew's bottom lip was quivering.

"Don't you cry, Andrew. Don't you dare cry."

The earl hauled himself to his feet. His heart had not burst, the horse had not trampled him, and he had not died of fright for the boy, to his own amazement. He sure as

Hades was going to kill something though. Still seeing in his mind's eye what could have happened, a red haze clouded his vision.

"What the devil were you thinking, you imbecile?" he shouted at the boy, relief and reaction making his voice harsher and louder. "That had to have been the most want-witted piece of behavior I have seen in my life! An infant knows better than to get in the stall with an unpredictable animal. How could any son of mine be so stupid, for pity's sake!"

"Then you should have let the horse kill me," Andrew yelled back, his face screwed up with the effort to hold back his tears. "Then you'd be rid of me once and for all, just as you always wanted!"

"I never wanted my heir pounded into a pulp, dammit!"

"But you never wanted me here, and you're only going to send me away again anyway!" Andrew could not stop the sob that escaped from the depths of his despair. "I hate you!" With that, he turned and ran out of the stable, the puppy at his heels.

"Andrew! Come back here this instant!" But the boy kept running. Kenyon had not killed the boy, only his love. He swore, loudly enough to bring the grooms and stable boys racing in from the yard, then he picked Andrew's spectacles off the floor. Still cursing, he swung around and hit the wooden upright beam with his fist, which did not do much for the beam, his temper, or the knucklebones of his right hand.

He threatened to dismiss every single one of the stable crew for leaving his son unattended. He threatened to have the horse shot, and the dog, and his wife, for taking the boy away from the safety of school, forcing Kenyon to prove to her just what a poor parent he was.

"Cut line, Kenyon." Brianne was there, offering her handkerchief for his bloody hand. Royce was beside her, looking none too happy. "It was our fault Andrew got into trouble. We left him alone when we went up to the loft to . . . ah, to . . ."

"To check the roof for leaks," Wesley finished for her. "I thought Andrew knew better than to go near Thundering Avenger."

"Thundering Avenger? That's the brute's name? You let my son near a horse named Thundering Avenger? And you leave him alone while you go off seducing my sister? I'd challenge you to pistols, by Zeus, if I thought you were a gentleman."

"I know you're angry, Kenyon, but

307

shouting at Wesley won't bring Andrew back," his sister shouted back at him.

"No? But it will make me feel a great deal better to toss him out, along with his horse and his mangy dog, if I cannot call him out." The earl took a step toward Wesley, forgetting the highwayman was wounded, forgetting a lady was present.

The lady kicked him in the shin. "If Wesley goes, so do I."

"Now that's the best offer I've had all week."

Before the siblings could resort to name-calling, Wesley pushed Brianne behind him. "I apologize about not watching the lad closer. As for your sister, I intend to make her an honest offer."

"Honest? Coming from a highwayman, that does not reassure me!"

Royce had a bullet hole in his shoulder, but the earl was swaying on his feet and dripping blood down his pants. It would not be an even match, so the younger man held his arm up. "We will discuss this another time, Lord Windham. For now, instead of arguing, why don't you go inside and see your hand looked after, while Brianne and I go after Andrew before he gets any farther away?"

Kenyon jerked his head in agreement.

"That's Lady Brianne to you, sirrah. And you, Bri, get the straw out of your hair before anyone else sees you."

Soon was obviously not going to be tonight.

"You hit my son?"

"Andrew is my son, too, by Harry. And of course I did not hit him, Aurora. I hit the blasted stable, which is why you are pulling splinters out of my hand, not little boy's teeth. What kind of an animal do you think me, anyway?"

Never knowing anyone to take his anger out on defenseless buildings, Aurora did not answer. She just kept dabbing at the blood so she could see the wood pieces.

"Confound it, I shouted at him, was all. If you and everyone else hadn't been mollycoddling the boy, he wouldn't have turned craven and run. He was in the wrong, dash it, putting himself in danger that way."

Aurora pursed her lips, but still did not comment. She also did not probe quite so gently with her needle and tweezers.

"He'll doubtless be back by supper, if Brianne and the make-bait don't find him first, and I'll apologize for yelling if you think I ought. I was just so worried, and it was such a stupid thing to do."

"What, try to rescue his puppy? What would you have done, or Sir Timothy?"

Kenyon sighed, then gasped as she pulled a chunk of wood the size of a piece of kindling out of his hand. "I might also have shoved Brianne straight into the highwayman's arms."

"From what you told me, I thought she was already there. And I thought you liked Mr. Royce."

"He's a likeable enough devil, but not what I'd pick for my sister's husband."

"You did not get to pick her first husband either, recall. But what did you expect Brianne to do, tumble into love for a worthy vicar, or settle for a sedate squire? Wesley Royce will suit her fine. You'll just have to see about his inheritance so they can scandalize the *ton* from someone else's house. I'm sure you'll be owing him an apology for this day's work, too."

"Let him find the boy, and I'll kiss his feckless, felonious feet."

But Wesley and Brianne did not find Andrew, nor did he appear for supper. Together with all the servants, they searched the attics, the cellars, and the conservatory, the wash house, the ice house, and the nearest tenants' houses. Aunt Ellenette took to her bed, and Aurora's relatives took the pony cart back to their bog to see if he'd gone there.

"I wish Ned were here," Aurora fretted. "He'd know where to look."

Kenyon was trying to button his caped riding coat with one hand, getting ready to join the footmen and grooms and gardeners. "Nonsense, my dear. You might as well ask Frederick where Andrew is. Brianne and Christopher and I were raised here; we know every place a child can hide."

They also knew every local cottager and village resident. Andrew did not. "But it will be growing dark soon, and he'll be afraid." Neither spoke of the missing glasses, now in Aurora's pocket, and what unseen dangers Andrew could have stumbled upon. "Besides, neither you nor your brother are recovered enough to be riding cross-country like this."

"We'll do what we have to. If Kit weakens, I'll send him back, so tell the watering pot not to worry. And you try, too, my dear. We'll have him back. Soon."

Chapter Twenty-six

The bells were peeling for Andrew again, but not to celebrate his homecoming. Aurora had the estate fire bells rung to bring in the searchers, and the village church picked up the signal. Andrew was not found, and was not likely to be by the men on foot or horseback, searching roadside ditches and haystacks. He'd been abducted.

Aurora's former maid, Judith, who'd formerly been able to ride a horse, was so heavy with child she'd had to walk the distance from her cottage at the edge of the estate to report what she'd seen: a dark carriage hurtling past, a small face pressed to the window. Her husband had saddled up and ridden after it, calling back that he would send messages to Windrush as soon as he could give a direction. But he had one swaybacked horse; the carriage had four gleaming matched chestnuts.

Now they had to wait for word, which was harder than scouring the countryside. At least then they'd been doing something, anything. Now Kenyon was pacing. Nialla was weeping into Kit's handkerchief while he sat, exhausted after his ride. Brianne and Wesley were warming themselves with the aged bottle of brandy they'd unearthed from the wine cellar, and Aunt Thisbe was joining in, to settle her nerves, while Uncle Ptolemy was stroking a lizard. Aurora did not drink, did not pace, and did not find petting an amphibian at all soothing. She was sewing a shirt for Andrew to wear when he got back. She'd only stitched the lawn fabric to her own skirts once, and jabbed the needle into her finger three times, she was that calm.

Aunt Ellenette came downstairs to see what the new commotion was about and started wailing about Gypsies carrying the boy off. They'd be stealing Frederick next!

"We'd never be so lucky," Kenyon muttered under his breath, but reminded his aunt that the carriage was an elegant equipage, not a Gypsy caravan. "Besides, I know all the Gypsy families who camp near Windrush. They are decent people who have traveled this way for years. They might borrow a chicken or two, but they would never jeopardize their welcome." He was desperate, so asked, "Does Frederick have any thoughts on the matter?"

Frederick thought he'd like to sample the spirits, but he'd settle for the salamander. Uncle Ptolemy tapped the pug on its flattened nose, which had Aunt Ellenette up in the boughs, then up in her room, with the dog. Kenyon nodded his appreciation to the older man and resumed his pacing.

"Do you think Lord Phelan could be behind Andrew's disappearance?" Aurora asked when no one seemed to have a better idea, white slavery and chimney sweeps not being better ideas, to her thinking.

"What good would my son be to Ramsey?" Kenyon replied. "And he has to know I would spend the rest of my life tracking him down if he harms the lad. No, I cannot see Lord Phelan committing a crime so likely to get himself killed."

"Do you think Andrew is being held for ransom?"

He shrugged. "Where is the demand for payment, then?"

"Besides, a kidnapping is usually planned," Wesley added, leading Kenyon, at least, to speculate on how Royce knew such a fact. "No one could have counted on Andrew running off on his own, or what direction he'd take, to have a carriage ready to hand. This smacks of someone already in the vicinity snatching a golden opportunity

when it ran past. Do you have other enemies, my lord, who might seek revenge?"
Wesley sounded positive the glowering earl
must have a few.

"No one who does not fear me more than
hate me — with just cause. I will not tolerate
having my family threatened. I would suspect that mawworm Podell, but he is too
much the coward. And he prefers to vic-
timize women, not children. No, I have no
idea who would have done such a thing, but
he will pay, you can be assured."

"You'll pay him to get Andrew back,
though, won't you, if it is, indeed, a plot to
extort money from you?" Aurora had a
dread of her furious, impetuous husband
exacting retribution instead of paying the
ransom.

"What, do you fear I'll tell him to keep the
boy if the price is too high?"

"No, I fear you'll throttle him before he
tells where he's taken Andrew." Aurora had
to cut apart the two sleeves of Andrew's
shirt that she'd just sewn together.

"I do not let my emotions overrule my
reason, madam wife," he replied, which had
Brianne scoffing and Aurora raising her
brows. "Well, this afternoon was different. I
had good cause to be upset, dash it." He
went back to his pacing. Aurora sewed the

sleeves in upside down.

Christopher could barely stay awake, so Kenyon sent him up to bed, in case he was needed fresh in the morning. If they had no word by then, Kenyon intended to deploy riders in every direction, asking after the dark coach with chestnut horses. Brianne challenged Wesley to a round of billiards in the game room rather than sit watching her brother wear out the carpets. Nialla went to check on her cat, and, making Aurora promise to call them if there was news, the McPhees also retired, since they had been up since daybreak, counting croaking frogs. The earl would not heed Aurora's advice that he seek his bed, despite his bone-weariness. He'd never sleep, anyway. "But you should rest, my dear, for you've been exhausting yourself for weeks, it seems, with your nursing."

Every dread possibility was waiting for her upstairs, like monsters under the bed. Aurora knew her imagination would haunt her, picturing Andrew's fear in vivid, glaring colors. But Windham would not let anything happen to his son, she kept telling herself. Kenyon was strength and safety, so she needed to be near him. "No, I'd rather stay here with you."

He came and knelt in front of her, taking

the mangled shirt out of her clasp. He brought both of her hands to his lips. "We'll get him back, I swear it."

The note came long after midnight. A boy from the village livery stable brought it, but he said a stranger had paid him to deliver it, then rode off. Kenyon tore the page open with his bandaged hand, swearing.

"Is it from Judith's husband?" Aurora wanted to know. "Did he say where they were? Or what direction they were heading?"

"No, it's from the kidnappers."

Aurora was relieved that this was a matter of greed, not vengeance. Extortionists would never harm the boy, not if they wanted to see their money. "How much do they want? And where can we get it this time of night?"

"They don't mention money, just that we need to talk. The note says to be at the Jolly Cricket in Kings Lynn, on The Wash in Norfolk. They must think they are far enough ahead of any pursuit that we cannot overtake them before they reach the harbor."

"Sounds like they are headed out to sea as soon as the business is completed." Back from the billiards room, Wesley thought they'd be wise to do so, from the look on Windham's face.

Brianne was outraged. "Unless they think to take the money and the boy both! They could sail anywhere, and we'd never find them."

Windham handed the note to Aurora. "No, I'm sure they'd only be taking Andrew to France."

Brianne and Wesley stared at him as if he'd become as queer in the attics as Aunt Ellenette. "How in the world have you come to that conclusion?" Brianne demanded.

"Because the note says '*Il faut que nous parlions.*' That's 'We need to speak,' in case you've forgotten all those lessons at your expensive finishing school. Where else would Frenchmen run to? Not that that will save them, of course. And Norfolk is still a long way from Paris."

Aurora was studying the message as though another reading would offer up more information than the two lines contained. "But what would a Frenchman want with Andrew, if not money for his return?"

"If today was an example of your skills at diplomacy, brother, perhaps you made enemies across the sea, too." Still holding her cue stick, Brianne stabbed at the carpet with it. "I never could believe you were part of the peace negotiations committee."

Kenyon ignored her, except to tell her to straighten her gown. Wesley took the stick out of her hands before she attacked the knickknacks on the mantel. "I'll wager it's Genevieve's family, then," Brianne said. "They never liked her marrying an Englishman, and might have blamed you that she ran off with the duke and died in France. Though what you could have done to stop her I cannot imagine."

Aurora was hopeful. Genevieve's family would never hurt their own flesh and blood. "Perhaps they only want Andrew to go back to France with them for a while, to see his mother's homeland?"

Kenyon shook his head. "They are all dead, the ones who did not settle in England. Only an aunt and a cousin or two remain, that I know of. They could visit Andrew anytime they want. I've told them so many times, sending on his schools' addresses, not that any of them ever has. And they don't need money."

"Who else could have an interest in Andrew?" Aurora asked the question they were all wondering.

"It might turn out to have nothing to do with the boy at all, except as a bargaining tool. Someone wants something from me, that is all I know." They followed him to the book room, where Kenyon fumbled to open the safe with his bandaged hand. Wesley offered to help, but received such a foul look that Brianne took offense.

The earl withdrew a pouch filled with money, even though the kidnappers had not mentioned a price. "Dash it, this is not enough. Who knows where I'll end up or how soon I can get a draft on my bank?"

Aurora gasped. "I knew I shouldn't have spent so much on the banana trees!"

"Banana trees?" Kenyon paused in his counting. "No, don't tell me. But don't be absurd. None of this is your fault." He stuffed the money in his inner pocket, then withdrew the velvet pouch containing the Windham diamonds from the safe into another pocket.

Brianne's protests turned to a whimper when Wesley pinched her. She shrugged, remembering that she wouldn't be wearing the necklace again, anyway.

Finally, before closing the safe, Kenyon took out his Mantons.

Aurora watched him clean and load the pistols. "I am going, you know."

He didn't even argue, but warned that he intended to sleep in the coach, driving through the night, stopping only when the horses needed changing. Aurora nodded. She would not have it any other way. Wesley volunteered to start out cross-country on horseback to see if he could intercept the coach before it reached the coast. It was a long shot, even if Judith's husband had left messages along the way, but worth the try. And no, Wesley would not let Brianne ride along, no matter how bruising a rider she was. She could not keep up with Thundering Avenger, to say nothing of what would happen to her reputation if she was alone on the roads with him for days and nights.

Considering the disarranged state of her clothing after a simple billiards match, Kenyon thought it was surprisingly thoughtful of the cad to be worried over Brianne's good name.

Brianne agreed to stay behind and relay messages, especially if any further communication arrived. They did not wake the others since there was nothing anyone else could do, but hurried to pack. Aurora threw a few things in a valise, a change of clothing and her nightrail, her toiletry items and her Bible. Then she packed for Andrew: clean clothes, his favorite book, and some of the willowbark fever medicine, just in case. She also packed a hamper of food so they would not have to delay at the coaching stops longer than it took to put fresh cattle in the traces.

Kenyon also packed: a knife, a rifle, and a small ivory-handled pistol that fit in the pocket of his waistcoat.

Wesley's horse was out front, stamping on the ground while Royce made his farewells, which seemed to necessitate disarranging Kenyon's sister some more. Lord Windham decided it was a good thing the dastard was riding out; otherwise he'd have to lock the blighter up, the way he did Frederick after the pug expressed his frustrated affection for Royce's dog on the vicar's leg.

Then they were off, with two coachmen to share the driving. Mere minutes had passed, though it seemed like hours. And it seemed like days since either Aurora and Kenyon had slept. Both drowsed in the coach. Rousing briefly when the carriage wheel hit a bump, Kenyon saw how Aurora's head was bent at an angle guaranteed to give her a sore neck. He pulled her over to his side of the carriage, half onto his lap, then tucked the carriage blanket around both of them. He could smell the rosewater in her hair and know her softness, even through their layers of clothes.

Settling against his chest, Aurora felt

Kenyon's heartbeat, the steady power of this man. She knew he'd get Andrew back. "I love you, Lord Windham," she whispered when she thought he'd fallen asleep again.

"I love you, too, Lady Windham," he whispered back, before starting to snore.

Chapter Twenty-seven

Aurora was his anchor. Without her by his side, Kenyon would have run aground, or amok. On the other hand, of course, he would not be in this fix if she had not meddled. Neither would he have known his son. Now she believed he could find Andrew and bring him to safety; therefore, he could.

Wesley Royce met up with their carriage before they reached the rendezvous spot. He'd never encountered Judith's singular soldier on the road, but he had located the abductors, although not in time to halt their coach outside of town, not without jeopardizing Andrew. Once they'd arrived at their destination, right where they said they'd be waiting, three middle-aged men with French accents had taken a private parlor at the inn, as bold as brass and dragging a reluctant Andrew between them. There were two older men in worn but expensive clothing, and another, a long-haired servant who had an ominous bulge in his pocket. Not wishing to be seen, Wesley had stayed outside, but, according to the innkeeper, the oldest of the men had signed the register as R. DuBois. Both Wesley and Aurora looked expectantly toward Kenyon, hoping he'd be able to explain, but the earl knew no one by that name, not that criminals who stole children were wont to use their real identities.

The innkeeper had also mentioned to Wesley, for a price, that Monsieur DuBois was taking his orphaned nephew back to France, now that the war was over, since the boy had been expelled from every decent school in England for lying and stealing and fighting. As proof, DuBois had shown a bitten thumb, while the servant sported a black eye.

"Good for Andrew." Kenyon was helping Aurora down from their carriage, some distance away from the inn. They'd walk, rather than arrive in the crested coach, hoping to catch the abductors unawares. "But of course the innkeeper would not listen to his pleas for help after that. This DuBois shows a modicum of cunning."

Wesley disagreed. "If DuBois is so wily, why is he just sitting in the parlor taking tea, when he knows you're on his trail?"

"Because he knows I would not enter the parlor with my pistols blazing, not with

Andrew in the room. Bullets have a nasty habit of missing their targets, so remember, there is to be no shooting." Despite his words, Kenyon checked the dueling pistol in his greatcoat pocket, and the smaller one in his waistcoat. Wesley felt behind him, where his own weapon was tucked into his waistband under his coat, and nodded. He left to take up a position outside the partially open window of the Frenchmen's parlor.

Kenyon tried to get Aurora to wait near the carriage or outside the inn. Then he tried to convince her to stay in the inn's lobby, the public room, or an upstairs bed-chamber. Finally, he tucked her arm into his elbow, and together they walked into the inn.

"Monsieur DuBois is expecting us," he told the bowing innkeep. "You do not need to announce us." He tossed the man a coin for minding his own business, and they went down the hall to the room Wesley had described. "You stay here until I say to come in," Kenyon instructed Aurora, who nodded, then followed right behind him as he kicked open the door and strode in.

The three men were sitting at the table, but Andrew was in the corner on the floor. He jumped up and ran to Aurora, who gathered him in her arms and her skirts and her tears. Kenyon, meanwhile, was inspecting the men. Even with his glasses on, he did not recognize any of them, but he did recognize the pistol in the long-haired servant's hand, aimed at Andrew's head. He bowed slightly and said, "I do not believe we have been introduced," in English.

The man who appeared to be in charge smiled, stood, and bowed, as if they were at an embassy dinner. "In good time, *mon ami*, as soon as you have put down your weapon."

Kenyon shrugged and placed the Manton on the table closest to him. "You are no friend of mine."

"No, and for that I apologize. If times were different . . . who knows? Would you like to sit? *Comtesse*, can I offer you tea?"

Still clutching Andrew as if he would fly away if she didn't keep a tight hold, Aurora shook her head. Her stomach lurched at the thought of making polite conversation with these monsters who would threaten a little boy. Now was not the time to be sick, though. She did take Andrew to a sofa against the wall, trying to place the two Frenchmen at the table between them and the man holding the gun. She kept her arms around the boy, ready to shield his body with her own if she had to.

Kenyon did not sit. "Your intentions, sir?"

The Frenchman studied the cup of tea he held between blue-veined hands. "They say you are a formidable negotiator, my lord. I have a — how do you say it? — a deal I wish to make with you."

"I do not bargain while you have a gun pointed at my son's head."

DuBois smiled again, flicking his fingers at the servant, who lowered his weapon but did not put it down. Then he said, "But is he your son? That is the question."

Kenyon was losing patience. "Who the devil are you, and what do you want?"

"You really do not know?"

"And I really do not care." Kenyon reached into his pocket — the servant's gun came up again — and pulled out his wallet. He threw it on the table, and then opened the velvet pouch and tossed the Windham diamonds alongside the money. "There, that is all I have. Take it or leave it, but my wife and my son and I are leaving. If you think you can stop us, you might want to look out the window."

When all three Frenchmen turned, Wesley waved, his pistol in his hand.

"And my coachman is at the rear of the

inn, and my groom at the front. All armed."

"Ah, you have misunderstood the nature of the bargain I wish to make, no?" DuBois reached into his own breast pocket — Kenyon took a step closer to his pistol on the table — and pulled out yet another drawstring pouch. He upended it next to the diamonds. Rubies, emeralds, and pearls spilled out, a pirate's bounty.

"What the devil?" Kenyon stepped closer, picking up a ruby pendant. "This looks familiar."

"It should. Your wife brought it to France, hoping to buy Napoleon's favor. You were asking about your family heirlooms just last month, no, while you were in Paris? Here they are. The sapphires would complement the *comtesse's* blue eyes, no?"

Kenyon pounded the table, then winced as his injured hand throbbed. "Enough. Tell me what you want and have done with this fustian nonsense. My wife is tired, and the boy is upset."

"*Très bien.* Let us begin at the beginning. I am René DuBois, *si'l vous plaît,* and this is my brother, Jean-Claude. Our sister was Nicole DuBois, who became the wife of Raoul, le Duc D'Journet, your wife's lover."

"Nicole died in childbirth."

"But her son, Henri, lived. Henri is now

the duke, of course, not Raoul's usurping cousin Lucien who is this very moment claiming the title and the estates."

"But Henri died in the crossing to England. I wrote Lucien, and I know he received my message even with the war going on, for Henri's name was inscribed on the family tomb. I went to check when I was in Paris."

"*Oui,* we know you did, and that got us to thinking, *n'est ce pas?* Perhaps you went to pay your respects to the memory of your own dead son. Or out of guilt, for claiming the duke's son for your own."

"What?" Aurora gasped. "My lord would never do such a heinous thing. Andrew is his son!"

The earl finally sat down, letting the ruby pendant swing from his left hand. "But now I understand. If you can produce Henri, then you can have yourself named as trustee and get your hands on whatever remains of D'Journet's properties, or what you can steal back. And you thought I would trade these" — he grabbed up a handful of necklaces and brooches — "for the boy."

DuBois nodded. "*Exactement.* Everyone knows you despised Genevieve and Raoul for the scandal, and everyone also knows you never acknowledge the boy. This is the first time you have seen him in, what, six years? In your heart you do not think he is yours, *monsieur*, do you? But these," he said, shoving the Windham diamonds closer to the pile of other treasures, "these are yours."

Kenyon swiped his hand across the table, sending the jewelry flying. "How dare you think to barter for what is mine, with what is mine. Andrew is my son, do you hear? My son. Even if he were not, I would not give him to a fool who'd think the paper-thin peace will hold. Napoleon is not finished, and what happens to the duke's estate then? France will never go back to the way it was, with soulless aristocrats like you in command. The people will never let that happen. You do remember the people, don't you? The starving masses who had to overthrow the king just to eat? I would send no child to such a living hell. And I would never trade my flesh and blood for these cold stones."

"Prove it, *mon ami*. Prove you are the boy's father. He does not resemble you. He did not run to you when you so gallantly rode to his rescue. You would not look at him since he was an infant."

All his doubts, all those years of wounded pride and willing negligence were coming back to haunt Kenyon. Still, "He is my son," he insisted.

Aurora spoke up. "A man does not have to prove he fathered a child. Can you prove you are brothers, Monsieur DuBois? You do not look alike, yet your birth records would show your parentage, the same as Andrew's shows his."

"But we have a sailor who was on the smuggler's ship, ready to swear that the boy who drowned was Windham's heir."

Kenyon muttered, "What did you trade for his lies, his mother's life?"

"Look, *monsieur*." She took Andrew's spectacles out of her pocket and put them on his face. "You see? He has his father's eyes."

DuBois smiled as he picked up the fallen jewelry. "The priest at my church wears spectacles, and he did not father this child either. Poor eyesight proves nothing."

"Very well, then, listen to this. We have locks on the grates of the nursery fireplace at Windrush. I noticed them when I was having the rooms refurbished for Andrew. Do you know why?"

Windham didn't know why, or if the locks actually existed. He nodded encouragement to his plucky little wife anyway.

Aurora did not wait for DuBois to ask.

"Because when he was learning to walk, Andrew knocked against the screen and fell into the fire. He was burned on the foot, and has a scar to this day."

Kenyon glanced toward the boy's feet, as if he could see through the sturdy boots Andrew wore. "He does? That is, he does."

"Yes, he does. I saw it myself when he was recently ill, and the nursemaids can verify the rest of the story."

"The ones who Genevieve did not dismiss for being so careless," Windham added. "But enough. You cannot prove that Andrew is Henri without my cooperation or you would have taken him away."

"But you will give this cooperation, this consent, no?"

Three pistols were aimed at Andrew suddenly. Kenyon could not chance going for his own weapon. He made sure Wesley did not fire by holding both of his hands up.

DuBois went on. "You will sign the paper here, that you knew Henri survived, but adopted him as yours since he could not go back to France."

"I regret that my writing hand is too injured." Kenyon made sure DuBois saw the bandages, and made sure the weasel understood that hell would freeze over before he signed such a document.

DuBois gave a Gallic shrug, without lowering his weapon. "We are at an impasse, no?"

"No!" Andrew burst up from the sofa and raced over to Kenyon. "He is my father! No one else is. I will not go with you, and I will not tell those lies you told me to say. My father loves me, he does! Otherwise he wouldn't have cared if I got trampled, and he wouldn't have come after me."

"Then why did you run away from home?" DuBois asked.

Andrew raised his chin. "Because I have the Warriner temper, the same as he does, and the same as my Aunt Brianne! Uncle Christopher is too sad about his arm to be angry, but when he recovers, you better watch out, 'cause he's a hero who's already killed lots of Frenchmen. And if you don't let us leave here, I am going to become very, very angry. Besides, if you shoot me, not only will my father and Wesley kill you, but you still won't have any heir to bring to France."

While Andrew was speaking, Aurora had reached under her skirts for Brianne's pistol strapped there above her garter. "Andrew, stand aside," she said now, directing the gun's sight right between Monsieur DuBois's eyes, she hoped. "I have heard enough. This boy is no blood relation of mine whatsoever, and I would never claim otherwise, but he is as dear to me as any child of my womb could be, and I am not leaving without him. Kenyon, pay the men for the jewels if you want them back, or not. I do not care. But I shall shoot the first man who blinks. If you are thinking that I will not pull the trigger, *monsieur,* understand that I have already shot the man outside once" — Wesley tapped his pistol lightly against the open window — "and I can shoot a man again."

Kenyon did not put his son down until they were at the carriage. He handed the boy up to Wesley and turned to hug Aurora, lifting her off her feet and twirling her around. "You were magnificent, madam wife, with the merest tinge of green in your complexion. But my stomach was in my own mouth, to think of you carrying a loaded pistol like that!"

She smiled. "Who said it was loaded?"

Chapter Twenty-eight

They stayed overnight at an inn near Sleaford, about halfway home. Kenyon took two rooms, one for him and his wife, and one for Wesley and Andrew to share. Andrew needed one of his parents nearby, though, Aurora declared, ordering a cot prepared for him in her room.

Kenyon was still grumbling about it the next morning. He might owe the highwayman a heavy debt for his assistance, for guarding their backs as they left the Frenchmen, but the earl would be hanged — like a highwayman, b'gad — if he wanted to share a bedroom with the fellow, let alone a bed.

"What are you complaining about, Windham?" Wesley asked, tying his horse to the back of the carriage. "You're the one who snores."

"I do not snore!"

Aurora giggled, a sweet, girlish sound that had Windham wishing the Frenchmen had kept Andrew and Wesley both, so he could have his wife alone, for once. "Such disloy-alty shall not go unpunished, wench," he growled, though they all knew Aurora had proved her loyalty and her bravery and her love, many times over. She giggled again and winked at Andrew.

Kenyon shook his head. "Nor such a lack of respect. As the head of this household, I hereby issue the following command to all of you: there will be no more escapades or alarums. I swear my hair will turn gray before my next birthday, otherwise, if I should live so long. I cannot survive more panicked palpitations of the heart. I will have peace in my household. Is that under-stood?" If he attained a degree of sanity and serenity, it would be for the first time since the day he'd met Aurora. He did not regret that day, not in the least; he just wished havoc did not follow her around like Nialla's cat, waiting to pounce.

Aurora smiled at the others. "Poor dear, I fear his nerves are overset. But we promise to be good, don't we?"

Andrew nodded. "No more trouble. Cross my heart."

"Good," Kenyon approved, looking at Royce through his looking glass, needing to know he'd given up the life of crime.

Wesley saluted and said, "On my honor."

"Hah!" But Kenyon was satisfied. Everything was right in his world and getting better by the day. Then night fell. They reached home.

"Bloody hell."

Aurora clapped her hands over Andrew's ears. "My lord!"

Servants were running in every direction, dogs were barking, Aunt Ellenette was in a swoon on the sofa, and Nialla was, naturally, soaking Christopher's shirtfront with her tears. The monkey was hanging from the chandelier, and any number of creeping, crawling things — things Kenyon used to think of as bait, not pets — were scurrying across his Aubusson carpet, with the McPhees on hands and knees in close pursuit. And his sister, daughter of an earl, darling of the *ton* at her come-out, was using one of his fencing sabers to hold at bay that most infamous of intruders, most threatening of trespassers, a middle-aged Cit. Nialla's father had come to call.

Welcome home, my lord.

Christopher, it seemed, had written to Noah Benton expressing his intentions toward the man's daughter. Having intentions toward such a goosish little female was bad enough, but announcing them to her ambitious father was foolish beyond permission. Kit's honor, however, demanded that he ask the coal merchant for that very permission, proving to Kenyon that bravery had little to do with wisdom. But the chit was underage, and in effect unwed, so she was technically under her father's control, although Kenyon distinctly recalled being informed that Benton had tossed the chit out when she faced disgrace. That was, of course, before she became involved with the brother of the Earl of Windham. Suddenly, the little redhead was a valuable commodity again.

Benton had hied himself to Windrush, but Nialla and Kit and Brianne were driving around the neighborhood, trying to find what strangers had been spotted before Andrew's disappearance. Benton spent the afternoon ingratiating himself with Aunt Ellenette by fawning over Frederick. Since the merchant also had a pushed-in nose from early days in the coal fields, protuberant eyes, heavy jowls, and a physique that resembled an ale keg, it was no wonder Benton admired the pug. And Aunt Ellenette admired the paving stone-size diamond he wore in his cravat. They were as close as inkle-weavers when the young people returned.

"My precious darling," he had gushed to

Nialla, holding his arms wide. She clung to Christopher. "You didn't find the boy, did you?" Benton asked with inordinate eagerness. "Captain Warriner would be next in line to the earldom then, wouldn't he?"

That was when Brianne locked the nabob in the conservatory. She couldn't push him down the stairs to the wine cellars, or roll him out to the ice house, but she could lure him to the glassed rooms with the promise of meeting a true Incomparable, one of the nobility's noblest — Sweety. She locked the door behind him. The aristocracy could have their little jokes, Benton chortled, until darkness fell and he grew hungry. When he had to fight the monkey for an orange, Benton decided he'd had enough and broke out, using Uncle Ptolemy's brass telescope to shatter the glass door. Brianne grabbed Kenyon's sword. Heaven only knew what she intended to do with it, or the mine owner.

Wesley did not wait to see. He reached over his beloved's shoulder and removed the sword. "I'll take that, love."

"Oh, hello, darling. Will you skewer this midden rat for me, please?"

"Of course, sweetings. As soon as I've had a kiss."

"Bloody hell!" Kenyon shouted again.

Aurora giggled as she waved a vinaigrette under Aunt Ellenette's nose.

"This is a fine way to treat a guest!" Benton blustered. "I've a mind to leave and take my little girl with me."

Christopher took the sword out of Wesley's hand.

"Cease!" When the Earl of Windham yelled, the walls shook. Even the toads stopped in their tracks. "You, sir, come with me." He jerked his head toward Benton. "And no one else."

"But it's my intended he's threatening to carry away."

"And it's my intention to make sure he does not. You're a soldier, Kit. Leave the talking to me. I brought Andrew back, didn't I?"

"With just a hint of help from Lady Windham," Wesley reminded Kenyon.

"You, sir, can unhand my sister and see about getting the blasted monkey down from the chandelier. I shall deal with this monkey's uncle of a mine owner."

The negotiations took two hours and two bottles of wine. In the end, Kenyon agreed to keep Brianne from murdering the merchant. Nialla's dowry was restored, and she was reinstated as Benton's heiress. Benton would also finance a project Kenyon and

Kit had spoken of on the long journey home from France — a small manufactory employing out-of-work soldiers. A natural leader of men, Captain Warriner would manage the new venture, so he had a livelihood without being dependent on either his wife's money or Windham's. The earl, for his part, agreed to deed Kit and Nialla one of the lesser estates that had come through his mother's family, as he'd always intended. He also agreed to let Benton visit at Windrush once a year — and pay court to Aunt Ellenette.

Kenyon opened another bottle of wine to toast Kit and his bride-to-be, who spouted tears of joy, of course. Benton raised his glass to the title he hoped to buy for his first grandson, and Windham drank to seeing the last of Frederick. Then he excused himself to tell the happy news to Aurora, who had taken Andrew upstairs long before. Peace with France was hardly as sweet as this deal, and Kenyon could not wait to share the details with his bride. After that, he'd share some of his dearest wishes and his deepest feelings.

Unfortunately, Aurora was already asleep, and sharing her bedroom with his son.

"Bloody hell."

Everyone wanted to hire Ned Needles —
Bow Street, the earl's solicitor, the Earl of
Ratchford's solicitor, and Lady Anstruther-
Jones. Ned, however, was content to remain
in Lady Windham's employ for better pay
and better working conditions, at least until
he finished his education and could become
the best and brightest Runner Bow Street
had ever seen. Wasn't he already living like
a prince at the earl's London town house
after he found the starchy old butler's
missing choppers? Besides, the little nipper
needed him. Tiny chap with specs like
Andrew needed looking after. Who better
than Ned to show the earl's heir around
London, how to defend himself against bullies, and how to cadge extra sweets out of
the earl's London chef?

It was Ned who had found Lord Phelan,
just as he'd promised. Not Bow Street, not
the investigators hired by Mr. Juckett, the
earl's man of affairs, not Lady Anstruther-
Jones's spies. No, it was the street urchin
who'd sent word around Town that he had a
check to deliver for the low-tide lord. The
address of Lord Phelan's sister was forthcoming. Bow Street was keeping an eye on
the shabby place on London's outskirts
until Lord Windham arrived.

Ned had also located Inky Devine, master forger with minimum scruples. Inky had written a new will for Wesley Royce's half brother, for a price. For a higher price, he was willing to deal with Lord Windham. He would not testify against Baron Alford, naturally, since doing so would put him out of work, and out of the country, likely, aboard a prison ship bound for Botany Bay. But Inky was willing to write a new note, in the previous Lord Alford's handwriting and dated the day after the forged will, stating that the baron had had a change of heart on his deathbed and was leaving one-third of his fortune to his beloved second son, Wesley.

Windham was taking the posthumous posting to White's that evening, sure to find Alford at the gaming tables. They had arrived in London that afternoon, in response to Ned's message. Deciding she had to put the whole issue of her parentage and inheritance behind them once and for all, Aurora insisted on joining him in Town. So Andrew had to go along, of course, and the monkey. Aunt Thisbe and Uncle Ptolemy were staying behind to see about planting cranberries from the Colonies in the swampy section of Windham's property, and Christopher was taking his fiancée and her father to inspect his new estate. Aunt Ellenette was going along as chaperone for the young couple, and Frederick was dogsberry for the older. Wesley had been threatening to kill his perfidious half brother in a duel, so Windham sent him and Brianne off to Scotland to wed, threatening to kill the highwayman himself if he did not stop compromising the earl's sister in the billiards room, their bedchambers, and everywhere in between.

They'd taken the boys to Astley's Amphitheatre that evening, and, much as he hated to leave his wife alone, Kenyon was now on his way to confront his new brother-in-law's betrayer. The mission did not take long. Kenyon took the man aside at the august club and showed him the note from his deceased father, just found. If it was not just found, he stated matter-of-factly, Alford would be ruined. The forger had confessed, the original will had been preserved, and Windham would not permit his sister to marry a pauper. If Alford should happen to die suddenly, Wesley Royce would inherit everything, did he understand? Since the earl's hands were at his throat, it would be hard for Alford to misinterpret. "Strange," he hoarsely croaked, "your finding m'father's note that way. The solicitors will straighten the whole thing out in the morning."

So Windham left White's with a jaunty step. The evening was still young, and his warm and willing wife was waiting up for him. One more hurdle in the way of his domestic tranquility was crossed. He crossed the street, and his head exploded. That's what it felt like, at any rate, before he fell flat on his nose. Before losing consciousness, Kenyon did manage to lift his head an inch off the cobblestones in time to see his attacker running down an alleyway, her skirts flying. A woman, b'gad. It figured.

Chapter Twenty-nine

The scene was tender. So was the back of his head.

Aurora was kneeling on the floor beside the sofa where the footmen had carried him. "Don't die, my darling. Oh, Kenyon, I don't think I could live without you. I know I have not been a good wife to you, but I swear I will do better in the future, if you have one. Please, my beloved, don't leave me, not when I have yet to become your wife in deed."

He sat up, clutching his head. "Now? You want me to consummate the blasted marriage now?"

The butler coughed. Oh, lud, Kenyon groaned. Now all of London would know the Earl of Windham hadn't bedded his bride! At the moment, he did not care. He did not even care that Aurora was leaning over him, her entrancing décolletage just inches from his eyes. That's how badly his head hurt. "I am going to murder the bastard who did this."

"Wesley's brother?" Aurora guessed.

"No, there was no time for him to act. And not DuBois or his servant, either. The man I paid to watch in Kings Lynn sent word that all three of the Frenchmen sailed right after we left."

"Weren't no cutpurse," Ned put in, " 'cause you still had your wallet and ring and sparkler in your neckcloth."

"Then who? Who would do such a terrible thing?" Aurora was wringing her hands, instead of the damp cloth for his head.

"I think it was Phelan Ramsey's sister."

"But Lord Phelan does not have a sister."

"Exactly."

"I knew you'd come."

Lord Phelan was not a handsome man, being small and spindly, with a large nose and blackened teeth. He was a really homely woman. The gun he was holding was not terribly attractive, either. In fact, Lord Windham was getting deuced sick of having every malfeasant malcontent point a weapon in his direction. His skull ached, he was the laughingstock of London, and, instead of waiting in the carriage as he'd ordered, his bride was right beside him in this filthy boardinghouse parlor, facing a foxed felon with a full budget of grievances.

"Of course I came, Ramsey. What was I supposed to do, wait for you to bash me over the head again?"

Phelan drank straight from the bottle of Blue Ruin on the littered table in front of him. "The tap on the brainbox was to encourage you to call off your hunt for me. I figured you'd ought to leave me in peace now that m'nevvy knows about the bloody will. He'll honor it, the nodcock, so you've got the baggage and the bounty. I've got bill collectors after my blood. Didn't need you leading them to my doorstep."

"Too late. They're here, along with Bow Street, the magistrate's office, and assorted others in the legal professions. So what do you want? You know you'll never get your hands on Aurora's inheritance no matter what you do, so why attack me?"

"I wanted to see you dead, you demmed meddler, so I could find someone else to wed the chit. May Podell rot in hell for lying to me about being a bachelor. I should have taken the wench to the Fleet and married her m'self. Now that won't work."

"I'm afraid not, Ramsey. There's no way out of here that does not involve pistol balls or prison. The choice is yours, of course." The house was surrounded by Runners, constables, and a whole regiment, it seemed, of Aurora's rescued veterans. "You'll never get out of here alive if you so much as sneeze."

Lord Phelan took another swig. "I'm a dead man anyway, might as well take one of you with me. She" — the gun barrel swayed in Aurora's direction — "is just like her mother. Wouldn't have me, you know. Begged her to, I did, even knowing she was carrying m'brother's child. She chose that muckworm Halle instead, then had the gall to name me godfather to my brother's bastard, and ask me to get the brat back to England. I did it, didn't I? And never got a groat for my trouble. M'life was never the same after. Yeah, the wench ought to pay for that."

Kenyon was losing patience. "You know, I was going to suggest to your nephew that he ship you out of the country so no one would be embarrassed by your ravings. We could keep everything private between the two households that way. I was even going to offer to help pay your way. But no one threatens my family, do you understand?" He took a step toward Phelan, which had the man redirecting his aim away from Aurora.

"Kenyon, no!" she cried. "Let him leave

the country, please. He did help my mother, and he cannot hurt us anymore."

"See?" Lord Phelan snarled. "M'niece loves me. So I think I better take her with me." He lurched up out of his chair and tossed the bottle of Blue Ruin at Kenyon's head. The bottle painfully grazed the previous injury and, worse, knocked the earl's spectacles to the ground. So he couldn't quite see Ramsey grab Aurora by the neck and put the gun barrel to her temple, but he could feel it in his gut. Aurora was struggling, but her strength was no match for the maddened Phelan, and no one would chance shooting the dirty dish now, not with Aurora in his hold. Ramsey's grip was so tight she could not even scream.

"Damn it, woman, I told you to stay in the coach!"

"Good idea, Windham. Mayhaps I'll borrow your carriage, too. Wouldn't want your little ladybird getting tossed around in a hired hack."

"My wife and my carriage?" Kenyon shouted. "Never. Besides, you wouldn't want to travel with her right now. She gets sick to her stomach when she's overset. That's right, isn't it, Aurora?"

Taking her cue, Aurora made gagging noises and clutched her stomach. Phelan shoved her away from him in the same instant Kenyon dove at him, just as Ned and two footmen burst through the front door. Phelan's pistol discharged, Aurora screamed, and Kenyon cursed as the Runners and the constables crashed through the back door. The bill collectors' bullies smashed through the windows. And the ceiling, mortally wounded, rained plaster down on all of them.

By the time Phelan was carted away, no one had to worry much about what he was going to say, not with his jaw broken. And he wasn't going to have to worry about his blackened teeth anymore, either, or his too-large nose.

It was over. Lord and Lady Windham went home.

The town house was quiet — incredibly quiet. The servants had all been given the evening off. Ned and Andrew were spending the night with Lady Anstruther-Jones, who was also entertaining a rajah and his seventeen children. Two more would not matter. Ned was likely teaching them all to pick pockets or something, anyway.

Kenyon missed the piped hot water at Windrush. The buckets that filled his copper tub here were already cool by the time he'd rinsed the last of the plaster dust out of his hair. Then he had to decide what to wear. Getting dressed was foolish. He had every intention of disrobing within minutes of entering his wife's bedchamber. His nightshirt was too fusty, a towel too casual for the momentous occasion. His dressing gown had blood on it from last night's head wound. Not very romantic. But that Hindustan prince with his harem had seemed to fascinate Aurora, so Kenyon wrapped a sheet about himself, tucking the ends over his shoulder. Deuce take it, he was as fluttery as a schoolgirl at her come-out.

Aurora had spent an age in her tub, too, worrying. She feared that, after waiting so long, Kenyon would be disappointed in her inexperience. She knew he'd be everything she ever dreamed of, and more than her poor maiden's mind could envision, but what if she did not please him? Legions of Lolas loomed in her imagination.

Not if she could help it. Aurora wasted more time dithering over what to wear. Her choice was easier than Kenyon's, since she already knew she'd be waiting for him in her bed, rather than exposed. She might have lovemaking on her mind, but she still had a modicum of modesty. So she wore the Windham diamonds.

Which landed on the floor atop his sheet before the first candle sputtered out.

"Have I told you how much I love you, Lady Windham?"

"Not that I recall, Lord Windham."

So Kenyon made love to Aurora with words, and she replied in kind. Truly their marriage was the happiest day of their lives, until tonight. She had given him back a soul, and he had given her his heart. Now they were both complete.

And then they were one, complete.

A short time later, Aurora laughed as his tongue touched her ribs. "That tickles, my love. What are you doing?"

"Inspecting my wife for identifying marks in case anyone ever tries to claim her, of course. I haven't found any birthmarks or scars or tattoos yet, but without my glasses I have to be that close in order to see, don't you know. A gentleman does not wear his spectacles to bed."

She giggled. "I wonder if such rules are written in Lady Anstruther-Jones's pillow book."

"We'll write our own book."

"Hmm. I am a very good researcher, my lord. But I did tell Lady Anstruther-Jones about Phelan, you know. I thought it only fair, since she helped us. And if word does get out, at least she will tell people the truth."

"Hmm." Kenyon was busy learning every inch of his wife, trailing butterfly kisses down her ribs, tasting, touching, savoring the scent of her, the silkiness.

"While I was there, she took Sweety back, but she gave us another gift."

He paused for a moment of misgiving, then resumed his exploration. "She must have had a large library of such books in her heyday." Right between Aurora's ribs, beneath her breastbone, he could almost touch her heartbeat. His own quickened.

"This gift is not a book."

Kenyon had reached his wife's firm belly, with its indentations and soft swellings. His Aurora, his dawn, was vibrating to his touch. The whole bed was pulsing with their rising passion. He did not want to talk about Lady Anstruther-Jones's gifts or gossip. "God, I love it when you purr like that."

"And I love what you are doing, Kenyon, but that's not me purring."

Barbara Metzger is the author of over two dozen Regency romances, and the proud recipient of a *Romantic Times* Career Achievement Award for Regencies.

When not writing Regencies or reading them, she paints, gardens, volunteers at the local library, and goes beachcombing on the beautiful Long Island shore with her little dog, Hero. She loves to hear from readers, care of Signet or via E-mail: Bdriftwood@aol.com.